THE NI
OF THE PEARLS

Copyright © 2025 Giuliana Arena
All rights reserved.
Editorial realization: studio pym / Milan
Cover Image: © ChimE / Adobe Stock
Graphic design: © Cristina Giubaldo
ISBN Code: 9798289605207

Any reference to actual events and/or real people is to be considered purely coincidental.

Giuliana Arena

THE NIGHT OF THE PEARLS

*To my grandparents Giuliana and Gigi,
Who have given me so many stories
and the desire to tell them*

CECILIA

1

Sils Maria, Summer 2010

It was a night of perfect silence. There was a faint, almost imperceptible lapping sound with every step she took. As the white silk of her nightgown wrapped around her legs, Cecilia hardly felt the biting cold of the water. She walked slowly, looking ahead into the darkness, only interrupted at times by the sudden parting of a cloud, which let the pale stars of that September sky peek out for a few moments.

She could not make out the outline of the peninsula, which lay somewhere on the lake's still surface.

Perhaps because of the many pills she had swallowed in one gulp, she did not feel the pebbles at the bottom hurt her feet. All she had left was to keep walking and let herself go until she no longer felt or thought anything.

When the water reached her waist, she jumped forward as if to swim, but she did not gasp; she kept her arms steady along her body. She felt the bun loosen, and her hair lay like a floating spider web behind her. A few more steps and she would touch no more. She did not notice the moment when the air stopped entering her lungs. No time for even one last thought. Only, finally, peace.

SAMAR

2

Algiers, 2010

When my father was diagnosed with stomach cancer, it quickly became clear to me that he would not have it for long. He came home from the hospital and sat on the old kitchen chair, placing a white envelope on the table and, without saying a word, pushed it slightly with his fingertips toward me.

My father was a man of few words, yet he could get to the centre of things and people's hearts, or at least mine. That day, too, he didn't need to speak. His dark eyes moved slowly under long lashes, now on me, now on my mother, intent on scrubbing the kitchen countertop as if the sparkle of that surface might reflect the direction our lives were taking.

I quickly looked at the papers in the envelope in that unreal silence that needed no explanation. I flicked through them, glancing at those lines of data, numbers and values, lingering on the last words of the diagnosis. I stared at those papers until tears prevented me from focusing on them. I stood up and leaned forward to hug him, leaning my face against his, as I did as a child. He must have been shaving; he always shaved when he went to the doctor. I noticed that because I did not prick myself, as I did then. We would not have laughed together at the red dots that would remain on my skin for a while. When I returned to look at him, his smooth cheeks suddenly seemed earthy. Without daring to utter reassurances that would have sounded circumstantial, I struggled not to sob until the pain that had filled my eyes was too strong to be contained. Then, I left for my room and went to the little balcony overlooking the rooftops of Algiers. I barely made it in time to hear Dad whisper, "I'm sorry, Samar," as if it was his fault, as if he wanted to protect me from what was happening to him.

That corner of the casbah was my refuge. From there, I could see the tangle of alleys, the clothes hung out to dry on the rooftops, and the infinite number of dishes that crowded the facades of each house like so many unlit moons. That evening, the air was still, but in the previous days, the wind had brought red desert sand, which had settled on the balustrade and the floor. With my bare feet on the tiles, I felt its grains: I liked to think how tiny pieces of immensity could break away and reach the labyrinthine streets where I lived. My father said he loved Algiers because it is a city where, on certain evenings, the sea and the desert seem to find a meeting point, two spaces equally vast and yet so different, almost opposite. It was one of those evenings. But there was no room to think about the desert and the sea, only the emptiness of a dull ache looming on the horizon, which I still did not fully understand.

A knot clutched my throat as never before: it was a lump of memories that had remained in the corner of my mind for so long and were now coming back to me. It was the two of us in the car heading toward the sea, with the road edged with red earth on one side and sand on the other and the palm leaves flickering. The queues to get to the sea, my restlessness at every traffic jam that forced us to stop, and his gaze in the mirror inviting me to patience and then leaning over the newspaper he held against the steering wheel. The vanilla ice cream we loved so much. In the evening, the white lines of salt on my skin, which I couldn't wash off because, on the way back, the taps would gurgle without letting out a drop.

And then he would tell me it didn't matter, that I would carry the sea on my skin a little longer. Then, in the middle of the night, he would wake me up, pick me up and put me half asleep under a trickle of water because you had to make the most of it when it was there, as well as the electricity. But the electricity, he said, was not a problem because if there was one thing that was never missing in our house, it was candles, since making them was his business. And when I had to do my homework, he would arrive smilingly with candles and light them one by one, illuminating the piles of crumpled photocopies that were my books.

His mother, my grandmother Nour, would have wanted him to be a lawyer or a doctor, but he preferred not to go to college and instead devote himself to the family business. I don't know why he chose this way; we never talked about it, but I think he loved manual dexterity, dipping his hands in kerosene, watching it melt and then pouring it into the moulds, preparing the wicks by dipping them several times in wax, searching for essences. He was focused and precise, his movements quick and expert. Now, he was annoyed that candles had become more decorative than functional objects.

He was a practical man, my father, which is perhaps why I loved even more the moments when, unexpectedly for those who did not know him, he proved capable of being suddenly overwhelmed by emotion and leaving room for imagination, as when on one of his trips to buy wax in Bugia – the city in Kabylia that gave precisely the name to candles (bougie in French) due to the large production that has always taken place there – he met my mother, Fatima. This beautiful girl had married him and followed him to Algiers. Or, as when at my birth in 1985, he chose the name Samar for me, which evokes long conversations in the evening.

Now, I thought, the flames of yesteryear would be extinguished forever, dampened by a breath that would take my father away from me, who would never again pour wax, wait for it to dry, choose colours or essences, who would never again bring me a candle to make me smell its scent or its smooth, shiny surface.

    I would have forever missed his ability to make everything fun and adventurous with just a few words. My heart clenched to think that now, in his situation, he would find no footholds to do this magic again. He would have no escape. His lost eyes, unable to ferret out hope, his once dry and strong body now only frail, hurt me. Besides, no one would understand me the way he did; no one would ever be able to contain my restlessness.

    The noises of the city preparing for the night came to me in one sound: the clattering of dishes and crockery for storage, the thud of shutters closed one after another, the meow of stray cats fighting over the last bite of the day. And then, the lights dimmed one by one. The night for me would have been long and painful.

    I always considered myself lucky to have my little wrought-iron balcony overlooking an alley, rare in the casbah. My childhood mostly took place in the inner courtyard, decorated with yellow and blue majolica tiles, which was also overlooked by the house of another family, friends of mine.

    They had a son, Mehdi, a few years older than me, with a large mass of dark hair that, as a child, he never wanted to cut. So, when I looked out at the courtyard from the balcony, I would see his brown, curly head bent over a red ant or a little paper boat that he dreamed of sailing into the fountain basin the day the water would start gushing again from the small stone palm tree that topped it. When he would notice me, he would look at me for a few moments, his slightly elongated cut velvet eyes, and then widen his mouth and the whole face in a smile I still find in him today, and he would beckon me to come down waving his hand in broad gestures. I would spend entire days with him, playing in the yard and running around the central fountain until my mother and hers would call us by looking out on their shared balcony.

Although outside that courtyard, the terrible 1990s, bloodied by extremist terrorism, gave Algeria no respite, childhood had left me with many happy memories that, that evening, I seemed to file in the past forever. And so next to the pain of my father's illness lay that of the end of a world that, I realized only then, had remained alive within me until that day.

My mother constantly criticized me when she saw me smoking because it was not a "good girl" habit. But now, she would not see me because she had slipped quietly into her room. I felt tears fill her light brown eyes and then go down on her beautiful face until they wet the orange bedspread. I lingered over the brief crackle of the lighter, hesitated momentarily, but then did not go to her because I knew it was difficult for us to be authentically close. There was no attunement, and the rare displays of affection lacked momentum. I couldn't say why, perhaps simply because since I was no longer a child, I spoke a language too different from hers.

She, who had educated me about freedom, lately changed her mind. Now, she would often return to talk to me about engagements and marriage as the only lifeline for a girl in 2010 Algeria. I didn't necessarily see a husband on the road I hoped to find, sooner or later, for my future. She claimed that the fact that I had gone to language school had influenced me in this regard, putting the ideas of Western girls in my head. For this, she blamed Dad, who had instead been happy with my choice.

I believe that the long period in which we lived with the constant fear of bombs, the darkness of curfew and the constant distrust of others never left my mother.

When that very hard time was over, Algiers had suddenly awakened, wounded but teeming with life. And while existence resumed, bars and restaurants opened everywhere. Those who could sew shortened skirts, and we teenagers, threw ourselves into the world, but my mother stood still. Perhaps that was why she wore brown, grey, and black. She indulged in a floral tunic only on exceptional occasions. Dad teased her, mispronouncing the saying "when the desert blooms," which indicates a very rare or impossible thing, into "when mom blooms."

Instead of laughing, she walked away, annoyed. I don't know if it's more because of the comment or our complicity. My father was not like her; he had managed to look forward, and his business had grown. He was now also selling some candles abroad through an association of artisans. He had started smiling again, even outside the house; he had managed to enjoy the change. He would read the newspaper, rustling the pages and shaking his head because it was all still to be done: Algeria might never have changed all the way; then, when he closed it, tapping it on his knees vertically to make the pages fit together, he would inhale at length as if to prepare himself for action, and I seemed to catch a glimpse in his expression of the satisfaction of even being able to think that helping to create a new country was possible. Perhaps their different attitudes toward the new situation, my father's desire to act and my mother's apathy had contributed to digging a furrow of silence between them, a silence in which there was not resentment but misunderstanding.

Mom's only recreation was going to the hammam with her friends. Sometimes, as a young girl, I had accompanied her, too, remaining silent in the warmth of the orange – or mint -scented steam emanating from the tubs, watching women of all ages, some with large flabby breasts, others with small toned breasts, talking about their husbands, sons and, more often, their daughters and the weddings they would arrange for them. Now that I was no longer accompanying her, I imagined her on the sidelines, staring at the finely inlaid columns, a little ashamed of me, of that girl who was "going for thirty" (that's what the women at the hammam would have said), not promised to anyone, that had studied and perhaps dreamt of going "over there," to the foreigners, the enemy, the colonialists. In a word, to France. The idea that I, too, wished to go to France had come to my mother when she heard that Mehdi had obtained a visa and would be leaving soon. He had asked me to follow him, to find maybe a course of study or a master's degree and set out with him. But that idea scared me more than it tempted me. After all, Mehdi's adventure would also be a bit of my own: I would follow him from a distance through his stories, which I imagined to be vivid and enthusiastic because no one could tell a story like he could.

I put out my cigarette, crushing it in the small amber ashtray, and heard my mother's suddenly hoarse voice calling to me. I descended the narrow staircase from the small terrace inside. I found her before me, her eyes swollen with tears, a few strands of hair escaping from her veil, and her mouth tightened. At that moment, she looked old, much older than forty-five. I ran to embrace her, trying to put into that gesture all the spontaneity and intimacy that I supposed must exist between mother and daughter, and murmured to her that perhaps, with our savings, we could pay for the necessary care. But she shook her head as if I had said something stupid and exclaimed, "Your father doesn't want to get treatment because the doctors say he's going to die anyway; he only has a few months left, maybe a year. Now come, he wants you." My mother always spoke like that: abruptly, without any sweetness.

Thinking back to that conversation with my father today, I felt my life was changing forever as I listened to him. I may have built up this memory later after many things happened. Yet, I have glimpsed a new possibility, a gift from Dad, his last one. The idea that I could look for another path for me, for my existence, and find it.

He began to speak in a low tone, almost pulling away from encrusted and meagre words within himself.

"Do not waste money on impossible cures," he had begun in a low voice, almost begging me, "My last wish is not to delay my death for a few months. My wish, Samar, is to find out the story that brought me here."

I gasped. We had talked occasionally about why I had blond hair and light-coloured eyes, and by now, I didn't even think about it. Even all the people who knew me were not surprised by my it; I was living the life of all Algerians in an Arab family and had minimal relationship with the small European community, mainly French, which was still present. My father had somehow relegated his French origins to the corner of the library, where, since childhood, I had drawn volumes upon volumes, letting myself be enraptured by the literature of a distant and wonderful world. "Dad, we know that your origins are European, that you were brought here by a French family, and then when your parents returned to France, they entrusted you to their maid, Grandma Nour, who raised you … and here we are." A few more words and my voice would crack. He raised his hand slightly, motioning me to be silent. His gaze wandered beyond that room, far beyond. I suddenly sensed him distant and resolute. I began to torment the cuticles around my thumbnail. I used to do this when I was nervous and couldn't smoke. I would focus on that little spot of me and channel all my anxiety there.

"Yes, of course, that's part of the story we know," my father continued, not minding my tension or perhaps not noticing, "but a few years ago, your grandmother Nour, before she died, told me that in fact, the Vernet family had, in turn, adopted me. My mother, your grandmother, only learned about this in the 1980s, when Maurice Vernet confessed it to her in a letter, in which he recounted that, unable to have children, he and his wife had gone to Switzerland during the war and had managed to adopt a baby only a few months old, about whose origins they knew almost nothing.

To prevent suspicion or gossip, as soon as he had a chance to work in Algeria, they hurriedly moved and stayed here for many years." He drew in a deep breath as if every detail of that story, made by speaking slowly, with the concentration needed to find the most appropriate words for me to follow that intricate thread, had stolen some of his energy.

I suppressed those words for a while, realizing that I had never really considered the deep pain that Dad had carried within him all his life, ever since his parents had abandoned him in Algiers as a child.

I concentrated on retrieving the stories I had heard so many times from him and my grandmother. I had paid little attention to those tales, which is the typical attitude of those who, having their whole life ahead, have no time to look back. I knew that my father was the son of a colonial administration official who came from Paris, Maurice Vernet. He and his wife Françoise returned to France at least a couple of times a year and, on those occasions, left little Gérard in the care of the very trusty Nour, the Algerian maid who had always worked in the service of the occupants who had succeeded each other in the large house on the elegant boulevard Laferrière facing the sea, in the shade of the tall palm trees.

They had begun to leave the child in Nour's care for more extended periods. When the war against the French began in 1954, after one of their trips to the motherland, they simply did not return. Nour had hoped day after day for their return, but then weeks and months passed, and she received only money from Maurice Vernet. Soon, she abandoned the affectionate but detached attitude of the housekeeper and, in a slow process, almost without realizing it, put on the role of mother for little Gérard. After some time, while feeling a little guilty, she had begun to hope that the Vernets would never return.

When she had met one of the leaders of the movement for

liberation from the French colonists, who was to become her husband, she had not hesitated to tell him that she considered that little French boy, the very son of that enemy they wanted to get rid of, to be her son. So much so that after the wedding, he, who understood Nour's love for the child, had managed to procure Algerian documents, and Gérard, now Fadi, became their son for all intents and purposes. Then Nour decided to forget his true origins, gave no more thought to the possibility of a return from the Vernets, who had not sent money for some time, and, forced to leave the beautiful house built in the French part of town, moved to an apartment at the very beginning of the casbah hill. That move had dispelled any sense of guilt in her.

When, in late 1962, the French left Algeria, which had regained its independence after more than a century of foreign domination, Fadi was an 18-year-old boy with dark, curly hair and large brown eyes. He spoke perfect French and Arabic, and he called Nour "mom."

My father and I remained silent, absorbed probably in the same thoughts, and we only recoiled the moment Mom entered the kitchen without looking at us and began to prepare tea. We turned our eyes toward her, who, after throwing a handful of dried mint leaves into the boiling water, contemplated them stirring in the pot. Then, after straining the brew, she handed us the boiling cups. Dad drew a deep breath and leaned back, looking up at the ceiling. "This story is also about you, Samar. Just think when you were born with such fair skin and blond hair – what a scandal, what a shock!" He smiled and glanced at me as if a beautiful thought had hooked him away from the darkness.

"Fortunately, your grandmother Nour, who enjoyed great respect in Algiers for the role she and her husband had played during the war of liberation, had silenced the gossip by passing on the rumour that your features were derived from who knows what distant ancestor. No one could believe that the granddaughter of one of the most active revolution leaders was of French descent. At the same time, Fadi's story, my story, was soon lost in the confusion of the war. The rumours and murmurs of the time had become increasingly evanescent until they disappeared." He smiled, shaking his head, admiring and amazed at how well his mother could paint reality in the tones she liked best.

I, too, smiled because the memory of Grandma always filled me with tenderness. Then suddenly, I stopped, frowned, and wondered why my father was telling me all this.

He read my mind and resumed explaining in an almost didactic tone: "In the same letter, Maurice Vernet wrote that his wife, unexpectedly, had then given birth to twins, and so they no longer felt like keeping me, their adopted son, too." That idea seemed horrible, unbearable, even as my father retraced his story like one who lingers with his fingertips on an old scar, which by now no longer hurt; at most, it gave a bit of discomfort.

"But how long have you known all this? Why didn't you go to Europe in the past years to find out what happened then?"

"Grandma Nour kept Maurice Vernet's letter from me until her death a few years ago. It was the only weakness she had. Maybe she was afraid of losing me, of destabilizing me, of making me suffer again. When what I thought of as my parents left me here permanently, I was already ten years old. Although I had never seen them much, I felt rejected in an intolerable way for a child." He emphasized the last words angrily, then, to himself in a low voice, "Abandoned by Mom and Dad," he whispered, brooding over what his childhood had been. "I didn't miss them so much because they had always been distant, far away, but I did miss the idea of them. I was trying to convince myself that something had happened, that they could not come back for me. But Nour knew that was not the case. We tried to contact them, sending a few letters and calling on the phone, but no one answered. Eventually, I gave up and, tired, challenged by an unjust childhood and a pain too great to handle, I surrendered to Nour's love, clung to it and decided that she and her husband would be my mother and father. However, following the revelations in Vernet's letter to Grandma Nour, I often promised myself to go to Europe on the trail of my origins, but I never did. We always believe that we have time for important things and that the right time to put aside every day and search for ourselves will come. After studies, after young children, after work. But it doesn't. My time is running out now, and I have no idea who my parents were. My real parents, I mean. I grew up with the thought that I had been abandoned. Only a few years ago, I discovered those were not my parents, but just a couple willing to do anything to have a child, except leave him here. Perhaps I was also held back by the fear of having to confront that woman who wanted to be my mother simply for a while, to fulfil a whim or that pusillanimous man who could not defend a child, a small child who called him daddy. And then I was afraid that the twins might accuse me of having financial demands or wanting to interfere with their lives...."

I widened my eyes in disbelief, wondering what I could do to unravel that thread and get to the bottom of an affair that appeared increasingly convoluted and disturbing.

"Who were my parents?" he asked himself, in a slightly lower tone of voice, but with more energy, insistently, tormentingly, as if I might, indeed should, already have an answer to give him.

Then he drew a sigh again, cast a glance at my mother, who from behind was surveying the now-empty pot of tea, and then, once he had gathered courage, all in one breath said, "I would like you to go to Europe, to France, meet the Vernet twins and try to find out more about my heritage. Then, yes, I will hold on. That will be my cure: not wanting to die before I know who I am." Now I recognized him: he had come straight to the point without hesitation. He wanted me to do what he did not have the strength to do. My heart began to beat faster. Dad was dying and was asking me to give up spending the unrepeatable time he had left with him, to go away for days, weeks or perhaps months that we would never be able to recover. And he was at the same time offering me the chance to leave, putting me on a path that I would otherwise hardly have had the courage to undertake, not least because, in recent times, facing the world and moving alone in the spaces of my life had paradoxically become more tiring. Confrontation with others had begun, in my eyes, to always go against me. After all, I had been out of college for almost two years and still could not give my life a clear direction.

As I pursued these thoughts, hovering between courage and fear, Mother, who had heard our words, sobbed in the corner of the small room, clutching her cup of tea as if to warm her hands even though it was not cold. The useless buzzing of a fly banging against the window punctuated the silence.

Even though my heart was bursting in my chest, I said, "I will leave, Dad; I will leave as soon as I can and find out the story that led you here, yours and, therefore, my origins."

I would have liked to feel as strong as I had tried to prove by uttering that sentence; however, I clearly felt I had found a goal that would take me far. I would be leaving on a journey to Europe and within myself, searching for my past and looking toward my future. I had been standing in front of him all that time. He invited me with a nod to lean back in the chair; I leaned my weight on the arms, and he took my head in his hands and kissed it as if to thank me as if he was too tired to speak and had no energy left except that gesture.

That night, I could not sleep. I got up, returned to the small terrace and, sitting on the wrought-iron chair, lit a cigarette. I watched the embers glow red and fade quickly into darkness.

Leaving would not have been easy. Getting a regular permit for France for a girl of Algerian nationality from a modest family could take a long time. My father once told me that Algeria is a huge waiting room because everyone in this country is waiting for something. I was well aware that many kids were waiting for visas to France, and it was not even given that they would get them.

However, Mehdi had made it and would soon join relatives in Paris, where he would film a documentary with the support of a Sorbonne professor.

He could have helped me or at least explained how to untangle the rivulets of bureaucracy without wasting too much time. Mehdi always knew his way around, always knew the right people, and thought the world was a simple place within his reach.

Only in the last period had I realized how unbalanced our relationship was: he had become a confident man, and I had remained a little girl, or, at least, that's how it seemed to me. But I had the feeling that deep down, he hoped I would remain so that he would not lose his role as leader or older brother.

The transition from darkness to light was so sweet that I did not even notice that it had begun to dawn. Then, when the voice of the muezzins calling the faithful to prayer from the minarets of the citadel's many mosques travelled across the rooftops and alleys of Algiers' casbah, I was brought back to reality. A sense of poignant melancholy pervaded me, of belonging and foreignness at the same time, for it seemed that without my father, that country and that city would never be the same again.

I had to think about the visa and try to leave as soon as possible.

I called Mehdi very early: he was already in the university library, intent on consulting a film history text. I imagined him concentrating, hunched over the volume, wearing one of his Korean-collared linen shirts, his gaze on the pages and his mind already elsewhere, projected on making his first documentary. "I'd like to go with you if I still can," I had begun without tergiversation. I had heard the creaking of the chair; upon those news, Mehdi must have stood up to avoid disturbing the other readers.

"I'm leaving in not even a month, Samar; the visa will take a while. Don't ask me to postpone the departure; I can't wait for you." I hoped he could help me get my visa as soon as possible, I could not waste time, and the idea of going to Europe alone terrified me.

"I would like to leave with you, Mehdi; I need your help to get the visa as soon as possible, but also not to be alone." I thus admitted my fragility, my fear. I relied on him, and I knew it would work. After all, Mehdi loved to feel indispensable and think that I could not be there without him. When I had told him I would not follow him to France, he had feigned indifference, but he had resented it, I was sure. He was silent for a while, perhaps expecting an explanation. "Then I'll tell you why it's important that I leave," I told him, " I'll explain everything."

He hesitated, almost weighing my words, doubting whether it was worth trying to understand right away or not. Soon after, I heard him regain his usual confidence: "Of course, I'll help you, Samar; we have to make an appointment and then go together to the French embassy to apply for a visa. Someone I know works there too…" He had set off, already chasing for a solution, already getting busy for me. "Join me here right away," he had then said urgently.

As he ended the call, I realized my heart had accelerated slightly. I swallowed, feeling a mixture of fear and excitement for that departure that was desired and feared with equal force.

I quickly got ready, pushed open the heavy black door, and went out. I looked at the white, light-flooded sky.

I walked down to the centre through the alleys, skimming over the vases, bowls, and bronze dishes displayed outside the many stores along the zigzagging stairs that connect the casbah to the rest of the city. Whenever an opening between the houses allowed, I glanced at the sea's blue strip.

The air was so still that the green-and-white flag over the university building's front door hung unusually lifeless. I entered the courtyard and passed among groups of students wearing leather shoes or imitation Nike and Adidas, engaged in conversations about the future that, as I knew well, oscillated between the desire to leave Algeria behind forever and the desire to build a different and better country.

I looked around and found Mehdi sitting astride a small wall. As soon as he saw me, he stood and waved. "What's going on?" he asked, a little alarmed.

We started walking in the courtyard as we had done so many times, and I told him everything. Mehdi slowed his pace and looked me straight in the eye to listen better. He was sorry for my father and impressed by my determination. He was not used to seeing me as brave and resourceful, and it seemed that it did not please him. He loved to feel that he was leading the game, and I knew that my being submissive, timid, and dependent on him filled him with pride. In any case, I forgave him for his possessiveness toward me because I traced it back to our childhood friendship and noticed how vigorously he strove to keep it at bay. I had known Mehdi too well, too long. Besides, his desire to protect me, which he considered a duty, drove him to bend backwards for me.

When I finished my story, we went back to the little wall where Mehdi was standing just before. He opened the folder in his hand and began to unwrap it. "First, you have to prepare the application file," he said, showing me a form.

"Hi Mehdi, we didn't even say hello," I smiled at him, reassured by hearing that my friend had already gotten into the thick of the matter and that it seemed much less complex to him than to me.

He responded to my greeting briefly, without taking his eyes off the form and pointing to one line in particular: "We have to decide what kind of visa to apply for. I have one for study, but you, not being enrolled in any courses, cannot. The only option is to apply for a short-term visa for ninety days. To get it, you have to show that you have sufficient resources to support yourself for your stay. You will be able to stay with my aunt and uncle for a while, who will have no problem declaring that you will be their guest; then, we will see. In any case, within those three months, you could also work without a work permit." I merely nodded and grabbed my pen to fill out the form, placing it on the clipboard. "You will need some passport photos and, of course, your passport, after which we ask for an appointment at the French embassy to deposit everything; they will take your fingerprints, and then you will be put on standby for your visa. The important thing is to get the appointment as soon as possible."

That very afternoon, I went to take the passport photo on a white background, which was required for the visa. Four photographs had come out of the camera, and I still have one. I keep it in my wallet as a relic of the person I was before departing. My eyes are wide in the photo; the neon lamp had turned them a pastel blue. Grey under-eye circles stand out against my fair skin; my lips are thin and tight, my freckles are hardly visible, and my hair is pulled back in a ponytail. I don't like having my picture taken. If necessary, I prefer to stand halfway in profile without looking directly at the lens so that at least a little bit of my upturned nose, of which I'm very proud, can be seen. In any case, that day, there was no room for vanity, only the anguish of taking, by taking that shot, a first step toward a journey I wasn't sure I knew how to accomplish.

Thanks to Mehdi, I could make an appointment to deliver the file with the request in about ten days. He insisted on accompanying me, and I was grateful. We crossed the threshold of the boxy building of the French embassy without speaking. Still, once we had hurried through the checkpoints and left our cell phones at the entrance, Mehdi moved within those walls perfectly at ease and seemed to know everyone. He spoke to the official at the counter as if they were lifelong friends, accomplices in who knows what transgressions. Standing behind him, as nothing about that conversation concerned me, I heard him explain that he had accompanied me because I was his dear family friend. I saw him turn toward me, almost leading the other's gaze toward something that deserved that small favour. I was embarrassed to passively be the subject of their conversations. At the official's invitation, I laid my clipboard on the counter and began pulling out all the documents and forms as he requested.

Then he took the prints of both my hands. I laid finger by finger on the machine, moving on to the next only when the green light came on.

I was nervous, and when the official finally dismissed us, I took the receipt and left with my heart in my throat, fearing that for some reason I would not be granted a visa and at the same time fearing that I would be able to get one and would really have to leave. Mehdi walked behind me, flaunting an optimism that I was not too keen to share.

The days that followed the visa application seemed endless. Anticipation and uncertainty dilated the minutes and hours. Every now and then, I would glance at my father, trying to catch some sign that I hoped I would still have him for a long time, against all odds. But he was always home, and that showed how much strength had left him. He, too, looked at me with eyes full of expectation, as if merely applying for a visa was an essential step toward the truth he sought. He, like Mehdi, was sure I would get it and urged me not to waste the time that seemed to me never to pass but to prepare myself, to look for the directions I should follow once in France. But I did not know where to start. Every time we crossed glances, my mother would shake her head as if to emphasize that I was about to do something crazy and that I would have to dissuade Dad from his purpose. And that, in the end, I would accomplish nothing. Squeezed between my father's grief and my mother's disapproval, I would leave the house and walk down the casbah, almost running, then pass by the monument of Emir Abd el-Kàder, who drew his sabre uselessly to the sky and I would lock myself in an Internet café.

    There, I would get lost on the Web, asking the search engine for the answers I sought. Like a fool, I would stay pinned to a chair, compulsively typing the name "Maurice Vernet," hoping to see a black-and-white photo or even an address pop up. Instead, there was a guy looking at me from his social profile picture, a smiling dentist with a practice in Rouen, and a manager in a suit and tie. So, I would add "Algeria" or something like "French colonial administration" next to that name, but nothing came up. Maurice Vernet had evidently not been a relevant enough personality to see his biography consigned to the Web. At other times, I would search for Françoise Vernet, or "Vernet twins," and in front of the many faces of strangers that showed up on my screen and that clearly had nothing to do with the people I was hoping to find, I felt lost in a meaningless maze and realized that I had no trail to follow. So, I would type "Vernet" on the "Pages Blanches" site in Paris, and several pages with names and addresses would appear. I would only dwell on the female names. It was a long list, but I could not be sure the Vernet I wanted to trace was included. I would jot down those long lists of names and addresses on a sheet of paper, which I would then fold to show Dad. I knew he would love to have something tangible, to clasp in his hands a small, concrete step in the right direction. I would nibble on the cap of the Bic pen with no idea how I would then ascertain whether the people I was looking for were hidden among those lines. Occasionally, I would interrupt myself and inhale the fresh air for a few minutes. And suddenly, I would realize that those long, useless days were not endless but piled up behind me in greater numbers and stayed there like so many small units of time lost forever. Days that brought me closer, yes, to the loss of my father but not, it seemed to me, to the answer about his past.

When it became clear that the Internet would give me no guidance, I told myself that I should look for books on the history of French colonization in Algeria. I tried the university library database. There was a lot of information on the history of the French conquest and the liberation war. Still, there was also no shortage of books about the decades in between. I requested more recent ones and began to check the name indexes, but no Vernet came up. Then, I flipped through the pages devoted to the period immediately following World War II. I was having difficulty concentrating, scrolling through those lines without knowing what to look for. Finally, I decided to look at the notes that accompanied the text. I had the feeling that I was finding a thin thread to grasp: it was clear that the documentation for the pre-liberation period was kept in the Archives National d'Outre-Mar, in the south of France, in Aix-en-Provence.

There had to be some trace of Vernet there, and perhaps, I might even find some indication of his daughters or the places where he had lived in France.

Here was a possible starting point. I made a few photocopies and returned the books, finally somewhat relieved. I arrived home with bated breath, clutching my trophy in my hand: a photocopy with an address in Aix-en-Provence highlighted in yellow. From there, I would begin and perhaps achieve my goal.

When I showed it to my father, he thoughtfully tightened his chapped lips for a few seconds, then placed a hand on my shoulder and squeezed it tightly while nodding slightly, "Good girl Samar, that sounds like a good idea."

I saw hope shining in his eyes and his smile, a pride that seemed disproportionate, like when, as a child, I could quickly tip over the bucket full of wet sand and pull it up slowly, gently, bringing out a perfect tower.

I learned by heart the address and hours of the archives, especially the structure of the documents. The war records were still sealed, but the personal files of the colonial administration after forty years could be consulted unless they contained personal information that was described as "highly sensitive." There were also files on individual local administrations in all French colonies.

Unfortunately, the inventory was not online; I would have had to wait until I was there.

The visa came with a phone call at 9 a.m. A voice said only, "The visa is waiting for you."

For the first time in many days, I felt light-headed, so I went straight to Dad's kitchen with the good news.

He looked tired, his head slumped back in the chair, his sunken eyes half-closed. But when he saw me, he understood at once without needing me to say anything. He then seemed to revive as if a wave had passed through him. He stood up. He was tall, my father, and that day, I noticed that his thinness, though usual, was as if changed: once bringing out his energy, now an unseen fragility. He clasped my shoulders with his hands, looked me in the eye and said, "I knew it, Samar; now run and pick up the visa, and then take a ticket right away," he moved his head forward toward the entrance as if to urge me to go immediately. He returned to his seat and waved as I took the front door.

As soon as I was outside, I called Mehdi and imagined his smile widening as he said, "Let's leave together."

I walked briskly, at times running, toward the French Embassy, for once not thinking about anything other than the first step of the adventure I was about to begin. I put away the fear which would take me nowhere, not thinking that the days ahead would inexorably mark the end of my father.

Outside the offices, I looked at the visa: ninety days, three months, to find the truth and bring it to him as a last precious gift.

That afternoon, Mehdi suggested that we go to the botanical garden. I could not even remember the last time I had been to what he thought was the most beautiful place in the city. The lazy gaze of habit meant that all I saw of Algiers were the potholes that made me jerk when I rode the bus, the pigeons that crowded the squares, the countless construction sites or the din of horns at rush hour. Now, however, I knew that only a couple of weeks later, that city would be a little less mine and suddenly seem more beautiful. My father used to say that you must look at things from a distance to appreciate them. This was true, according to him, for everything, even memories. And if you looked at some moments of your life from a distance, they became sweeter, even if you had once experienced them as painful.

We walked for a long time along the avenues made of old trees and twisted trunks, then decided to return home, but just before leaving the garden, I stopped and rested my hand on the bark of a large fig tree that must have been many years old. I then wondered if, by chance, one day, Françoise Vernet or her husband, Maurice, had touched that same tree. The bark was rough, and at that moment I felt my father's pain scratching me too. Who knows if that lost mother and father had ever loved him?

Mehdi turned to wait for me, and I caught up with him by running. We proposed again to go to the Martyrs' Monument in the following days, on the hill overlooking Algiers, to look at our city – from which we had never really left – all at once. But we didn't actually go because the day of departure came in a flash without my having time to realize it.

That morning, I hugged my parents. Mom remained rigid

and responded to my greeting by clutching me briefly, her lips contracted. She did not want me to leave. My father, on the other hand, although looking lacking in strength, encircled me vigorously to himself. I promised to take care of myself and not stay away too long. I did not want to be escorted to the airport, partly because my father's gaze was sunken in large, purplish dark circles under his eyes. The ever-increasing grey hair peeping through the glossy dark brown spoke for him and told me how ill he was.

Before crossing the threshold, I paused and closed my eyes, imagining the familiar rustling of the newspaper pages he used to flip through. I inhaled deeply to take in the faint whiff of mint that always hovered around the house. For a moment, I lulled myself into the illusion that this was just another day, like any other. And those days, those years always the same, not at all surprising, seemed to me in that instant memorable, beautiful, exciting. I went out quickly, walking through the endless maze of small streets, without turning around, without really looking at the white walls and the clothes hanging out, without listening to the sounds of life that would have continued to flow in those narrow streets even without me, without inhaling all the way through the smells of spices and sea and, it seemed to me now, of desert sand brought from far away. I did not want the desire to leave to give way to the most poignant melancholy. I felt my throat tighten into a knot of courage and fear, simultaneously.

Mehdi's sunny, open smile as he waited for me at bus stop number 100, which leads from Place des Martyrs to the airport, heartened me a little.

It was the first time I had ever set foot in the departure area of the airport: it had happened only a couple of times, years before, that I had gone with my father to the arrivals area to pick up some acquaintance returning from France, usually for a wedding, of course.

Now, I was the one leaving. This reversal of perspective, being "on the other side," on the side of those leaving, made my presence at the airport almost unreal, unbelievable, perhaps because it had all happened too quickly.

I found myself beyond the sliding departure doors in an instant, nervously clutching the handle of my trolley. Mehdi was excited, looking forward to boarding the plane. We did indeed show up at the check-in desk, which was still closed, but he didn't want to leave the first line we had conquered at the cost of an unnecessary uphill struggle. We walked the few meters in front of the desk in small steps, without stopping, and as soon as the girl in charge arrived, Mehdi placed his passports on the counter, with the frenzy of someone about to miss his plane. Having passed the controls, he wanted to go straight to the gate, even though it was a long time before boarding. I followed him a few steps away, trying to look at the store windows, which sold refrigerator magnets and jewellery, cigarettes and dates. I clutched a large green cloth bag and occasionally fumbled in it with my hand to feel if the pack of cigarettes was always in place, along with my papers, boarding pass and cell phone.

At the gate, we sat and waited on the pitted metal seats. As I pondered how quickly human destinies can change, following unexpected trajectories, Mehdi left me to fetch a small bottle of water. I saw him get lost among the speeding people, pass under the monitor showing departures and arrivals, and disappear.

In that instant, I understood the meaning of the word "loneliness." I pronounced it in Arabic and then in French within myself. I was alone. And Mehdi's presence, with his enthusiasm and hopes, would not tear that loneliness apart, for that strange journey was just mine.

And then I remembered, perhaps by one of those bizarre tricks of the mind that help one endure too harsh reality, when, as a young girl, I had gotten lost in Bejaia. I had gone to the big city with my father, who had to sell candles to the traders waiting for him at the port. I arrived in the van he had used with other men from our neighbourhood in Algiers. While he haggled the price, I watched the fishermen's boats on one side and the bustling activity of the industrial area on the other. Bejaia had become a major centre thanks to the oil trade, and the port, once small and frequented only by fishermen, was now a major industrial and commercial centre where oil companies carried on lavish interests. The fishermen were being pushed further and further into a corner. Without realizing it, I started walking to watch them as they returned with their nets loaded with fish.

I had walked along the main pier and entered the network of small docks, observing the boats and their lanterns, now extinguished after a long night's work. When I turned back to check if Dad had finished, I did not see him where I thought I had left him. I had retraced my steps and returned to where I had started. He was not there. I had tried to recognize the merchants he had talked to earlier, but they all looked the same to me; no one cared, while huge cranes and a large oil tanker moved slowly by. It all seemed too big, and I felt as alone and lost as I had ever felt. As I stood motionless amidst the teeming life of the early morning harbour, the stench of fish and the oil fumes mingling in an acrid, pungent, nauseating scent, I thought of my home, the warmth of the fire, the spices with which Mother was probably preparing lunch. And I had longed for nothing more than to find myself within those safe walls. I had felt tears filled my eyes when Dad had encircled me with his arms, smiling and relieved after the fear that he had lost me. He had never seen me again and had gone looking for me in the alleys behind the harbour that teemed with stores. I was safe again.

But this time, Dad would not be there, would not show up young and smiling behind my back to protect me. This time, I was the one who had to lead that man whom I loved so much to himself and to an understanding of his own history.

Mehdi returned and sat beside me, handing me a sip of water. Then, they opened the boarding gate.

I had never been on a plane before, but the flight did not scare me. I took my seat, turned off my cell phone, tucked my cloth bag under the seat in front of me, fastened my seatbelt, and sketched a smile at Mehdi, who was waiting restlessly for takeoff.

When the engines finally started, I squeezed the armrest until my knuckles turned white and closed my eyes. My heart bounced in my chest, and I regretted agreeing to go; I thought the task my father had assigned me was too difficult, perhaps impossible.

At the exact instant, I felt the wheels come off the track, the emotion of the last few days melted away in a warm, silent cry. Mehdi vigorously squeezed my hand for a moment. We had left our land and would reach Paris a little more than two hours later. The tension of the last few weeks and then of departure eased. I squinted my eyes, leaning my head against Mehdi's shoulder, who, on the other hand, was nervously flipping through a book, sometimes through the Air France magazine, unable to concentrate because of excitement.

3

Paris, 2010

The roll of wheels on the runway surprised me in my sleep. Mehdi lightly shook my shoulder and stood up to retrieve his backpack from the hat rack long before he received permission from the cabin crew. As soon as the doors opened, he motioned me to move as if he could not stay up there even a second longer. We walked down the jet bridge and arrived at the belt to wait for our luggage. The Charles De Gaulle airport appeared to me like an immense spaceship aboard which I would come to distant and unexplored worlds, to unknown and mysterious lives different from mine. Knowing French comforted me a little and helped me to feel less like a foreigner than I already was. After the last passport checks, following dazed Mehdi, I walked past the most beautiful boutiques I had ever seen: immense perfume shops, from whose glittering entrances a thick, sweetish perfume wafted; luxury jewellery stores, from Cartier to Bulgari, displaying necklaces, bracelets, and earrings I would never even have dared to dream of; and then the great brands of French and Italian fashion. From the windows glimpsed beautiful salesgirls, creatures from another world, with carmine-red lips and long bare legs, hands with lacquered nails and gaudy jewellery.

Outside the airport, I let Mehdi guide me as he slipped into the subway and took off down the corridors without hesitating, as if he knew the route from having done it a thousand times. He changed lines without pausing even for a moment to check the destinations or read the signs indicating the stops; he untangled himself in that maze as if he had lived in Paris all his life. On the subway, as I quietly feigned calm and confidence, I saw several women with their heads covered and heard Arabic spoken often. After almost an hour spent in the underbelly of Paris and walking down very long escalators, dragging our trolleys, we returned to the surface. I was looking forward to the outdoors and, more importantly, to walking around the city, which I had always fantasized about. It was the city of promise, of the future, of those who could make their dreams come true. Accompanied by these thoughts, I first glimpsed a rectangle of the grey sky at the top of the last flight of steps, and then my smile could do nothing but fade in the face of the squalor that stood before me. An anonymous, boundless suburbia contrasting with the glittering promises Paris made to girls seeking a different future. I snuck into a phone booth – there were still some in Paris at the time, thankfully – since calling home by cell phone would be very expensive. I slipped my credit card into the slot and dialled the number. At the same time, Mehdi waited impatiently outside, not even thinking of calling his parents. My mother answered, flaunting great relief as if I had waited too long to tell her that I was alive, that I had arrived and was okay. She told me that Dad was precisely as he was that morning, that is, quite ill, resting and couldn't put me through. I seemed to catch a vague reproach in her tone, cold and hasty, as if that trip was not Dad's wish before it was mine, as if I was just being selfish. I did not linger too long thinking about her; I waved goodbye, pretending not to have picked up on her disappointment. When I came out of the booth, Mehdi took me by the hand, perhaps because he was aware of how difficult it was for me to relate to her or maybe because he sensed the stinging disappointment that had run through me when looking at the neighbourhood we were in, despite my efforts to disguise it so as not to hurt him. As I walked briskly to keep up with him, I was ashamed of my thoughts about the squalor of those suburban boulevards. In fact, what had I expected? For Mehdi's relatives to live on some glitzy boulevard in the most fashionable neighbourhoods of the French capital?

"My relatives live here in the council apartments built in the area that once belonged to a car company," Mehdi explained suddenly as he pulled me along with him, still holding my hand. "It's not the best, but you have to think it's just a starting point for you and me. Tomorrow, I am going to the Sorbonne to meet with the professor who will follow me in making my documentary on Algerian immigrants in France. And you – you will be able to start your research...."

I always liked his optimistic outlook, so I tried not to get carried away by his concrete plans, which always seemed easily achievable. "I would like to get a job, first of all. I don't want to burden your relatives' shoulders for long; that's impossible," I said.

Mehdi seemed more astonished than I was by this peremptory statement, this sudden desire to assert myself, to be independent, which I had never thought of before. He was not very pleased; he cut it short: "Now, don't worry. Let's go home, have something to eat, and you'll see we'll be fine. You can stay as long as you want."

The small apartment was neat and tidy, and Mehdi's aunt and uncle, a very affable middle-aged couple, had prepared a cot with immaculate cotton sheets for me in a corner. I gave thanks, thinking that I should find the Vernet twins as soon as possible and complete my task. We ate excellent spiced couscous with vegetables. Mehdi was a flood, talking about his documentary, the professor he would soon meet, me, my father, and what I had come to do. I remained mostly silent, grateful to Mehdi for explaining what I feared might seem too absurd. We all went to bed very early, and I, despite my unfamiliarity with my new surroundings, fell into a dreamless slumber.

Mehdi's relatives in Paris ran a bakery near Rue Mouffetard. They baked baguettes and all sorts of bread nonstop, filling the quaint neighbourhood with a warm, enveloping aroma – so much so, in fact, that not only many Parisians but also numerous restaurants and eateries on the lively street stocked up on them.

They would get up when it was still dark, leave hot coffee in a thermos for us, and at dawn, they would come from the suburbs to their workshop, after an hour in the subway mazes, and start baking bread.

Mehdi immediately contacted the Sorbonne professor and several compatriots who had been in Paris for generations and began working on his project from day one. I felt utterly lost when he left to go to the university, leaving me alone in the small apartment. Then, driven by the idea that every minute was precious, I took courage and went out too. I walked for quite a while before reaching the nearest subway stop, following the directions Mehdi's aunt and uncle had given me. I looked at the colourful weave of lines on the boards displayed in the station for a long time, and with two changes, I managed to get to the Gare de Lyon. I wanted to buy a train ticket to Aix-en-Provence, where I planned to travel the following week, doing some more research before leaving. I scrolled through the timetables on the ticket machine screen and chose the first train of the morning, the one that left Gare de Lyon at 5:45 a.m. I would arrive in Aix shortly after 9 a.m. and by bus would reach the Archives, which remained open until 4:50 p.m. I would return very late in the evening, hoping to finish everything in the day.

Over the next few days, I decided to take another look at the volumes in the library specializing in contemporary history, which was located a little outside of town, not far from the house we were staying in. I hope to arrive at the Archives with an idea of what to look for to avoid wasting too much time in Provence. Arriving next to the large automatic glass door of the Bibliothèque, I had to move my arms several times to be noticed by the sensor. I convinced myself that I was like a ghost in that city. Undeterred by that somewhat ridiculous thought, I introduced myself as a student researching Algerian colonization and the fates of the French who had administered the colonies. The librarian, a kind young man with thick-lensed glasses, pointed me to several volumes on these topics. I had already consulted many in Algiers, and those days in the library only confirmed that the archives I was interested in were in Aix.

In those early days, I saw little of the French capital. One afternoon, leaving the library, I took the metro and headed downtown. I walked along wide boulevards, crossed gardens surrounded by the golden-tipped railings, admired the Seine and the elegant buildings overlooking the river, looked at boutiques and hotels, and felt so out of place, so foreign that I was surprised that the shop windows reflected my image. I felt like I was nobody, even more insignificant than usual in that glitter. So, at one point, I decided to squeeze into the subway, elbowing my way among a group of tourists who were climbing the stairs following the guide.

I had not been able to fully appreciate the beauty of that city I had dreamed of so much. Perhaps it was because my mind was only getting lost in my father's story, or because of the anxiety of my inadequacy regarding the task I had to face.

As I drove home, compressed in a train car going fast underground, I thought wistfully about Algiers, about the Algiers of downtown, the stores, the trendy cafes, the upscale restaurants, but also about the Algiers of endless construction sites and dust, of the upper part of the casbah, dilapidated and in a state of disrepair, with its destroyed, crumbling houses, almost an offence to the history and the former beauty of the neighbourhood that

Grandma had loved so much. And it seemed to me that in Paris, where I had come in search of a history that might really be my own, of my true roots, I could never really find anything of me. And in the crush of people returning home pressed into the belly of the city, I ran out of air, thinking that if I found nothing in Aix, I would not know in what other direction to look: the money would run out. I would have no choice but to return to Algiers to watch my father die without having given him any answers. If just thinking about a life without him was painful enough, the idea of disappointing him and seeing him go before I had found anything of my own roots was unbearable.

One evening, I spoke to Mehdi about how lost I felt in Paris, how it had also disappointed me, and how nothing I had seen so far, which certainly was not much, left me thinking that it could never be "home" for me. He replied with a smile and then told me that I had not understood anything about Paris, that Paris was also so much more, that that very evening we would be going out with friends to a totally different area, made up not of grand boulevards and fancy stores, nor of anonymous to dingy suburbs, but of streets full of life, of clubs, of things to do, of people to meet. Then, after a few moments of silence, he added, slightly uncomfortably, that his aunt wanted to propose that I go to work in the bistro of a certain Madame Thérèse Gourmand, whom she supplied with bread and croissants. In the same building as the Bistrot, on the top floor – he continued, keeping an eye on my reaction – there was also a room where I could go to stay. He specified that no one wanted to send me away. Still, it would be better for me to feel independent and not worry about money. That job would leave me time for everything else. I did not feel offended at all; on the contrary. It seemed like an excellent opportunity. Even though it had only been a few days, I was already starting to feel over my head in Mehdi's aunt and uncle's apartment. I enthusiastically welcomed the idea, and he seemed a little bewildered, as if he had not expected a genuine desire for independence from me.

That evening, we went to a club frequented by many foreign students, Arabs but not only. A narrow, steep staircase led to a sort of basement where, despite prohibitions, the boys smoked cigarettes, hookahs and weed. All the while, they talked about movies, politics, and literature. As the evening faded into night, I understood that Mehdi would stay in Paris forever, that that was his world, that his life would take shape there, among those intellectuals and artists who dreamed big but who, I thought, would not get very far. I, on the other hand, felt slightly out of place. Not entirely uncomfortable, but not in my "natural" habitat either. I was restless; I seemed to sense the ticking clock of Dad's life without me reaching my goal. While Mehdi enthusiastically threw himself into his new dimension, I was stuck, still, motionless. I did not know how to take charge of my existence because, unlike my friend, I did not know exactly what to do with it. I felt like I had already spent too much time sitting in the library with a book in front of me, endlessly wrapping long strands of hair around my right index finger. I was happy that I would finally go to Aix only a few days later, but I also knew that if I didn't find anything, I wouldn't know where else to look.

Occasionally, Mehdi glanced at me, almost as if checking that my silent presence was still beside him. But then he didn't bother to engage me in conversations or include me in the circle of friends. I don't know how he made it in those few days. Mehdi's personality towered over me. That could be why, I reflected, going to live above the place where I was going to work was an excellent opportunity to take back some of my space.

The following day, Mehdi's aunt introduced me to Madame Gourmand. She did so gently, perhaps not to give the impression that she was throwing me out and then ran off to work.

The small bistro, located in the heart of Rue Mouffetard, served croque monsieur and croissants, baguettes and salade, coffee and hot chocolate. Behind the white wooden counter towered the owner, always wearing a floral apron and a sunny smile. Inside were only a few stools for those who wanted to stop and chat with her. In front of the entrance, a small veranda, heated in winter, was filled with wrought-iron tables with the tops each decorated differently, so small that it seemed impossible to fit more than three plates on them and so close together that it must have been impossible to serve the courses without asking customers to pass them from table to table. Nothing escaped Madame Gourmand's taste: cups and tableware, all in the Provençal style, were each decorated with a different floral pattern. Even the glasses were of various colours. Pictures of beautiful gardens, flowers, and her smiling face behind her counter were on the walls. That's how she greeted me, with that unreserved smile that I would get to see many times in the future.

She immediately told me that she saw herself a little bit in me and in my lost demeanour. She recounted how she had had the same expression when, just 18 years old, she had moved to Paris from a small Breton village. Granted, the trip had been shorter than mine, but those were other times, and to her, it seemed as if she had landed on another planet. Having had no one to lean on in the capital had been so hard, and only after a long time had she really felt at home.

When I told her that I would only be able to work for a few days because then I would have to go to Aix, she did not bat an eye or ask me for an explanation. Still, I felt compelled to open up to her briefly and tell her about my mission.

She listened with interest, not stopping to look at me even as she simultaneously passed a rag over the counter. "What an adventurous reason to come to Paris!" she said enthusiastically.

Then, pointing his head to the corridor leading to the stairs, she added, "Come on, I'll show you your room."

She accompanied me to the fifth floor, slowly climbing and panting. With a broad hand movement, she opened the attic door and invited me in.

It was really the smallest room I had ever seen: a bed, a small table, a small stove, and a tiny sink. The window looked out onto a small balcony embedded in the slate roof. The bathroom was in the hallway, and as soon as the other room on that floor was rented, I would have to share it with someone else. I immediately liked the little balcony because it reminded me of the one in Algiers. Of course, there wasn't even a chair there, but I could still stand in front of the open window at night, letting the view sweep over the rooftops of the French capital.

That very morning, I returned home to my few belongings. Mehdi, who had been the one to propose the move to me, seemed struck by my haste to go, as if he had not expected such enthusiasm.

Perhaps he was bewildered because our being in Paris had further unbalanced our relationship. Mehdi, who was used to considering me somewhat dependent on him, found it difficult to relinquish his big brother role. However, when he offered to accompany me, he pushed back his possessiveness and was happy with my new arrangement. He also hoped to have a similar one soon.

That night, I could not sleep; it often happens when one is in a new room and bed. I realized that that trip to Paris might have put a perhaps unbridgeable distance between us, probably because we had completely different goals and objectives. What for Mehdi was a way of detaching himself from his origins, becoming an outside observer of them through documentary filmmaking, for me, it was instead a journey to the heart of my and my family's history, a trip at the end of which, I thought, I would be rich in the knowledge of my father's origins and thus my own.

I simply said I was okay in the occasional messages I sent to my parents from my cell phone. I did not immediately tell home about my new arrangement; I knew Mom would disapprove, and I feared that in Dad's eyes, the two new things, the job and a room of my own, might seem too final and represent my surrender or failure to the mission. I did not call until the evening of my first day of work at the bistro from a booth that was not far away. As I listened to the phone ringing, I imagined it lying on the small table in the lobby and hoped my father would answer. Instead, as expected, I heard my mother's voice. "You finally showed up!" she scolded me without asking how I was doing.

"I also have a cell phone," I replied, as if to tell her that she could call me if she wanted to, then decided to soften the tone of the conversation. I told her about the job, the small apartment, and Madame Gourmand, hoping she would feel better about the idea that I had someone besides Mehdi and his relatives to care for me. Phone calls were always contracted due to the high cost of overseas calls; however, when I finished talking, she said only a "Take care", in which I sensed a note of sweetness. Then she put me through to Dad.

"Samar!" he exclaimed enthusiastically when he heard my voice, stretching out as he always did the last *a* of my name. I told him every detail of what had happened up to that moment, especially about the Aix archives that awaited me two days later.

"Meanwhile, tell me how you are," he asked, putting off the question of my research.

However, I did not stop. "Dad, I'm afraid I won't be able to move on. What if I can't find anything in Aix?"

He cleared his voice without being able to make it less hoarse and then tried to reassure me that there had to be some document on Maurice Vernet. "You have to be systematic, Samar, sift through those archives sheet by sheet. And you'll see that the name we're looking for will turn up." Using that plural made me feel close to him, and I felt strongly that I was with him in that search, not alone. I wanted to ask him for a thousand pieces of advice. Still, I restrained myself because I wanted to show him that I knew how to move independently, and I did not want to burden him with the task he had entrusted me with.

"I miss you, Dad," I said quickly because we were used to always taking our feelings for granted out of that strange modesty that sometimes prompts us to keep the strongest ones to ourselves.

"I miss you too, Samar," I was afraid his voice would break, but fortunately, he managed to contain his emotion. "You'll see you'll make it; I'm hanging in there in the meantime." The faint sound of his smile reached me, along with the tenacity with which he did not stop summoning up any remaining energy.

When I hung up, I felt lighter. I pushed open the little glass door of the cabin, and the squeal of the rubber doors seemed lighter than before. I looked around, and Paris appeared full of promise—for the first time, the city I had always dreamt of.

The next day, as I waited tables, all I did was repeat in my head all the information I would need the next day at the archives: the history of the French occupation of Algeria, the year the Vernets arrived, the organization of the documents, the times of the train I would leave on, and the times of the possible trains to return. I feared my father's disappointment if I found nothing, and more than anything else, I feared that even if there was a chance to discover that truth, I would lack time. Time all my life had passed slowly, giving me the illusion that nothing would ever change, and that now seemed to run relentlessly, taking me to an unknown elsewhere that frightened me.

The night before my departure, I did not sleep. I tossed and turned in bed until I surrendered, opened the window and lit a cigarette, being careful not to let the smoke in.

I arrived at the station well in advance. It was still dark, but I did not sit and wait. I stood looking at the light board until the train platform bound for Aix-en-Provence appeared. Once it left, I abandoned my head in the corner between the seat and the window. I stayed that way for the entire trip, looking at forests, green meadows, cultivated fields, lavender bushes that would be long lilac rows a month from now, and then, suddenly, the sea. A wave of nostalgia swept over me; I thought I could fly on that blue all the way to Algiers at that very moment to embrace my father and rewind the crazy tape that had become my life lately and return to my predictable, slow, monotonous days.

Then, as soon as I heard the train pull on the brakes and come to a halt as the loudspeaker announced my stop, I wondered where I would be when the lavender bloomed.

Upon my arrival, the Archives had recently opened. I briefly explained to the person at the entrance the purpose of my research. She asked for my ID card, gave me a form to fill out with requests, and took me to the paper inventory, where I was to search for the exact location of the documents I needed.

I took to scrolling with my fingers through the many folders kept in the little drawer dedicated to French personnel stationed in Algeria during the war and in later years. I could request no more than two folders at a time and no more than six per day; it was essential to choose the right ones: burning those few attempts would have meant one more day in Aix, one more day in which my father would live without his truth. I marked on the form the markings that referred to the folders entitled "Colonial Administration Personnel Algeria, Careers, V" I handed it to the desk and stood waiting in the silence of the reading room, interrupted only now and then by the rustle of leafing papers.

When the attendant brought me two bulging cardboard folders, I inhaled deeply, trepidatiously pulled the string that held the first one closed, and unwrapped the flaps.

As my father had already told me, Maurice Vernet, as a colonial administration official, had always been concerned, in essence, with the economic relations between the colonies and the mother-country. Basically, I told myself, the unequal exploitation of our resources.

I immersed myself entirely in the research, opening each folder and scrolling through the files individually, remembering my father's words, "You have to be systematic, Samar, sift through those files sheet by sheet." I handled that light, yellow paper as gently as possible. I saw names, dates, journeys, stories, and faces flowing through. Different handwriting, lines typed in faded ink, notes of all kinds. About halfway through my work, I found a sheet of paper with the thinnest of papers, yellowed by time, indicating dozens of surnames, all with a V, in alphabetical order with brief indications of their movements and careers. I quickly scrolled through the letters, drawing a deep sigh to take a few extra seconds. What if he had not been there? What if I hadn't found anything about him? How could I have presented myself to Dad without a result? What if, instead, I would have located Maurice Vernet's address and found his two daughters, which was already not a given? What would I have asked them? How could I have asked the Vernet twins if their parents had ever abandoned a child in Algeria?

I did not have time to linger too long in those thoughts, and when I saw the lines about Maurice Vernet typed, they seemed to me a thin thread that my father's past, and therefore mine, threw me beyond the years, beyond the lives spent without knowing anything about our history.

VERNET, Maurice
born in Paris on October 25, 1901
Guadalupe from 1930 to 1934
French West Africa (Dakar) from 1935 to 1941

France (at Ministry of Colonies) from 1942 to 1943
Temporary leave from 1944 to 1945
Algeria from 1945 to 1954
1954 Returned to the motherland and hired at the Ministry of Economy.

This was followed by a series of codes that referred to another folder.

As my heart sped up slightly, I asked to consult it: I hoped to find an indication of a private address. Each file referred to an official, so I quickly went through them, one by one, until I found the one with the number relating to Maurice Vernet.

As soon as I opened the file, I saw him. The man who must have been my father's adoptive father was looking at me from a passport photo attached to a packet of light paper with a rusty paper clip. He was handsome with a pronounced nose, dark hair pulled back with grease, and thin lips contracted into an uncertain smile. I watched him for a long time, looking for traces of his thoughts in that distant image. He must have been about fifty years old in that picture; he had probably already abandoned my father in Algiers by then, and perhaps the guilt that would later lead him to write to Grandma Nour to tell her everything was already beginning to work its way inside him. Maybe the thought of that child made it impossible for him to really smile with his whole face.

Tormenting the edge of my thumbnail with my forefinger, I slowly went through the numerous papers, carefully scrolling through them individually. I hoped to learn more about him, his family, and his private life. Maybe about his wife Françoise, but it was mostly communications related to his work with the French ministry and accounts of the situation in Algeria. Toward the end of the folder, however, were indications of his retirement and an address:

Maurice Vernet, Rue du Bac 20, Paris.

The papers were all typed and initiated with a fountain pen by Vernet, with a signature I considered inwardly round, redundant, even cheerful: it did not look like the signature of someone capable of abandoning a child. I thought of the hands of what I had always imagined as "my French grandfather" touching those papers. I wondered how he might have never felt the need to contact that distant child of his. I would have liked to keep running those pages through my hands as if I could only understand more of the man's life by touching them, but I could not wait. For a moment, I was tempted to slip the photo off the paper clip and slide it into my pocket. Still, then I realized that seeing him again, even if only in a picture, would only renew my father's pain over that distant abandonment. I fastened the webbing on the folder and returned the material to the archivist. I left for the station, passing through the centre of the charming Provençal town and re-proposing to visit the South of France someday.

On the train, I compared the addresses of all the Vernets in Paris found on the Internet with those of the Aix Archives. None of the Vernets in the online directory lived on the Rue du Bac. I let myself go against the back of my seat. I had been in Paris for more than a week and was at my starting point. Arriving at the station, I decided, before going home, to go and see the Vernets' old address anyway. From the Gare du Nord, I took the Metro line 4 to Saint-Germain-des-Prés, and from there, I walked to the beginning of the elegant street. I took it and arrived at number 20, where there was a real estate agency. I looked up: there were probably apartments on the upper floors, and my father's adoptive parents must have lived in one of them. This, however, did not help me find the Vernet twins, who might already be dead or living who knows where. I walked along the street, brooding incessantly, wondering what other attempts I could make. I noticed that to almost every building on that elegant street were plaques commemorating artists, writers, politicians, and scientists, whose names mostly told me nothing. Yet, stopping to read about those lives made me feel part of something big, of a universal storyline. I found in those stories a meaning to my search, a reminder of the importance of recovering the past, of sinking down to the roots of general history and our own small, insignificant individual history.

It was as if my father had asked me to write his plate, to reconstruct the lines that would prevent him from dying as the son of a lie, from becoming the son not only of a mother and a father but also of a story, a path, a place – the son of a true belonging.

The fear of not being able to give my father the gift, the meaning of which I now fully understood, plunged me into a well of melancholy. I suddenly wished only to be in my room above the bistro. I still didn't dare to call home; I would do so the next day when I might have some idea how to go about my research.

By the time I arrived at the café, Madame Gourmand had closed and was probably in her little apartment in the back. I ran up the steep staircase to my room. Once there, I started scrolling again through the list of Vernets in Paris that I had printed out at the Internet café, even though I knew it by heart then. Nothing. No Vernet on the Rue du Bac. Sitting in the wooden chair, I stretched my legs forward and, looking up at the rafters of the sloping ceiling, gathered my hair into a bun made of a thick knot. I stayed like that for a long time, overcome with exhaustion but unable to move to the bed to try to get to sleep. I fell asleep very late, unable to get any real rest.

As the scent of breakfast croissants wafted fragrantly up all the stairs, I called home from the bistro phone, the pride of Madame Gourmand, who had had a telephone drawn on a wooden sign and had also hung a beaded curtain in front of the compartment where the device was located to give those who wanted to use the old-fashioned phones, and not the cell phones she still eyed with suspicion, a semblance of privacy.

To my amazement, this time, my father answered. He seemed to have a cheerful voice, or perhaps he was trying not to worry me. He asked how I was doing, and I searched for the words to tell him that the task was proving complicated and that I would probably have to go home empty handed.

"Samar…," he repeated, leaving the sentence hanging as if to express all his disappointment, perhaps at the lack of response, but more likely at the surrendering tone I had used. Then I told him about Maurice Vernet's handwriting and how rounded and beautiful it was. This seemed to me the only concrete detail to offer him. His voice came to me hoarse after he had cleared it. I imagined he had gotten a knot in his throat hearing about the handwriting of what he had once called *Dad*: "Go ahead, get the list of the Vernets in Paris back, cover the photocopies of the documents; maybe we missed something." Once again, he was bringing the responsibility for the progress of the search back to both of us and unjustifiably shouldering some of it made me feel less alone and disappointed.

Madame Gourmand saw me slowly unwrapping the long rows of beads to get out of that makeshift booth, and she immediately knew that I had not communicated good news. I told her about my trip to Aix the previous day, and she listened to me concentrating, moving her contracted lips all to the right. Then, after a few seconds of silence, she asked me to follow her as if she had some brilliant idea. Madame Gourmand was a simple woman, but not clueless and endowed with practical and forthright intelligence, as evidenced by her bistro management.

We went down into a cellar I had never seen. The smell of mould was powerful, and nothing could be seen until Madame, feeling the wall, managed to turn on a light bulb that hung dimly and lonely from the ceiling. She moved some boxes, looking at the metal shelves and lifting objects until she uncovered two large volumes in one corner. They were two old telephone directories, the kind they used to use in the old days, with pages as thin as tissue paper and tiny print. "Everyone, but really everyone in Paris used to be here, my dear. Let's see if there are any Vernets on Rue du Bac 20." She was delighted with her idea and gloated at the thought that old directories might be more useful than the Internet. I followed her up the ladder leading up and sat at a small table, flipping through those big books since the place was still empty. I turned the pages slowly because if I didn't find any clues, I wouldn't know what other attempts to make, and I didn't think Madame Gourmand might have any other ideas.

The only Vernet on the Rue du Bac was a certain Isabelle, but she was not at 20 but at number 35. Urged by Madame Gourmand, who encouraged me to overcome shyness, I tried to call, but no one answered. However, the number was not nonexistent. That same evening, I went to that address. There was an elegant building with numerous luxury store windows facing the street and then three floors of housing. I observed it by putting myself across the street to look up to the typically Parisian attic. I didn't know if the Vernet twins lived there. Passing the front door, I glanced at the golden intercom button panel. Still, there were only offices or numbers and no last names.

As I was returning to the subway, my cell phone rang. It was Dad again. The first few days, I had always been the one to call him. I knew he didn't want to be on my case, but maybe he sensed my need for encouragement. His voice was tired, but he was not in a bad mood. He told me that he was sure this had been a good day for my research.

"Actually, Dad, not so much," I said, pressing the phone to one ear and a finger to the other to try to hear despite the noise of the train. I'm not making much progress. There doesn't appear to be a Vernet at number 20 Rue du Bac. There is a Vernet at number 35, but I have no idea if that's who we're looking for."

He did not seem displeased; in fact, he seemed almost amused to hear me in that unprecedented role as a detective. "You will find your way, Samar. I never thought of it as an easy quest. It is normal for it to take some time, and I will try my best to wait for the truth," I heard him smile.

That sentence brought tears to my eyes. I wondered if it might not have been better never to find that truth because then perhaps Father would live again and again. But I knew instead that I had to hurry and come up with something to unravel that thread as quickly as possible. I gave myself three days to determine if one of the Vernet twins lived in that elegant building. Of course, I could not be sure that at least one was still alive. Here, if they had both died, all would have been lost. When I would end up at the bistro, I would lurk there, stroll back and forth down rue du Bac, look in the windows, stare at the doorway hoping no one would notice me, praying to see someone with a feature pop up that would make me say "yes, it's her. It's definitely her." But nothing. I tried to go there very early on Thursday before the bistro opened. I slipped under the still-half-masted shutter of a café that was opening then. Everything else was closed, the windows dull and lacking their usual sparkle.

A few people were walking hurriedly along the sidewalk, perhaps on their way to work or the station, clutching their briefcases. I stood at a small table looking out, taking small sips of lousy coffee. I lowered my eyes to check the time on my cell phone, and just as I raised them again, the door of number 35 opened. A Yorkie on a leash popped out first, then a tall, thin woman with a long grey braid slung over her right shoulder and an ankle-length black trench coat. I looked at her, searching for some clues. She paused for a moment beside the doorway and then began to walk in step with her little dog. Within moments, she would be out of my sight. It could have been anyone. However, the age fit. I leaned over a little to look at her again, and then she disappeared, and I abandoned myself in my chair, not knowing what to do. I could hardly follow her and ask her if her name was Vernet and if she was the Vernet I was looking for, the one whose mother had abandoned a child in Algeria. I was about to pay for my coffee and run to the bistro when the door opened again. No dog this time, just a woman dressed in bright colours and short hair.

    I had a thump in my heart because, although very different in dress and bearing, more youthful and less sullen than the lady before her, she looked strikingly like her. I looked closely to ensure I didn't see what I longed to see, but there was no doubt that the two women had to be twins. I quickly paid for my coffee at the cash register and went outside. I looked in the direction the women had gone and noticed that the latter was walking briskly as if to catch up with the former.

    Now, I had to find a way to talk to them, and I couldn't imagine anyone better suited than Mehdi to come up with it. I called him from the bistro calmly, thinking that the slight tension I had felt on the phone last time would vanish if he understood that I still needed him. I could hear that he was at the university, someone was calling him. He sounded in a hurry, but I knew he would listen. "Samar, I am making a documentary about the French of Algeria; if it is them, it will not be difficult for me to make an appointment. And then I can use my professor's name; they will definitely receive you." *You will see:* he always used this expression as if he could predict good things for me.

    I took the afternoon off and went to the Sorbonne, where Mehdi had a small studio with some doctoral students. As I had imagined, he moved about the university with the naturalness of someone who had worked there for years, as if he had a leading role in the ancient French academic institution. He said calling from the Sorbonne was ideal to give respondents an idea of professionalism. I knew that taking me into what had become his environment and showing me how comfortable he was within those walls also gave him great satisfaction. But I found nothing wrong with that; on the contrary, I greatly valued his ability to be casual in any situation and in the company of anyone. It was a valuable skill that I envied him somewhat and felt was beyond my reach. In the book-filled study, I leaned against one of the tables and handed Mehdi a slip of paper with the apartment number at 35 Rue du Bac. I was a little sorry to delegate that call to him, but I was sure that he would be much more convincing than I, whose mouth was already feeling dry with excitement.

Mehdi let out one of his best smiles on the first ring as if he could get right to whoever would answer on the other end. A few seconds and he was already speaking professionally and persuasively, recounting in full the purpose of his work and pointing out the names of important families he had already interviewed, with the idea that even if the person on the other end did not know them, he would be ashamed to admit it and would sketch it out. Shortly thereafter, I heard him say that he might not be able to go "that day" but that he had a valuable collaborator, who was also busy at the Sorbonne making the documentary, who could do the interview for him. I flinched from the table I had been leaning on and waved him off, widening my eyes, terrified that I would have to go alone. But he put his index finger to his lips to tell me to be quiet and then waved cordially, handing me the post-it note on which he had noted "day after tomorrow 2 p.m."

"I think you have to go it alone, Samar. Moreover, I don't know the story thoroughly, which is quite complicated from what you told me; I wouldn't know what to say. You'll see; you'll do just fine. Besides, lately, it seemed that you didn't want me around anymore; I was surprised when you asked me for help contacting the Vernet twins." Mehdi was a flooding river, talking fast, without stopping, perhaps because he did not want us to find ourselves in the awkward silence. "In any case, the lady I spoke to was nice; she said she doesn't think she has much to tell you about her people in Algeria, but she will gladly receive you."

I felt a little displaced; all that talk sounded to me like a slightly stymied "now get over it," I hadn't expected that; in fact, I was sure he would be happy to come back and take care of me with that big brother attitude he always had. Instead, something had changed. Perhaps, I reflected, I had wanted that change; maybe I had really wanted, in the weeks before, to fend for myself or at least without him. To be autonomous. Undecided about what interpretation to put on that contradiction, I nodded as if to agree with him and then said, "Thank you, Mehdi", with the sincerest gratitude.

On the day of the appointment, my mother called me early in the morning, before I started serving breakfast, and I came out of the club to answer. "Come back, Samar. Dad is sick." She started talking like that without greeting me or asking how I was doing.

I shivered at the thought that my father had already ended. "But how bad?" I asked anxiously, praying that Mother was exaggerating to force me back in. "I don't want to come back empty-handed, and now I'm on to something." I kicked one of the many cigarette butts people were throwing on the sidewalk.

"I wish you had never left," she added almost angrily. Then, she realised I was smoking, "You could spare me your smoking while we talk on the phone! You'll never find a man if you act that way."

"Mom, please. Tell me about Dad; you can't start out like that and then attack with the usual story that I shouldn't have left. How is he?"

"He's sick, you know how he is, and I don't find it right that you're there."

"But has it gotten worse? Can you get him on the phone, please?"

"He's resting now, Samar, I can't put him on." So he was not in the hospital; he was like the last time I had heard from him, weak, tired, but not yet at the end.

"I have to go back to work now," I said, cutting it short and rescheduling to talk to him as soon as possible.

"We made you study with great sacrifice, so why are you standing there in a bistro as a waitress?"

"Ah, did you make me study to get married and lock me up to raise children and clean the house?", I could no longer keep quiet, as I had learned to do when she apostrophized me in that tone between annoyed and victimized.

As I threw the cigarette to the ground and put it out by crushing the butt under my right foot, I almost paid no attention to his last sentence, "I knew going over there, to the French, would hurt you. Your father was reckless."

I said goodbye to her without answering and hung up, annoyed. My mother, as usual, only amplified my insecurities and the anxiety of not succeeding, and she had always managed to make me feel burdened by the desire to be independent, to seek my own way beyond any conditioning, as my father had wanted. I dreamed of a different life, but I felt fragile: I had known until then nothing but my own world, made up of an Algerian family, lifelong friends, and studies at the Faculty of Letters and Foreign Languages that I had loved so much, even though I detested confrontation with professors and the moment of exams, which I faced with shyness and a deep sense of inadequacy.

I sighingly reentered the bistro and went to the kitchen to put on my pink apron, the same as Madame Gourmand's but less than half as wide. As I knotted it at the waist, I realized my mother had not even told me how Dad was doing. I proposed again to call him later, trying to zero in on when she would not be home.

As I waited tables at the petit café, I repeated in my mind

what I knew so far: the existence of the Vernet couple who had abandoned my father to Grandmother Nour in Algeria and then had twins, still living together, on the Rue du Bac. The thought of meeting the Vernet sisters made me a little anxious. What was I going to tell them? How would they take it? I was going to visit them that afternoon. I prayed I could get some helpful information, assuming they had any.

Leaving the bistro, I walked through the neighbourhood streets to reach the subway. It was market day, and I passed among the fruit and flower stalls, noticing how the sounds, scents and colours, though vibrant, were less intense than those in Algiers and how people here were more hurried and distracted.

Arriving at the Quai Voltaire, I observed the elegant buildings with their characteristic slate roofs, the bridges connecting the two banks of the Seine, the *bouquinistes* and the students passing quickly by on bicycles, making me think of Mehdi. I imagined navigating the entire course of the river, getting to the sea and then from there to home. At that point, I was reminded of my mother's words almost shouted at me during our last phone call: "But you, what do you really want? You don't know; you simply have no idea. And being there will only confuse you further." I took on task Dad assigned me as if it were *my own*. In fact, I perceived it to be just that, and I told myself that if I could come to unravel the skein my father had put me in charge, I would also be able to find my place in the world. This was not an entirely rational thought but rather a feeling, an intuition I could not fully grasp.

As I saw Rue du Bac, I realized my heart was in my throat: I almost ran. Then I hoped to catch a glimpse of Mehdi waiting for me somewhere, with his unkempt beard, dimples in his cheeks, and eyes shining with irony. But no sign of him. I felt my stomach clenched, perhaps from running or excitement, but mostly from fear of failure. If the two women had nothing to add to the picture

I had painted for myself, I should have returned to Algiers empty-handed and with the confirmation that I was not worth much.

As I rang the intercom, I noticed my hand shaking slightly. The door clicked the instant I spoke my name. I looked around the large lobby and called for the elevator, which arrived immediately in its wrought-iron cage. As I reached the fourth floor, I thought that building, with its marble stairs and shiny dark wood doors all alike, was the most beautiful I had ever seen. When I was on the balcony, I immediately noticed a door ajar, which, as I approached, opened. A black girl in a white apron greeted me and led the way.

I walked in, and the little dog I had seen with one of the two sisters on the street began to prance around me without barking. I bent down briefly to stroke it and then looked at the room where I was standing. It was a hallway overlooked by a few rooms with heavy curtains drawn to shield the light. The bright day outside seemed to find no place in that house. I clutched my shoulders, shivering. It was cold.

As my eyes adjusted to the soft light, I caught sight of two women sitting on a worn dark velvet sofa. Above them, the twisted arms of a large chandelier with its many extinguished bulbs. One wore her now completely grey hair pulled back into a long braid resting on her right shoulder; she was very thin, somewhat sullen, and dressed in dark, just as I had seen her on the street. She looked at me through thin, metal-rimmed glasses. The other woman had hair that was bared and still, perhaps thanks to a dye job, a dark colour. She was slightly rounder than her sister and wore more colourful and showy clothes. They greeted me with a hasty smile, clutching a cup of tea. I introduced myself, flaunting professionalism as Mehdi would have done. I explained what he had already said on the phone, namely that we were looking for information about the French occupation of Algeria to make a documentary. One of the two women smiled at me, "Of course, your colleague told me on the phone; just ask," she said, jingling two large colourful earrings. "Although I don't think we could be of much use to you even though both our mother and father often told us about that period, which is also when we were born." With a quick count, I calculated that those women must have been about sixty years old, maybe less. A young age to stand there, locked in the family home, sipping tea on that early spring day. They looked very lonely and bored, perhaps they would have wanted to entertain themselves for a while, I hoped in my heart. I wondered where to begin.

The short-haired woman introduced herself as Pauline and said, "Have a seat. Where are you from?" I recounted that I was the daughter of a Frenchman from Algeria and was busy with university in Paris. I did not like to lie: my hands suddenly started sweating.

The other, more sullen woman, who had remained silent until then, absorbed in sipping her tea, took the floor. "My mother had us late. We were born in '55, and she was already forty-two."

"So you have never lived in Algeria."

"No, no. Our parents moved to Algeria during World War II. Our father worked in the colonial administration; he went back and forth a couple of times a year," Pauline explained, taking the floor again.

"Have you guys ever been there?" I asked her, hoping to bring the conversation to the familiar terrain of my city.

"No, we have never been there, partly because our mother, after returning to France, never wanted to go back; the French from Algeria were never well-liked, of course," she replied.

I jotted Algeria in my notebook, made a circle around it, and then made a cross to say they had never been there.

"Did they ever tell you what their life was like there?"

"Not much; our mother did not like to talk about it, and neither did our father. Over there, they had to endure the great pain of losing a son, a brother we never knew. He died when he was not even 10 years old. In fact, I think it was precisely because they had recovered from that trauma that they returned to France. Algiers was too attached to the memory of that first son. We were born shortly after their return, in '55".

I shuddered: this little brother, who died as a child, must have been Dad's age. I felt my mouth knead and could say nothing better than a matter of fact "I'm sorry," sketching a somewhat sad expression. Pauline shook her hand as if to say not to worry, that it didn't matter, and then continued, "When the war broke out, our mother was already married. Our father was fifteen years older than her and wanted an heir very much. I think that's why he had ended up marrying a young woman who had grown from a maid into the lady of the house."

A note of sarcasm did not escape me, and I felt embarrassed by that overconfidence. I tried to change the subject and asked when exactly they had gone to Algeria and why exactly there, whether it had been by choice or whether Maurice's superiors had somehow imposed it on him.

"I don't know exactly when, but I think after a couple of years after the beginning of the conflict. At the outbreak of the war, our parents had been married for some years, but our mother could not get pregnant. She and our father attributed this to the stress of the war and occupation; nothing had happened even before that. On someone's advice, they went to Switzerland, where they were supposed to meet a doctor they hoped could help them. Dad had many contacts, acquaintances, and family friends. I don't know exactly how long they stayed, certainly more than nine months, as they returned home with a beautiful baby. Evidently, the fresh air and tranquillity had helped. Just as they had decided to return to Paris, my father was offered to move to Algeria. Given the oppressive atmosphere in the French capital in those years, they went willingly. And they stayed until the child died of bronchopneumonia." I wrote "Switzerland" and circled the word, then drew an arrow to "Algeria."

"As you see, about the life of the French in Algeria, we can tell you very little," sister interrupted her.

I frowned as a doubt entered me, "I feel sorry for your mother… Did she never want to go back to Algeria?"

"Oh no, not a chance! I think she hated that place, with what had happened to her," the woman replied dryly, bringing her long grey braid behind her back in a firm, annoyed gesture as if to end the conversation.

"Our mother always hated everything and everyone. Come on, Isabelle," huffed Pauline, setting her cup of tea on the coffee table.

"I don't think this young student cares about your recriminations against mom, Pauline."

Thinking quickly, having let go of the initial tension, I was now perfectly clear-headed. I was rummaging through my mind, looking for the right questions. It was clear that the two sisters were willing to talk, especially one of them. They must have been very lonely, or so it seemed to me. "She must have been glad to have you, two beautiful girls, after that tragedy." "Yes, of course," Pauline replied, "although our father would have wished for a male heir. In fact, I think he basically loved us more than our mother did. She was not an easy woman; she was selfish and cold. He was good but completely incapable of taking a stand, she was always the one to decide."

"Pauline!" Isabelle nervously stopped her sister, "This student is here to learn more about French rule in Algeria, not to go into the boring history of our childhood!"

I was wringing my hands, which I had held in my lap since I had been invited to sit, in fear that the sisters' desire to talk would die down before I knew anything useful. I had placed myself on the edge of a chair covered in red brocade. The atmosphere in that cold house was growing stifling and tense. "Indeed, it is still interesting to know the paths that were followed by the families of the colonial administration. It must have been a great pain for your parents to lose a child like that in a foreign country…" I stammered these words while thinking about what more I could ask. I wanted to know more about that little brother: it could only be my father… or had they also had another child? No, that was the year of birth, and my father had no other siblings. A knot came to my throat because, after all, I had no concrete evidence in hand. Silence had fallen in the living room, and even the young maid who stood on the corner looked uncomfortable. Yet she must have been used to the bickering of the two sisters. "So, from Switzerland, your parents went directly to Algiers with a baby only a few months old."

"I don't know if they returned from Paris, but I don't think so; they went directly to Algiers with the very small child. Ironically, they felt that the climate in Algiers would benefit the little one much more than the climate in Paris. But evidently, that was not the case."

"So, about the kind of life they led in the Algerian capital, you don't know much…." "Oh no, but I can easily imagine it," Pauline continued, "the same one they then led here: our father always at work, our mother bored and completely disinterested in her son growing up in the hands of some maid." I thought of Grandma Nour. Based on Pauline's account, though lacking a valid lead, I was becoming more and more convinced that this child was my father and that the Vernets had justified themselves to everyone, upon their return to France without the son they had so longed for, by saying that he had died of bronchopneumonia. It was then that I thought it was time to leave. I imagined myself already on a plane to Algeria, pondering how I could tell Dad that his parents had told all his Parisian friends that he had died when he was ten years old and then never looked for him again.

Almost sure that I was unlikely to get any more confidence, on quick reflection, I realized that I had to cling to the only new information I had received during that brief conversation: the Vernets' stay in Switzerland. Then, staring at the word "Switzerland" that I had jotted down, I asked one last question.

"Do you remember where exactly your mother went to Switzerland?" Pauline, her eyes bright and sly, brightened, "Of course! I don't know where that doctor was from, but I do know that he used to send his patients to the Engadine, near St. Moritz, because of the good air. There, our parents' acquaintances resided during the war, and they let them stay in their chalet for as long as they needed to. I know because when Isabelle and I, as girls, were invited to Sils Maria, near Sankt Moritz, to ski, Mother prevented us from going because the place reminded her too much of our little brother. I'm sure that's what she said. Just hearing the names of those places drove her crazy." I wrote down those names: Engadine. Sankt Moritz. Sils Maria. I didn't know all the places, but the sisters talked about them as if I should, so I didn't ask any more questions.

I began to wonder how I could have gone to Switzerland and, once there, how I could have found the traces of that child whom the two sisters believed to be dead but who – I was increasingly certain – was not dead. However, now, he did not have long to live. Meanwhile, Pauline, after huffing noisily, apostrophized Isabelle: "With this story of the dead little brother... but do you really believe that she would have loved us more if she had not had that pain? And do you really think she was so grief-stricken? But come on, you knew her... she wasn't the type to love anyone to the end, not even Dad, who did nothing but please her all her life... He was a fool, too. Don't you remember the tantrums she used to make over the slightest thing? Or when she cut my braids just because I didn't put the doll away? Our father certainly wasn't bad, but that didn't save us. He was a succubus. I also blame him for the hellish childhood we had."

"Stop bad-mouthing our mother in front of a stranger!" interrupted Isabelle, turning to me, "Excuse me, excuse us. Unfortunately, my sister always tends to put the business of our family and childhood in the public eye." Isabelle sighed, took another sip of tea and slowly began to wrap some tobacco in a rolling paper. Pauline merely shook her head in disapproval, probably both at her sister's vice and her defence of her mother. Still, then, thoughtfully, she dared not retort.

I stood up, listening only partially to the discussion between the two, broke the silence that had suddenly plunged into the dark room with a few curt thanks, said my goodbyes, and looked to the maid to escort me to the door, away from the recriminations of the two Vernets. I needed to think calmly, to put all that chatter in order and derive from it a trail to move forward. The two women greeted me without even sketching a smile or gesturing to get up, and I left accompanied at every step by the creaking of the old parquet floor.

My eyes had become accustomed to the dimness of the Vernet house, and when I walked out the door, the sun almost dazzled me. I decided to take a walk through the center of Paris and walked toward the Seine promenade. After a few meters, I heard myself call. Turning around, I saw Mehdi running toward me, a little breathless. "So, how did it go?"

"What are you doing here?" I asked him, but I knew he wanted me to feel he was always there for me. However, as he answered me that he had not been able to resist and that as soon as he had freed himself, he had run to Rue du Bac hoping to intercept me. He had a slightly more uncertain smile than usual. We walked together, passed the Gare d'Orsay, and crossed the river, looking at the sparkle of that wonderful city.

I told him that the Vernet sisters had no idea that that little brother of theirs who died shortly before they were born was not actually the natural child of Françoise and Maurice and that if I wanted to find out more about that child, adopted and then abandoned in Algeria, I would have to go to Switzerland, to the Engadine and start from scratch. Maybe I could have inquired about orphanages that housed children during the war and searched, like a needle in a haystack, for traces of my father's origins. Or I could have given up, as part of me would have liked, and returned to Algiers with the bit of information I had gathered. Mehdi walked beside me, strangely silent. He seemed to be not listening to me and chasing other thoughts; I expected him to inundate me with words and assumptions, cheerfully flaunting his proverbial optimism, but instead, he seemed distant. When I stopped talking, I noticed that, step by step, the space between us had filled with anticipation. I strolled around absorbedly, fiddling with an unlit cigarette between my fingers, now thinking back to my conversation with the Vernet sisters, trying to decipher Mehdi's oblique gaze.

As we reached Place de la Concorde, I felt the absolute loneliness and abandonment I had experienced at the airport. I opened my mouth and drew a deep breath, lifting my rib cage as high as I could, then coughed briefly as if I had been out of breath for a moment. The Parisian traffic closed in a noisy, chaotic knot, with no order around the obelisk. I felt as lost and foreign as ever. I rummaged in my bag for my lighter. "Mehdi, how are you?" I found no more original words to break that silence, to try to retrieve Mehdi and bring him back to me from the faraway place where he was.

Mehdi simply told me he was working hard and hoped to gather all the material in the next few weeks and begin editing.

"How are you doing at your aunt and uncle's?" I asked him again, looking for a topic that would loosen the conversation and restore our usual confidence.

"I moved in with a French friend, to her house." He said it quickly, as if confessing.

I stopped at a red light without really knowing what to say.

"I'm glad," I said, looking toward the traffic light, not wanting to let the small weight I felt pressing on my chest to show through.

"Hey, she's just a friend."

" Mehdi, you don't have to worry. I'm happy for you, really. And anyway, I think I'm going to leave soon."

"And where will you go?" he asked in a tone that seemed to evoke the concern of my older childhood friend. I did not know, perhaps to Switzerland or, more likely, to Algeria. I merely shrugged. I was not jealous, just a little lonelier. Besides, hadn't I wanted Mehdi to stop taking care of me? Hadn't I wanted to feel independent and try to fend for myself without anyone's help?

We had arrived near the bistro. I checked the time on my cell phone; I had to go. We looked into each other's eyes and laughed. Perhaps we both, at the same instant, thought back to the afternoons we had spent together as children. Maybe laughing was the way we had found to say that, even if it came time to go our separate ways, we would always be there for each other. We hugged each other tightly, and I felt relieved. Something had changed between us, but nothing was lost.

As soon as I saw him turn around, I crossed the street, and a car, passing too close to the curb at great speed, brushed past me.

I entered the bistro where Madame Gourmand was already preparing dinner. Hot and ruby in her apron, she was busying herself between the counter, the tables, and the kitchen. She told me there was no time now, but I would tell her about it later. I set to work, not ceasing to repeat endlessly to myself every single word Isabelle and Pauline spoke. Once the place was closed, Madame, passing the rag on the counter, raised a questioning look at me. "Well?"

I told her everything straight.

"You absolutely must go to Switzerland!"

"I only have a visa to stay here, not to go to Switzerland!"

Thérèse looked at her thoughtfully, then brightened, "You need to find a job for the summer in Switzerland!"

"That would be easy, Madame!"

"Tomorrow morning, let's go together to Marc, the guy from the seasonal jobs agency. He sends young people halfway around the world who want to find a job abroad, maybe to deepen their language or gain experience...."

"I saw that the place where I should go is called Sankt Moritz; it is in Engadine, a region of Switzerland where German is spoken. I know little German. I only took a course during the first two years of college and have never spoken it..."

"You'll improve if you have to," Thérèse answered with an irresistible smile. "Now eat something and go to sleep. Tomorrow, you will feel more confident." I dared not retort, but I was not so optimistic.

I listlessly made a sandwich and sat on a stool, eating it in small bites, fiddling with the corner of the pink paper napkin Thérèse had handed me. "Don't you think I should go home? After all, if my father was adopted in Switzerland during the war, it would be impossible to trace who his parents were..."

"Oh, no, you must not return without results! You must give it a try. You owe it to your father and yourself. You've come this far; don't give up now," Madame pleaded, wrinkling her forehead and throwing her head slightly back.

I rested my chin on my right hand and, exhausted, sighed, "Thank you, Madame; Paris would have been even harder for me without you. I'm going to sleep."

I remembered my father's words, "You have to be systematic, Samar, sift through those archives sheet by sheet." I underlined the words Engadine, Sankt Moritz, and Sils Maria several times, almost leaving grooves on the paper. Then, I tried to fall asleep.

The next day, Madame Gourmand got me out of bed early and hung the sign on the door of the club:

CLOSED BECAUSE MADAME IS BUSY. SEE YOU TODAY AT LUNCH!
HAVE A GOOD DAY EVEN IF IT STARTS WITHOUT MY CROISSANTS!

I smiled as I read it and meekly followed Madame. We did not travel far and quickly reached the agency of Marc, a nice guy with red-rimmed glasses, a garish shirt and friendly manners.

"What a pleasure, Thérèse! Who have you brought me?"

"This is Samar, a friend of mine. She would like to find a job for the summer in Engadine."

Marc frowned, unbuttoning the cuff of his fuchsia shirt and rolling his right sleeve over his arm. I seemed to read in the boy's eyes what he was thinking, namely my inadequacy, petite and shy as I was, to work in the exclusive Swiss hotels.

"Are you studying German, Samar? We could look for something in Germany, in Munich or Berlin...."

"No," Thérèse intervened before I could open my mouth, "she wants to go right there, to Switzerland. And yes, she studied German."

"But my dear, the hotels in Engadine are very demanding; they are mostly luxury hotels, and I don't think they would hire a girl who doesn't speak the language well for the season."

I heard Thérèse's thoughts running through her mind at lightning speed, looking for a solution.

"But she speaks Arabic, she is Arab. There must be some big hotel hosting rich people from those countries."

Marc smiled first at me and then at Thérèse, looking, without finding it, for a way to say no to that woman of infectious cheerfulness, who, he knew, never gave up when she was passionate about a cause.

"And that's fine. I'll try, but I can't guarantee success. Currently, many big hotels are looking for staff for the season. If we want to focus on the Arab, obviously, we have to start with the exclusive ones, the five-star ones." He began to look around the Internet. I could see the screen reflected in her glasses. Madame Gourmand kept looking at me to reassure me.

"I know there is a village called Sils Maria in the valley," I said, thinking of the strange name of the place where Françoise Vernet had not allowed her daughters to go skiing as girls.

"I would focus on Sankt Moritz, where there are as many as four five-star hotels, which hire more seasonal staff and are more likely to be interested in Arabic as well, although honestly, that's a request I've never had...." Somewhat disappointed that I could not go to that place with the strange name I had diligently jotted down in talking to the Vernet sisters, I was distracted by the hum of the printer that threw out a short list of hotels and addresses.

Madame Gourmand held me close for a moment, leaned back in her chair, and wrapped her left arm around me. "Aren't you happy, dear?"

"Yes, of course, thank you," I replied, wondering how I would manage. I felt like running away, buying a ticket to Algiers that evening. Perhaps I had believed in myself too much. I had dreamed of leaving Algeria for France and Paris for years, and now that I was there, just where I had always wanted to be, I felt only a great sense of foreignness. At that precise moment, I focused on that feeling, and I told myself that perhaps my mother's longed-for marriage and the handicraft business of making candles could be a pleasant refuge, a peaceful retreat for me.

However, I did not dare to back down, and when Marc asked me to answer some questions and fill out a resume outline, I meekly obeyed.

Finally, Marc presented me with a paper to sign. I quickly scrolled through it and immediately read, "Fluent German."

"But my German – I don't know if I would call it fluent, Marc, let's say it's just enough, conversational," I protested then, increasingly agitated.

"Prepare your answers to the questions you are sure they will ask," he smiled, handing me a document that was supposed to guide me through that kind of interview.

I looked questioningly at Thérèse, who immediately encouraged me, "Sign, jump in, don't be afraid. At most, they'll take it out on Marc," she chirped while the boy huffed and smiled at the same time, waving his right hand as if to chase away a fly. "I'll let you know the day and time of the interviews, Samar." He said this by extending his right hand to me, which I shook with gratitude but also with a bit of fear.

That evening, the phone rang, Marc's singsong voice announcing that I was expected Saturday at the Majestic and two other hotels in Sankt Moritz. I tried to reply, but Marc greeted me cheerfully and hung up quickly.

Madame Gourmand paid for the ticket for the trip. I would leave on Friday afternoon and sleep on the train.

On Friday, having finished serving lunch, Madame wanted at all costs to accompany me to the station: she hung one of her signs on the glass door of the bistro:

TONIGHT, WE ARE CLOSED. COME IN THE MORNING, AND YOU WILL FIND MY CROISSANTS.

I remained silent because I was too afraid to hear the tremor in my voice and utter words that might betray the genuine panic. Thinking about what lay ahead of me, I feared that I would get stuck in the metro and no longer be able to move a step. I felt my legs getting heavier and heavier and a strange chill down my spine. The ceiling felt too low and oppressive, and my breathing was short. I tried to concentrate on counting the minutes between stops to deceive the negative feelings that gripped me. Arriving in front of the Gare de Lyon, Madame hugged me and took something wrapped in tissue paper out of her bag. She handed it to me.

"But Madame, what is it?"

"Open it!" I gently lifted the paper flaps, peeling off the bits of tape, and found a very soft yellow cashmere sweater. "It's cold in Switzerland. Not that it's always sunny in Paris, but you're going almost two thousand meters!"

"Thank you, Madame!" I spread my arms wide to hold Thérèse. I felt her buxom breasts against me and kissed her plump cheek with élan. I noticed her emotion and had a knot in my throat. "Now I'm going to set the place up for tomorrow morning; as of today, I am alone again...." She rolled her eyes and, a little dejected, walked away, leaving me at the platform, trolley in one hand, cigarette packet clutched in the other, yellow sweater on one arm, and a green bag slung over my shoulder.

Before boarding the train, I searched for my home number in my cell phone's address book. I hesitated a moment, I was sure they would be worried; Switzerland was somehow even less familiar to them than France, but it didn't seem right that they didn't even know where I was going. Mom answered as usual, she was strangely in a good mood because the doctor had found Dad "stable," certainly not improved, because that was impossible, but as if suspended in a balance of his own, however precarious. I told her I could hardly be on the phone and was about to leave for Switzerland. A long silence followed, which I dared not interrupt. Then she said only, "Be careful," but she did so with a certain fragility in her voice and genuine apprehension. I tried to reassure her, and as I boarded the train, I thought Mother's attitude toward me was not one of hostility but stemmed from her desire to protect me, or rather, her desire to see me happy and respect social conventions. I did not ask to talk to Dad as I usually would have so she would not think I did not care to speak to her.

I wondered if I should call Mehdi, but I didn't. I had to be alone for this new adventure. I would only notify him if I returned with something in hand. Like a few days earlier toward Provence, the landscape began to flow out the window, slowly at first, then faster and faster.

CECILIA

4

Engadine, 2010

At the same time that Samar was entering Marc's agency, Cecilia Alesini had finally arrived in Sils Maria. Now into old age, she knew she would not have much longer. She wanted to spend as much time as possible in the only place where she felt she truly belonged, the only corner of the world that contained her life's emotions and sorrows. Every year, contrary to the opinions of her doctors – including Albert, the Swiss cardiologist who followed her during the periods when she was on vacation in the Engadine, who advised her against going to the mountains at that height with her ailing heart – Cecilia felt that she still had too many unfinished accounts with life and that only there, with that cobalt blue lake and the slopes of the mountains covered with dark forests and the meadows dotted with flowers, could she close the circle and find, perhaps, some meaning to her existence. Loving that place had always been easier for her than loving the people whose lives had, over the years, become intertwined with hers. Only there, during the war, had she truly experienced what love was.

That year, she had decided to anticipate her stay in Sils and had not waited until summer. It was April, but the air was still cool, and a few patches of snow persisted in the shady areas. When the driver pulled up in front of the hotel entrance, Cecilia felt, as she did every time, great excitement and, at the same time, poignancy for the past that was gone forever. Spending long days there helped her stay connected to that past and those she had loved and lost irrevocably. The Brunne family, who now ran the hotel, were the owners' grandchildren at the time and knew nothing of her history. Cecilia felt almost compelled to go up there, to confront what she had done and what had happened. She had returned every year, for decades, in the secret hope of making peace with herself, of understanding what exactly had indelibly marked her life.

While she was lost in these thoughts, the driver unloaded the many suitcases. Then he opened her door and helped her put on her mink coat. She got out, grabbed the cane from the mother-of-pearl knob the man handed her, and began to slowly climb the steps leading to the entrance and the revolving door. She loved the fact that nothing had changed in all those years. She had not changed either: in her soul, she was still the same brave and indomitable girl everyone knew, and even her age had not made a dent on her character.

Leaving her bags with a bellhop, the driver greeted her with mock politeness and an imperceptible nod and left. He would return for her when she asked.

Once inside, Cecilia held her thin hand to the young man at the reception desk. He had been working there briefly, and he was kind. Of course, Marco was more elegant, more gentlemanly, more old-fashioned. Still, the hostility, disguised as matter-of-fact politeness that he had always shown her because of the events that happened then, did not make her regret Marco.

Even now that she was over ninety, it would not have been difficult for those who had known her seventy years earlier to find in her movements and features the young woman who had entered the same hall. Looking at her today, anyone would have remembered the petite girl with blue eyes and long, straight blond hair. As then, she was still a woman who knew no other dimension than loneliness. After all, her mother had died when she was still a child, her father had thrown himself under a train as a result of bad business dealings when she was a young girl, and she had grown up in Milan in a boarding school of nuns for orphans. She had, by necessity, learnt to fend for herself as a child, developing a great desire for redemption as she thought about her future. A few times, the orphans were forced to attend funerals of important figures, locked in their little black dresses, pitting rosaries with their fingers in a sad choreography. On those occasions, Cecilia would look at the ladies and their jewellery, their dresses made of precious fabrics, and told herself, murmuring as if she were intent on prayer, that she, too, would be like that one day. She was used to repressing her emotions, just as it had always been imposed on her, first by the roughness of her young life and then by the nuns. She had never been a misbehaving child. She sensed that to enter high society circles, as she dreamed, she had to acquire the impeccable manners of the ladies she admired. She read widely but struggled to understand some of the passionate and romantic characters in the novels she sometimes discovered in the college's large library. She was accustomed not to allow emotions to move her; she could keep them well locked inside her, so deep inside that she had forgotten their taste.

 She was good at school; discipline and hard work would later enable her to be free and have everything she wanted. Feelings seemed like a weakness she did not want to allow herself. When her classmates began to talk about love, she stood aside, dreaming of a different future of independence and freedom. When she turned eighteen, the nuns informed her that she could no longer stay there, except for a few months: just enough time to get a job. If the idea of leaving relieved and excited her, Cecilia carried high hopes. She dreamed of employment different from her peers, who aspired to be waitresses or sales clerks. One day, however, they proposed that she be an assistant to two great seamstresses. She, who, despite the sisters' efforts, had no skill with needle and thread, hesitated at first, then thought that, perhaps, this was the opportunity she had been waiting for. And so, gathering her few belongings into a suitcase, she moved into the small room above the downtown tailor's shop, where so many ladies of Milan's affluent took turns. Wives of hierarchs and men of power. One day, Emilio Alesini entered the tailor's shop. He was a polite, shy and gallant boy with long dark eyelashes and curly black hair. He was accompanying his mother, a wealthy lady and wife of an industrialist very close to the fascist regime. As soon as she saw him, Cecilia decided that he would become her husband.

With the feeling that would be her last arrival in Sils, Cecilia slipped the key into the lock of Room 225, as usual, as in the fall of 1943, at the height of the war. The memories flowed vividly, without interruption, as if watching the same film every year, an old black and white film, was an inevitable condemnation, a way to atone for her sins. Almost seventy years had passed since she first entered the hotel. She had not gotten there so comfortably then. There was war, and Switzerland was reluctant to take in too many refugees from the rest of Europe. But she was young and brave, and nothing could stop her.

5

Engadine, 1943

Cecilia had fallen through the net. On that freezing night, she had succeeded. Fortunately, her husband had arranged every detail through some of his contacts helping the thousands of people seeking refuge to cross the Swiss border to the only remnant of peace left in the heart of Europe.

Emilio Alesini did not want to leave his beloved wife in Milan. Especially now that she was expecting a child. Cecilia repeated to herself that the baby had served a purpose: at least her husband had decided to let her get away. Of course, with that escape into the night, that running and freezing, it seemed unbelievable to her that the little one was still standing there, too bulky a weight in her belly. She did not want him. She had never wanted him. And she had not been able to fully share Emilio's excitement at the news.

However, she had been pleasantly surprised when he had begun to make arrangements for her departure.

The truth was that after the early days when being loved was a great novelty, Cecilia realized that Emilio was a good but boring man, and she could not stand boredom. He could not stand up to her and would indulge her every desire. Any provocation or request from Cecilia was met with nothing but a meek smile. Initially, she had been pleased with so much love;

she was not used to being loved, and it had been so intoxicating that she had looked for nothing else but then never meeting any curb to her own demands, never having anything to conquer, no success to earn, had made Emilio much less interesting in her eyes: was it possible that he could not take a clear stand, to assert himself? He went from pleasing his mother to pleasing her without a flicker of impulsiveness, of imagination, a sudden decision. Everything in Emilio's world was orderly and precise, planned, but his desire for order never translated into imposing it on others; if he found disorganization, he would escape it to where he could feel comfortable. If someone wronged him, he would stand aside; if someone pushed to pass first, he would gallantly give way. When faced with injustice, he would rather pay than fight. He said losing out was better than engaging in long battles and that his peace of mind was priceless. Behind the tortoiseshell-rimmed glasses, his eyes expressed all the politeness and goodness of an extremely decent man. The wavy hair was the only jarring note, and Cecilia was sure he would have preferred it straight and easily combed. Perhaps that's why he persisted with Brylcreem gel: to have no detail escape his little world. Every morning, he would do his tie in front of the antechamber mirror, always the same precise gestures, in a flawless knot. It seemed to Cecilia that he followed the same movements every day to the millimetre. Even on the morning of her departure. The routine reassured him, while she, who by marrying him thought she would have an extremely bright life, realized more and more every day that no amount of wealth could buy her and that only a different character, more passionate, more adventurous, more unpredictable, could help her to find within herself all that she had striven for years to keep at bay. In short, to be happy. And Cecilia ended up forgetting his goodness, his kindness, his love. She realized day after day, with amazement, that love was not enough and could not reach the most vibrant and genuine part of her. And she felt herself sinking into a sense of boredom, immobility that she had never expected in what she had imagined as a happy life, which would make her find a new self. Despite that love given to her without reservation, she felt as cold as she had always been; nothing inside her stirred, and he had no strength to reach her. She realized she could not blame him for this but could not forgive him either.

Sure, he had worldliness and wealth but lacked imagination and real fun. He would attend the social evenings with his phlegm, be attentive to chat with everyone, not leaving anyone out, participate in the small talk, and then, at the same time, after saying goodbye, he would leave, taking Cecilia by the hand, who at that point was eager to go home and wondered why she had wasted so much time getting ready.

At that moment, however, she was grateful to her husband for thinking everything through and leaving nothing to chance, probably precisely because of his meticulousness and perfectionism: she would be helped by a customs officer and reach the Engadine, in a place called Sils Maria, which seemed a nice place. Not that Cecilia loved the mountains, but certainly, with the war, Milan was unliveable. Especially since, in Sils, she would be staying in a reportedly beautiful hotel where time seemed to stand still. She had just been able to look out on a lighter life than she had known until then, and the war had come, with its harshness, renunciations and sacrifices, taking everything away. She knew she was selfish, but it seemed she had suffered enough already.

"Now let's think about getting to our destination," she had thought as soon as she felt safe in Switzerland, "and then we'll think about everything else."

A car had come to pick her up. She had then spent a night somewhere near Lugano, and the following day, the same car picked her up and drove her to her destination.

The journey had lasted several hours, but Cecilia had not spoken to the man driving. She found him absolutely anonymous, not worthy of the slightest interest, as long as he drove well.

The constant turns had made her nauseous, but she gritted her teeth and held on: she did not want to stop; she wanted to get to Sils. Looking out the window, she already felt like she was at peace. Milan had become bleak. Cecilia hated the curfew and the difficulties in finding food. At the same time, social evenings were now almost just a reason to feel guilty. In Milan, war loomed every moment of the day; it hung in the air. And she, who was then twenty-five years old and had already experienced the harshness of life, now believed she had arrived at a haven of quiet. Instead, there was nothing but talk of the dead, the maimed, and the destroyed cities as the sirens forced her down into that fetid cellar and onto the damp floor next to her neighbours. She had not married Emilio to lead that life.

There, in Switzerland, just a few kilometres from the border, everything looked different. Quiet. Maybe she would never have to hear of death and destruction again. Perhaps she would be able to live again.

Around noon, the car reached the Maloja Pass. The sky, previously overcast, had become clear. To the right, the blue lake of Sils sparkled in the sun as a few white sails sailed across that lapis lazuli blue. On the slopes of the mountains, thick with dark pines, the light green grasses around the still lake looked like soft waves under the touch of the wind. A small peninsula was nestled on the lake, while just where the road to the village began were a few white houses that did nothing to detract from the magic of the place. Painted a pale pink, stood in a commanding position at the hotel where Cecilia was expected. She recognized it immediately: Emilio had described it to her over and over again. She had never listened to him carefully until he started telling her about it as his possible destination. Emilio wanted his son to be safely born. His wife to be safe, pampered by the hotel staff where he had spent the long summers of his childhood and where time had stood still, where the war would never make its echoes heard.

She got out of the car, nodding only in greeting to the man who had driven her there, then moved to the trunk, but she had nothing with her but the rumpled travel bag she had been clutching the whole time. She had gone through a hole in the net; her evening clothes had remained in Milan. At that thought, she paused, pulled out a small powder case and fixed her face with a few quick gestures. Then she looked at the entrance to the Hotel Maria. A few steps led to a solid wooden revolving door. She climbed the stairs after motioning the driver to go.

She slipped in through the door and pushed it open. Once inside, she paused for a few moments and looked around; there was no doubt that her husband had found the right place for her. She would be fine in that place, very fine.

Cecilia's lace-up shoes sank into the soft Persian carpets lying in the spacious entrance hall. On the right, a wooden counter with a black telephone profiled in highly polished brass above it and the many little boxes inside which hung, each in its own space, the keys to the rooms, with the key ring shaped like a large M, the initial of the hotel's name, Maria. Beyond the boxes, a small room, probably the concierge's office, could be glimpsed. Next to the counter on the left instead started a long staircase with a finely wrought iron railing. Cecilia looked ahead as she wondered about the key to the room intended for her. Beyond a wide crystal door opened an immense drawing-room, topped by the largest chandelier she had ever seen. The countless armchairs, carefully arranged in front of small walnut tables, were all but empty except for one, placed at the end of the room, next to the large circular window overlooking the woods. Cecilia, from the doorway, where she had been standing for a few minutes now, glimpsed the profile of a man intent on reading a book as his fair hair fell over his forehead. That image made her feel at home. But the moment was immediately interrupted by a gust of icy air and a male voice behind her. Cecilia turned around, and a gentleman in his sixties, tall and large square glasses, the friendly air, approached her, "I am Marco, the concierge of the hotel that, from today, will be your home," the man's face opened in a wide smile and, with an unmistakably Tuscan accent, he continued, "Welcome Mrs. Alesini." Cecilia reclined her head slightly, studying who was in front of her. It had to be the man her husband had told her about, the Italian doorman who had been working in Switzerland for a lifetime. She felt she could trust him, and taking off her leather glove after undoing the golden button, she reached out to him with her thin, off-white hand.

"We would have liked to have had you here at another time, ma'am, when we welcome people on vacation, not people fleeing war. But I'm sure you will still be comfortable with us. Herr Brunne and his wife Monika, the owners of this magnificent place where I had worked since the beginning of the century when I was a boy, try to carry it on, despite the war, keeping the rhythms and traditions of the hotel intact. This is home to them and their eight children, and they wish that serenity will not be lost despite the atmosphere into which Europe has sunk for too long now." On hearing of the presence of eight children, Cecilia smiled, simulating the smug look full of tenderness that her peers typically had in such cases. Still, inside, she thought it was madness. How could anyone bring eight children into the world? At the very least, she thought, if this Frau Brunne has had so many children, she will know how to deliver them and will be able to help me out when, supposedly in five months, the time comes. "Well, Marco, I am curious to meet Mr. and Mrs. Brunne and their offspring, but now I would like to be able to go to my room. The journey has been long and, as you can imagine, also too adventurous for a woman in my condition," she murmured, brushing her fingers over her only just-rounded belly. Evidently, that gesture had worked well, so to speak, 'appropriate'. Marco approached her with great thoughtfulness and gently took the bag from her hand.

"Lapo! Lapo, come here; you have to accompany a lady to room 225 on the second floor!" Out of the small door behind the counter popped the ash-blond, shaggy head of a little boy with somewhat shifty light eyes. "This is my son Lapo; he helps me at the hotel." Cecilia frowned at him as if something was amiss. The boy briefly uttered a greeting without looking away from the keyboard. "He's a good boy, ma'am; my wife gave birth to him and left shortly after; she was just forty-two then. He is fifteen, though in some ways, he looks much younger. One part of his mind stopped at a certain point, no one has ever understood why, while another part has developed enormously: he remembers perfectly all the names, birthday dates and passport numbers of anyone who passes through here, even for a single night" – she then smiled fondly. " He is happy here. These mountains and the lake are enough for him, he does not need more." Cecilia watched momentarily as the silent little boy looked down at his toes and walked toward the stairs behind him. As she climbed the first two steps, she rested her right hand on the handrail and turned to Marco, who watched her from the lobby, "Who is the man sitting at the end of the hall with a book in his hand?" Marco smiled as if Cecilia had asked him about an old friend: "It is Mr. Ashton, ma'am, our English guest." Cecilia was dying to ask what an Englishman was doing there in the Swiss mountains. Still, she did not want to give it away and, turning again, continued up the stairs behind young Lapo.

Arriving on the second floor, Lapo and Cecilia walked down a long corridor from the red walkway. The boy stopped before the last door on the right and introduced the large key into the lock. He slipped into the room bathed in half-light and peeled back the thick yellow brocade curtains from the large windows. Immediately, a beam of the brightest light came in through the windows and illuminated the large hexagonal-shaped space. On the right, a small sitting room opened with an armchair, an inlaid coffee table, a standing lamp, and a fireplace surmounted by a trophy of deer antlers. On the left, a door led into a snow-white bathroom with a beautiful ceramic tub with feet and gilded faucets. Cecilia appreciated the lovely room, with its three windows overlooking the endless prairie that veered from green to the warmer colours of autumn and ended in the blue lake. It was furnished with a light-coloured wooden closet decorated with Art Nouveau-style flowers, a bed with a satin backboard as yellow as the curtains, and a soft, puffy white comforter on top. On the walls, pale blue wallpaper and a series of watercolours in delicate tones. Cecilia had a flicker of happiness; she would have liked to throw herself down on the comforter and bathe her face in the warmth of the goose-feather pillow. But she maintained her usual demeanour and dismissed Lapo, "Thank you, the room will be fine."

"It's one of the most beautiful ones we have," the boy replied, stammering slightly.

Cecilia had no trouble believing it; it looked gorgeous. "Just one thing," she replied ruefully; however, "please remove that trophy from the parlour; I don't want anything dead here."

The boy nodded, backing toward the door without looking back. "And fetch me some salts and soap; I'd like to bathe if possible." Lapo nodded again as he opened the door. He hastily greeted her and quickly went out. Cecilia waited to hear the door click and looked around smugly. That place was great, she would fit right in. She would think about childbirth in a few months. That thought made her anxious, and she pushed it back, feeling a little guilty: she would have managed like all women always do; she would have managed too, even if she did not feel the desire to become the mother of the baby growing inside her. She slipped off her shoes without sitting down and, with a leap, was on the bed. Her clothes were muddy and worn from the trip, but if she had soiled the sheets, she would have had them changed. Now, she would also have to find a way to get her clothes from Milan up there. She looked up at the coffered ceiling. There, in that place, far from the war, her life was beginning again.

Spending her time between the soft bed and the cosy armchair by the fireplace, Cecilia had waited three days in Sils for before deciding to leave her room. When she needed something, she pressed the special switch on the bedside table, and in minutes, Franciszka, the petite maid with the smoothest red hair, showed up. Cecilia liked that the girl not much younger than herself never uttered a word more than necessary. Her little redhead with a starched lace peeped through the door whenever Cecilia rang and retreated as soon as she had ordered what she needed: boiling water for washing, soap, tea, a snack, a glass of milk or a cup of chocolate.

However, Cecilia felt like coming out of that state of torpor and loneliness and participating in the hotel's life. Indeed, everything seemed to take place there as if amid a vacation season. Meals were served in the large dining room on tables impeccably set with fine china plates, crystal glasses and silver cutlery. Every afternoon, guests were allowed to have tea in the main hall, and Franciszka brought a trolley of sweets to accompany it. Once a month, a pianist, a cellist, and a violinist entertained the guests. Some danced while others spent their time in the large, heated swimming pool, from whose windows one could see the surrounding forest. Marco, the concierge, explained this to her when he had gone to her room to personally deliver an initial letter from her husband. She had taken it, feigning more surprise and joy than she felt, placed it on the bedside table, and invited Marco in. She had asked him everything she wanted to know about the guests she wanted to meet and the customs of the hotel.

After Marco left, Cecilia opened her husband's letter, wondering how he had made it from Italy so quickly. She had recognized his straightforward, precise writing.

It was only a few lines:

> My beloved Cecilia,
> I miss you more and more every day, and I hope to catch up with you soon, at least for a few days. But, as you know, leaving and crossing the border is not easy. And anyway, I can't afford to leave the steel mills for too long.
> I hope the trip, though uncomfortable, went well and that you feel at home there.

I look forward to embracing you and your womb with our little creature.

I will try to get you a trunk with some extra clothes through my contacts at the border.

Always yours,

Emilio.

As she folded the letter, Cecilia could not rejoice at the idea that Emilio could join her there. It was unfair to him, who had sent her there to protect her, but now that she was away, she did not miss him and had the impression that she had already built a new dimension in which he wasn't present.

She had just decided that she would leave the room the next day. She had gone to the closet and pulled out the few clothes she had stuffed into the leather bag she had arrived with: a white blouse with a bow around the neck, a black cloth skirt, a pair of silk stockings, and a thick woollen shawl. As for shoes, she would have to make do with the lace-up ones she had arrived in. She pressed the bell and handed everything to Franciszka's diligent hands, "Try to refresh these clothes for me, if you can, and clean my shoes." The girl nodded and wandered off into the dark hallway. The next day, fully dressed, Cecilia looked at herself in the mirror. A little powder and red lipstick would make her look almost perfect. She couldn't wait for Emilio to get her trunk with her clothes and at least some of her jewellery. Now, however, was time to meet the other guests, before her belly would make it impossible for her to tie her skirt.

Cecilia descended the stairs slowly, her white fingers brushing against the wrought-iron handrail. She had almost reached the end of the staircase when she saw the fair-haired man she had noticed when she arrived. He stood with his hands in the pockets of his dark pants and clasped an unlit cigar between his lips. A short time later, he looked up and, taking the Cuban with his left hand, stepped toward her, extending his right hand. His face, with marked features, widened into a broad smile. "Madam, you have disappeared since your fleeting appearance three days ago."

On meeting the man's blue eyes, Cecilia instinctively contracted her abdomen and stretched out her hand in turn, "Cecilia Alesini."

"James Ashton," he replied.

It was then that Cecilia began to desire him. She would have him for herself, no matter what. At that same instant, James Ashton, an English journalist and photographer, knew this slim woman with fair skin and very blond hair would be his. And the fact that she was pregnant, a detail that had indeed not escaped him despite her obvious attempt to conceal it, would only require a little patience. The war would still be long, very long.

Marco, the concierge, a family friend of Emilio Alesini's, watched the scene from his station and thought that nothing good would come of it. Lapo, sitting in the office, separated from the reception desk, had finished at that instant adjusting a component of the small radio that he and his father occasionally used to listen to some music. He would not be distracted until he finished his work with infinite precision. When he polished the last valve, he closed the device with the small screwdriver he always carried. Then, he looked up at the key grate. Each time he looked at it, he could not resist the temptation to memorize, with a brief glance, which ones were missing. Certainly not because he cared to know who was in the room and who was not, but simply out of a desire, or even a need, to reconstruct in a flash any interrupted sequence. At that moment, he saw the lady he had accompanied a few days earlier to Room 225 through the grate on which the keys were hanging. She was standing in front of the English photographer. And Lapo was surprised to notice a slight tremor in her hand. He was hardly mistaken about people and would never have guessed anything in that cold woman could vibrate.

After the first few jokes exchanged with her at the bottom of the stairs, James had gently brushed Cecilia's back, leading her toward the large living room where, at that hour, tea was served. Passing through the glass door, she felt the warmth of the room and the faint whiff of the wax that, Franciszka, had probably given to the ancient, highly polished parquet peeping out between one carpet and another. There were at least thirty small tables, some round, some square, and only a few were occupied. Cecilia did not have time to observe who was about to have tea beside her since James motioned for her to sit in a small armchair, which she hastened to scoot over right next to the bow window overlooking the woods. She had not blinked, had sat meekly, gripped by an incredible excitement: she sensed his personality. She was dominated by it, as never before. Of course, she would not let him see it, but she felt less strong than the man in front of her, vulnerable and naked.

"You are lost in thought. What is it you are chasing?" he asked, in perfect Italian with a strong English accent.

She winced slightly, praying inwardly that he had not sensed what was going through her mind. Then, she regained her composure and flashed one of her best smiles, lighting up her face and slightly hollowing out the dimples in her cheeks. "I was wondering how you knew I'm Italian."

"When I see a beautiful woman, I always ask for information," he said, glancing at Marco, who had just then looked away from them to arrange some papers on his counter.

Part of Cecilia rejoiced to know that he, too, had noticed her a few days earlier, but she decided to feign annoyance at that stranger's curiosity and Marco's indiscretion, "Then they must have also told you that I am married."

"Of course," James replied with a smile, "and also that you are expecting a child, for that matter, which in any case, despite your best efforts, does not go unnoticed."

The reference to pregnancy made her uncomfortable. She stood up nervously, turned around and made to leave, not caring about Franciszka, who had just approached them with the dessert cart.

"Cecilia!" James called, also heedless of the girl who pretended, embarrassed by the scene, to arrange some cutlery on the bottom shelf of the cart. Cecilia turned slightly, and he added, "Are you familiar with Francis Scott Fitzgerald's novel *The Great Gatsby*? I brought a copy of the original American first edition of 1925 to the library."

She rolled her eyes, "No, nor do I care."

"You should read it; it would amuse you."

Cecilia sighed, showing indifference, and sat down on the other side of the room, not far from the four joined tables where, in that instant, Brunne's eight children took their seats. Next to those brats, tea that day would be far from what she had pictured. Especially since she had risked showing herself fragile in front of the man. As she tasted a slice of sacher served by Franciszka, Cecilia had the impression that a silent war had begun with that stranger, one which, for the first time in her life, she was not sure she would win.

Shortly thereafter, Cecilia heard a female voice calling her name. As she looked up, she saw a woman in her mid-30s, looking a bit frumpy, with wide hips, hair pulled back into an unmade bun, small eyes, and flushed cheeks, coming toward her.

"I am Monika Brunne, the owner of the hotel. I apologize for not introducing myself sooner, but we had some problems to solve. My husband and I are happy to host you. These days, it really is an island of happiness here." She said it quickly, as if acting. Cecilia seemed to notice something wounded, surrendered, and resigned in her.

Suddenly, as Monika Brunne spoke, Cecilia felt a slimy look upon her, "How do you do? I'm Joseph Brunne," a man thus interrupted his wife by carefully examining Cecilia's body, so much so that she felt almost uncomfortable. He was rough while giving himself the tone of a great gentleman. The well-cut clothes certainly could not hide his real nature from an intelligent woman like Cecilia. The pronounced nose, the too-short stubble, the thick eyebrows, and the off-white hair pulled back with brilliantine revealed a man who was not ugly, but decidedly unattractive.

"I guess you have already seen our children. It's impossible not to notice them, ma'am, isn't it?" laughed Monika, slightly guffawing.

"Of course, what beautiful children," Cecilia replied, without even turning toward the table of little ones, tenaciously forcing herself to exchange a few more words with the not particularly lovely couple.

"I wish you a pleasant stay here with us, Mrs. Alesini," Joseph concluded, glancing at Cecilia's belly. "I know you are expecting a baby, but you need not fear; my wife has baked as many as eight; she and Franciszka, the woman who welcomed you, will know how to help." He said this in a dismissive tone, as if he were talking about a head of cattle, the kind that was raised on the farms around there. Still, Monika did not stiffen or even notice the triviality of the verb her husband used to refer to her parts ("baking") and, turning around, took the knife from Franciszka's hands and began to slice one of the cakes for her children.

After that meeting, Cecilia thought that what Emilio had told her about the Brunnes must be true.

Monika and Joseph had grown up in the hotel. They were, in fact, the children of the two partners who had opened it in the early twentieth century, allocating vast sums of money to refurbish an old, disused building. Monika Brunne's parents then gave the hotel the imprint it retained to the day: a place of luxury, never excessively ostentatious, a house of great style, dedicated to a select and refined clientele. Joseph's father, a widower, had indulged the wishes of his partner and wife, not least because the Maria had become a destination for politicians and intellectuals from half of Europe: business was good, in short, and that was all he cared about.

Monika and Joseph had studied with a governess and had grown up together. After all, Sils Maria was nothing more than a small village with four houses where everyone knew each other. Monika was a sweet, intelligent child with her mother's taste. Joseph was a closed, capricious, overbearing child. However, it was already written as something inevitable and dutiful that they would marry. And so it had been. Monika, with her characteristic docility, had accepted her lifelong friend's marriage proposal: she cared deeply for the hotel that her parents had made with great sacrifice and did not want outsiders to enter management and ruin its unique imprint. Joseph, for his part, was more interested in profit, which, thanks to Monika's skill, would certainly be big. The wedding had been celebrated in the hotel's tiny chapel. Precisely nine months later, Monika had given birth to her first daughter. She was not yet nineteen years old. Over time, she had realized that bringing children into the world, nursing them, and caring for them was the only dimension of marriage in which Joseph could make sense. She had taken motherhood as a mission, a task that she carried out mechanically, without great impetus, but with diligence. Once her parents had entrusted her with the management of the hotel, passing away a few years later, she had continued to run it with her husband as they had done, carrying on its tradition and hoping that her children, or at least some of them, would do the same. Also, as a sign of continuity, Monika decided to carefully retain the valuable staff who had already worked there, first and foremost Marco, the concierge who had long played an essential role far beyond that of a simple concierge. She then had the proper insight into hiring the young Franciszka, the Polish girl assigned to various tasks, including lovingly devoting herself to her children.

Joseph, for his part, saw Monika solely as a mother, a kind of big belly capable of giving birth to his offspring. Despite everything, he delighted in his success with other women. He collected dozens of them, especially among the service girls or among the daughters of local shepherds, who often lent themselves to meet all his demands in exchange for little. Stuff that his saintly wife Monika would not have ever dreamt of. He always had a passkey with him, which he used to take his mistresses to vacant rooms without bothering too much about hiding.

And Monika, in fact, let him. She sensed that she could not satisfy certain cravings of her husband and did not even have the slightest intention of doing so. When her first female daughters had grown up a bit, she had caught, with great disquiet, some of his glimpses of them that she did not like, so she was all the more content that he had other interests and other adventures, and she had made it a point to keep an eye on her daughters.

Monika's beauty, sensitivity, and desires had thus faded. She had become enlarged, almost displaced, and no longer cared for her appearance as a hotel owner of that standard would require. With the outbreak of war, she found an excuse to abandon even the minimal self-care she had maintained. She argued that it was inappropriate to wear makeup or care what one wore in years when the rest of the world was sinking into suffering. By now, in her eyes, the Maria was no longer the refined vacation spot it had been since the turn of the century, but only a refuge for the privileged rich who nevertheless had a duty to keep a low profile, out of respect for the situation.

She was doing what she was supposed to: giving birth, raising children, and managing the Maria as her parents would have wanted. This was her life, and Monika had learned to accept it early, perhaps too early.

From time to time, as she looked at herself in the mirror, she told herself that her mother would suffer significantly from seeing her like this. Partly because of this, upon the arrival of the Italian guest, whom everyone said was beautiful and elegant, she had hesitated to introduce herself.

When she had seen her in the salon, so slim and refined, she had put aside with some effort a painful twinge of jealousy, rejoicing in the short duration of her conversation with her.

Having finished her conversation with the Brunne, Cecilia forced herself not to look in James' direction yet, and when, out of the corner of her eye, she looked for him for a moment, she found that he was no longer there. Her heart, which until that moment had been pounding in her chest, entirely out of control, calmed down. She leaned back in the tiny chair and relaxed, devoting herself to observing the other people around her. The Brunne children continued noisily making their snack; Cecilia looked at all eight of them, one by one. There were the first two girls, ages twelve and eleven, with long blond braids, then the two dark-haired girls, ages nine and six, the two four-year-old twins, and, again, two little ones, ages two and one. Unbelievable.

Not far from her small table sat an ordinary-looking couple of a certain age. Cecilia thought it was the Klimo, the Germans, that Marco had mentioned to her.

And then there were two girls, perhaps slightly younger than her, who pretended to be engaged in dense conversation but were actually, Cecilia had noticed, studying her with ill-concealed curiosity. In fact, Marco had also told her about the two French sisters, Louise and Béatrice Beauvent, hiding in Sils to escape the harshness of the occupation. Of the other people there, about ten or so, Cecilia knew little, probably because they were transient guests looking for different accommodations. Some looked bewildered and lost, their gazes bent over cups of steaming tea. They did not seem to be enjoying the rich snacks. Of those small groups of people, Marco had made no mention.

After serving tea, Franciszka sat at the children's table to help the two little ones with their snacks. Shortly afterwards, Lapo arrived and sat beside her, pressing his hands over his ears as if he did not want to hear the little ones' voices. Franciszka then urged everyone to lower their voices, resting a finger on her lips and adding a rebuke: "You know Lapo can't stand loud noises. Try to speak quieter."

Cecilia decided it was time to go. That was enough for that day.

Walking down the corridor, she strained her ear to figure out where James's room might be, in case she heard his voice. She hoped in her heart that it was on the same floor as 225, but she immediately banished that thought and quickened her pace, quickly slipping the key into the keyhole of his room.

For a few evenings after meeting in the living room, Cecilia carefully avoided James by having dinner brought to her room and going out very little, although she had to admit it cost her a great deal of effort.

One day, she went downstairs and, hoping to meet no one, slipped into the sitting room, where she intended to read a series of volumes stored in a not-so-small bookcase. Perhaps the definition of "library" on a brass plate screwed to the door was a bit of an exaggeration. Still, undoubtedly, there was no shortage of choice. Ceiling-high wooden shelves ran along all the walls and contoured the large windows and front door. The carpets on the floor were in shades of yellow, as were the comfortable armchairs. Fabric lampshades of the same colour diffused a warm light while outside the still landscape of pine trees reconciled silence and absorbed reading. It looked like a corner belonging to another century were it not for the large radio resting on a walnut cabinet with wavy mouldings. With its rounded shapes, polished wood, and four knobs, every night it became the beating heart of the hotel, Marco had explained, proudly pointing out how Lapo was the one who took care of it and intervened in case of breakdowns or technical problems. There he was, trying to pick up Radio London and catch a few words in the endless rustle of the radio waves. Cecilia brushed the polished wood with her fingertips and thought she would rather not have that window to the world and her former life, the real one she would have to return to at some point.

Perhaps this was also why she had not yet participated in the ritual of listening to the radio since her arrival.

Cecilia walked lightly over to the shelves and looked at them for a long time, searching for the volume suggested by James. Scrolling through the ribs of books, she heard a female voice behind her, "Cherchez-vous quelque chose?" Cecilia knew

French well and would have been pleased to be able to show it off. She turned and saw one of the two Parisian sisters. It had to be the younger one, Louise, who, while also fluent in Italian, out of courtesy, had been told to speak in her own language. "No, I'm not looking for anything in particular," Cecilia smiled, "I was just taking a look. I am Cecilia, and you?"

"Louise," the girl answered, showing an imperfect but sunny smile and wrinkling her nose. "It's nice to have a girl our age with us. Are you staying long?"

Cecilia shrugged slightly, "Until the end of the war, if there is ever an end, or at any rate, until the baby is born…"

"Oh, how nice, you are expecting a baby… but that's great! Of course, you will miss your husband very much…"

Cecilia felt mounting within her an uneasiness mixed with guilt that pervaded her every time someone got excited about her waiting for the baby: she just could not be happy about that waiting. Moreover, contrary to what that girl took for granted, she did not miss her husband. But, condescendingly, she murmured, "Yes, of course, but I'm here for the baby, for the baby's sake," uttering the phrase so often sounded by her husband: "for the baby's sake."

"You will see that you will be fine here. We can even become friends! We will forget everything together, and then we can take care of the little one when the time comes."

Cecilia clutched the pit of her stomach and whispered, "Don't run like that; just recommend a good read for now."

Louise began talking to her about French and Russian literature by reaching into the bookcase, pointing, grabbing, and flipping through volumes. Cecilia did not listen to her and continued searching for Fitzgerald's novel. Then, all of a sudden, her gaze landed on the very title she was looking for. "Maybe something light. I see The Great Gatsby there."

Louise looked at her questioningly, "I don't know what this is about, but wouldn't you prefer some good French novels, perhaps? I guess you have met Lapo, the concierge's son: he is the one who keeps the library in order and arranges the books according to rigorous criteria. They are divided by language and genre and placed in alphabetical order…" She rolled her eyes as if it all seemed too complicated and, in fact, added, "Impossible for me to understand that boy. The Klimo clearly thinks he is a fool, and in my opinion, they would be quite happy not to have him here, yet for some things, he is so brilliant…" Without listening to her, Louise continued to speak while Cecilia was already climbing up the ladder and leaning against the shelves. "Be careful, my sister Béa almost fell." But she had already gone down and clutched the volume in her hands. Louise suddenly realized that her chatter was unwelcome and again cheerfully chirped, "I will leave you to your reading then, but this evening we could have dinner together. I will introduce you to my sister, and you can tell us a little about yourselves. And then, perhaps we could call each other by our first names."

"Thank you, with pleasure," Cecilia hastily closed, sinking into a soft armchair far from where Louise sat.

When she opened the book, she saw a folded sheet of very light paper slip into her lap. Instinctively, she looked up to check if the intrusive Louise had noticed it. The girl was already absorbed in her own reading.

She opened it and gasped. She checked again and saw that no one was watching her and read.

I see that you have come looking for the book I recommended. I had no doubt that you would. James.

On the other side of the room, Louise, looking satisfied with the acquaintance she had just made, continued her reading, no longer addressing what she considered a new friend. Admittedly, she had seemed a little unfriendly, but her tendency to always see the good in people had led her to attribute this to being alone and away from her loved ones. She, at least, had Béa with her. She was curious to know what her sister would say about the young Italian, but she was sure she would be annoyed by her presence next to James Ashton.

That very evening, Louise, while preparing for dinner with her sister Béatrice, told her about the young Italian girl.

Béa did not listen to her much: it was typical of her younger sister to get excited about new acquaintances.

"She's wonderful, and she seems nice, too," she told her, setting herself aside to wait for her response. And she had murmured something in assent, in an indifferent tone, just to make her stop. "I think we could become friends," Louise urged her.

As she swiped carmine-red lipstick over her heart-shaped lips, Beatrice replied, "It is not easy to make friends here, and perhaps not even convenient. Soon, the war will end, and we will finally go back to Paris, to Dad. And we'll only come here on vacation, just like before."

Upon arriving in the dining room that evening, Cecilia paused briefly to look around. She immediately heard Louise's voice calling, "Cecilia, we are here! Come to our table!" Cecilia, who had not yet spotted James, turned in the direction of the voice and saw the French girl in a simple green dress, waving. Cecilia hesitated again but decided she could not deny the French sisters her company. Sitting next to Louise was another girl with her dark hair gathered in two thick braids, knotted in turn above her head. More beautiful than her sister, she must also have been a few years older and, indeed, Cecilia assessed, classier. Béa extended a manicured hand to her, hinting only at standing up. Cecilia, shaking that hand and looking into those big dark green eyes, felt slightly uncomfortable and immediately sensed they would never get along.

Louise took to telling about how glittering, happy, and fabulous her and her sister's Parisian life was before the war and how, when German troops had occupied Paris on June 14, 1940, they, finding themselves already in Sils Maria, remained there, while her widowed father, a very wealthy antique dealer, returned to Paris to salvage what could be saved.

While her sister was talking, Béa was studying Cecilia surreptitiously, who, in turn, cast an occasional glance at the entrance to the room so as not to miss the moment when James entered.

"Now eat, Louise," Béa suddenly interrupted her sister with a bored air. Louise, without a word, started meekly swallowing spoonfuls of soup. "Before we left, our father entrusted Louise to me," Béa said, addressing Cecilia as if to justify her attitude. Indeed, Béa seemed much more mature and aware than the clueless Louise.

Louise's eyes lit up with gratitude whenever she mentioned her beloved father. She did not hesitate to say that Béa, in those two years in Switzerland, had taken care of her like the mother she hardly remembered. Listening to her, one had the impression that she relied entirely on her sister. It had not escaped how Louise hung on her every word and made her sister's every opinion her own. After all, even at the table, Louise never chose a dish without first receiving Béa's approval. Cecilia immediately began to wonder to what extent Louise really loved her sister and to what extent, on the other hand, she simply depended on her. She did not seem to dare contradict her or much less criticize her; she only praised her talents, but every now and then, she gave her glances that Cecilia would have called envious. Indeed, Béa's beauty and grace were incomparable, and even if Louise had made an effort to imitate her, as in the colour of her dress, hairstyle and perfume, her blatant attempts were doomed to failure.

As Cecilia thought about the strange relationship between the Parisian sisters, she saw a rather elderly man she had already noticed approaching the table: he sat at another table with his wife, who had remained seated sullenly, squaring the scene nervously from a distance. The man shook Cecilia's hand with a wet and soggy grip and introduced himself as Walter Klimo, giving only a brief nod to the sisters. Then he turned to his wife and introduced her as Danielle. The woman nodded her head without smiling. Just as Cecilia was thinking how to end all those pleasantries with the unpleasant Walter Klimo, a beautiful, smiling brunette woman in her forties came to her rescue: Anna Zeller. A few steps behind her was her mild-looking husband, who had smiled at Cecilia and waited for Anna to introduce him: "This is my husband David, and they," she had added, pointing to two young boys who had just entered the room "are our sons, Andreas and Martin, ages twelve and thirteen. It is a pleasure to meet you; until now, we had not dared to disturb you." Cecilia had immediately felt in tune with Anna Zeller; she had seemed open, sincere, genuine, and somebody who could smile with her whole face. "Can we sit with you?" she asked in French with a strong German accent, looking at Béa and the four empty seats.

"Of course!" replied Louise, moving one of the chairs.

Anna took a seat next to Cecilia and smiled at her again. In the meantime, Walter Klimo abruptly moved aside and, after a moment, without saying goodbye, walked away to join his wife, who was disapprovingly watching the scene, with astonishment, with a grimace of near disgust, or so Cecilia thought.

The evening went on merrily, and Cecilia was grateful for Anna and her family's arrival because Béa made her uncomfortable, and Louise, no matter how hard she tried, could not really provide interesting conversation.

Anna had asked her if she spoke any German, and when Cecilia had said no, she had joked, "What a pity for you, Cecilia, you won't be able to converse with Danielle Klimo…we can call each other by our first names, can't we?" Cecilia laughed immediately, happy to have found complicity in disliking Walter Klimo's wife. "She speaks nothing but German," Anna continued under her breath, "after all, she is so proud of her origins that I don't understand why she didn't stay in Germany…"

"I have never spoken to her; she didn't even introduce herself; as for her husband, he seemed pretty slimy."

"Don't worry; now that they have seen you talking to us, they will stay away from you. We are Jews, and they are of those Germans who despise us."

Cecilia swallowed. They had often talked with Emilio about racial laws in Italy, Jewish friends, and Jews in Germany. To Cecilia, it had seemed absurd, but that, all in all, would never have affected her closely. As far as she was concerned, Anna was the best person she had met since arriving there.

David and the boys, who had sat next to Anna and Cecilia, listened to the conversation. At the same time, Louise and Béa asked the waiter for clarification on the composition of some dishes.

"How long have you been here?" asked Cecilia to start a conversation.

"Too long, too long," David had replied, his gaze veiled with melancholy.

Anna quickly changed the subject: "We could do some German lessons. I taught in Germany and would love to spend a few afternoons in your company. The days are so long sometimes here."

Cecilia enthusiastically welcomed the proposal and escaped Louise's gaze, suddenly clouded with jealousy.

"Are you also coming this evening to listen to Radio London?" Louise asked at the end of the meal. Lapo is great with the radio; he can almost always find the correct frequencies. The Klimo people think he's stupid, but he's actually an absolute genius."

Cecilia did not want to hear about everything she longed to leave behind, so she declined the invitation, saying she preferred to stay in her room that night. She regretted it when she saw Lapo go to the library, followed by James and shortly after by some other hotel guests.

A few days later, returning from a short walk in the woods, Cecilia saw a folded piece of paper in key box 225, opened it, and again faced with that typically masculine, angular but neat handwriting.

I expect you at my table tonight for dinner. James.
PS Have you started the novel I told you about yet?

Cecilia slipped the note into her pocket, determined to pretend she had not even read it. She felt herself flare up, and then, with an indifferent air, without stopping any further, she quickly climbed the stairs, wondering if she would accept the invitation, even though she knew the answer well in her heart.

That evening at the table, James had told her his story in a low, slightly hoarse voice, occasionally running his right hand through his blond hair, which was only slightly greying at the temples. Cecilia noticed once again how his presence filled the entire room, and she could not take her eyes off his thin lips, pronounced nose, and broad shoulders.

He had been born in London, but since he was a young boy, he had dreamed of travelling the world. When his father gave him a Rolleiflex, he knew the camera would be his travelling companion and working tool. In 1933, James sensed something important happening in Germany and went there. He had chronicled the rise of Nazism with hundreds of photos.

He was young then, and his reportage had earned him great fame. He had then returned often to Germany, tenaciously documenting the Nuremberg parades, the discrimination against Jews, and the involvement of the masses in a project that, he realized early on, would have ominous consequences. He could not rest easy until he would convince his own country of the supreme evil represented by the rise of Hitler. He tried to stay in Germany when the war broke out and continued his work. But a British photographer in wartime Berlin was really risking too much. When the SS had begun to openly hunt him down, James had fled to Switzerland. By '41, he had managed to return to Germany. He was brave. He wanted to understand what was happening to German Jews, that interested him. But when his photos of the violence and deportations appeared in a British newspaper, James again became an explicit target for the SS and decided to flee again. A daring escape had brought him back to Switzerland, and after some time in a refugee camp, he chose to stay in the hotel in Sils. He had no shortage of money, and then, as soon as possible, he would return to England.

The days were long for someone like him there, but he knew crossing Europe to return to his country was too risky.

Every so often, he would leave Sils to go and take his photos of Swiss landscapes or, more often, of refugees housed in labour camps. Sometimes, he would go as far as the border to document the plight of refugees trying to escape the war and enter the strange country that remained virtually unaffected. He had photographed families stranded at the border with Italy and others who had managed to enter Switzerland. Those weeks of work, which would allow him to acquaint the world with the war from that perspective, would then give him the energy to spend more time at the hotel without giving in to the temptation to escape, to run away, to go looking for other scenarios while taking considerable risks.

Having finished his tale, James thought that, given the arrival of the young Italian woman, he now had one more reason to stay in Sils. He found her fascinating due to the contrast between the elegant, haughty lady expecting a child and the wild girl he sensed in her. He liked her petite being, her cerulean gaze, cold at first glance, but that hid, he had seen, a vibrant, strong and indomitable soul.

James had had women since he had been there. He had always had some, after all. He remained bewildered by his success with the female gender but also by the tears he had unwillingly caused. From his point of view, things were straightforward: he was not unfaithful; as long as he was with a woman, he had eyes only for her. He sought freedom in his adventures, but only freedom. The pleasure of discovery, the search for the new and the beautiful. And then the feeling, priceless, of going away to something else. Just like in his work. He liked to be where things happened, where there was passion, vitality, and momentum. Then, when the passion died out to make way for small habits and routines gradually becoming more and more established, he felt the urge to move elsewhere. He could not explain how it could not be that way for the female gender; he did not understand the need to stop for stability.

It had been a few weeks since her arrival, and Cecilia had had to surrender to the fact that she could no longer hide her belly, which was growing daily. She had had Marco take her to a seamstress in Sankt Moritz, who had tailored a couple of dresses that fit her well.

Admittedly, for the first time in her life, she did not like to look at herself in the mirror. When she opened the door of the light-coloured wooden closet with the full-length mirror, she shied away from looking at her own reflection. Fortunately, the oval of her face had retained its usual appearance; indeed, her skin seemed brighter and clearer. That was what she was banking on when she saw James. After the evening they had had dinner together, Cecilia had wholly surrendered to the idea of spending much of her time with him. Not only because his presence was, indeed, unavoidable, but also because his company aroused in her the most extraordinary feeling she had ever experienced. Indeed, those encounters had become almost daily.

In those first few weeks, Cecilia, absorbed by James's charms, had also gotten to know the other hotel guests better and spent some time with them. Many kept to themselves and did not always come down every afternoon for tea or in the evening for dinner; there were, however, a few fixed appointments, which most of the guests never missed, such as Sunday tea, served with pastries flown in directly from a famous pastry shop in Sankt Moritz, or the party every third Friday of the month, attended by three musicians.

Anna Zeller often accompanied her on walks, and Cecilia giggled at the idea that Louise was somehow jealous of her.

Under the guise of German classes, they sometimes managed to leave her at home. They did not want to exclude her, but their chemistry was different. Cecilia was also curious of Anna and her family's history. Anna recounted it one day while they were standing on a bench made out of an old moss-covered log right next to a small fountain from which ice-cold, crystal-clear water flowed ceaselessly. The weather was getting colder and colder, and soon it would start snowing. Cecilia and Anna did not look at each other but stared at the valley below them, a distant point, because painful stories are hard to look into the eyes.

The "J" printed in red on his passport changed David's life. Not the deprivation of rights, not the looting of Jewish stores, not the expulsion of his children from school. But that "J," initial for "Juden," did. It had been a long time since his friends advised him to move to Switzerland, trying to save in the neutral country his wealth, bank accounts, jewellery and the Zeller family's art collection, the result of the passion of several generations.

For David, that indelible letter was the unmistakable sign of the need to flee. There was no longer a place for them in Germany, despite all he felt he had given to that country. From that moment, as he walked out of the police offices with his wife clutching his arm, he had begun to think about how to get into Switzerland. He could not imagine another place where he could wait for better times and hide his possessions. As he explained his escape plan to his wife, Anna, he discerned a kind of compassion mixed with astonishment on her face.

At the end of her husband's speech, she only said, "No, David, it seems you are unclear about what is happening. The 'J' in the passport will make it difficult for us to enter Switzerland. Don't be so naive to think that the Swiss authorities are there to welcome us with open arms. I have heard of some Jews being turned away at the borders. Don't think you will save your heritage; forget your paintings, sculptures, and collections. That's not what we have to think about now. We have to think of our children."

Anna had spoken expeditiously and with unusual lucidity, which had startled and unnerved him simultaneously: "What are you saying? Switzerland will welcome us, all right. We have two young children. We are a respectable family known in half of Europe. Do you want us to go away, leaving our belongings here? Are you crazy? We will have to take everything to safety. We will return it here as soon as this madness is over."

"Life, David, we have to save our lives and especially the lives of our children." Indeed, David had never had much practical sense and had found himself managing the family business without really being up to it. His two brothers, who lived in London, had always made the most critical decisions from a financial point of view, considering him the younger brother to lead: a controlling presence over businesses in Germany and nothing more. Perhaps because of his character, he had married Anna, a woman of pulse and great practicality.

Indeed, David soon had to admit that his wife was right. Not long after, their home had been ransacked and completely stripped of its art treasures. He had watched the scene helplessly, paralyzed in the face of violence he would never have thought possible. Objects that he had seen in his home all his life, first from his grandparents, then from his parents, had been taken away before his eyes. A businessman of no great value, he had good taste and a refined sense for beautiful things. That is why, among the brothers, he was assigned the most valuable pieces, favouring them over the larger shares that went to the others. As the SS ransacked the house, Anna had trembled, not with fear but with anger and outrage, clutching her two children to her. Perhaps at that moment, she had stopped loving her husband, who still seemed incapable of understanding.

Organizing the escape to Switzerland took several months, months in which conditions for Jews in Germany became increasingly difficult.

It was Anna who had contacted Marco, the concierge of the hotel in Sils where she had gone every summer, first as a child and then as an adult, with her husband and finally with her whole family. She knew him to be a good man and was not mistaken. Just before the vacation, Anna had her husband open an account in Switzerland, where they kept a certain amount of money. They could count for as long as they stayed there with that money. And then, if anything was missing, Anna did not doubt they could reach an agreement with Monika Brunne, the owner. Anna had heard in those last months about the sorting and labour camps organized in Switzerland since the beginning of the war. She also knew that children were usually placed with families who took them in, and she would not allow her family to be dismembered.

During the months when Anna was preparing to flee to Switzerland, David sat in an armchair all day. He did not answer letters from his brothers asking what had become of the Zeller factories. He listened to the radio from time to time, shaking his head. The factories had been 'aryanized', that is, basically expropriated. But sooner or later, he kept repeating, this madness would end. Anna occasionally glanced at him surreptitiously, and her anger mounted. She could not stand his immobility, his expressionless, passive face, abandoned to a fate of ruin that seemed not to concern him.

Anna recounted that Marco only gave her all the directions to seek refuge in Switzerland in '41.

Cecilia sighed. Even though she usually did not like to hear about the war and even though she had hoped to live off the grid, she was so honoured that a woman like Anna had chosen just her for this confidence. She could not help but be touched by that pain. And then she had the impression that, for some reason, the Klimo family also looked at her with the contemptuous look usually reserved for Anna and her family.

"So the Klimo treat you this way because you are Jewish?" Cecilia, the very instant she uttered those words, realized how stupid that question was: it was evident.

"Yes, of course," she replied with a shrug as if to point out the obvious. "It probably seems unbelievable to them that the Brunne's are hosting Jews, which, by the way, as you may have noticed, happens quite often with families passing through. I honestly don't know why the Klimos are here; if they are so happy with their Führer, they could stay in Germany with him, don't you think?"

"How long have they been here?"

"I think they are the oldest guests: they were already here at the time of the invasion of Poland. They had always spent about half the year at the Hotel Maria, arriving from Munich loaded with trunks and settling in, heedless of Germany's difficulties in recent years. After all, even the catastrophe following World War I had not affected their routine much. They were rich, quite simply. But rest assured that Danielle never felt guilty about her wealth, not even in those difficult years, for the simple fact that she thinks she deserved it: if, despite everything, they are doing well, it is because they have always behaved appropriately. Never a missed church service, never a behaviour outside the commandments that the world insisted on not following. Good Christians, that's how those two think of themselves, and that's why they feel entitled to all. Danielle is convinced that Hitler will set things right by ending the moral decay that has affected Germany in recent decades. I always felt German before I felt Jewish, and yes, for some years, Germany was in trouble. Hitler made people believe the war would end within a few months.

Now, Danielle must have convinced herself that, evidently, to atone for their sins, the German population has to suffer more than she had ever believed. And indeed, it was no accident that she and her husband sheltered in the Engadine at the outbreak of that cleansing conflict. In Danielle's worldview, God, whom she never ceases to thank, perpetually clutching the red-grained rosary beads you may have noticed, never does anything haphazardly and protects good people. So imagine how jarring our presence and the occasional presence of other Jews, mostly Italians, at the hotel is to her. Even now, after so long after our arrival, I sometimes fear that something might happen for which we would be kicked out of the hotel or even from Switzerland. That something might change in this balance, and that my and my family's protection might fall apart."

If Joseph Brunne had reconsidered, if the Klimo had complained more openly than they did, if somehow their presence had become unwelcome, what would have become of them? And, most importantly, of the boys? Anna inhaled deeply as if having spoken so long and so fiercely had caused her to run out of air. Then she took to staring at the fountain's jet of water. Whenever she thought that because of the Klimo, or perhaps an afterthought by Joseph Brunne, or for any other reason, the bubble in which they lived might burst, Anna trembled with fear.

Cecilia huffed and rested her hand on her friend's shoulder. She was not accustomed to tender gestures, but the irony and courage with which Anna told those terrible stories could not help but arouse her admiration and sincere solidarity.

Sometime later, one afternoon, as Cecilia was nervously reading yet another letter from her husband, abandoned in one of the library armchairs, Louise shook her by suddenly saying, "My sister had an affair with James Ashton, not bad, right?"

Cecilia struggled to keep her eyes on her husband's regular handwriting, but she could not resist the temptation to ask when it had happened and how long it had lasted for, as a blade of jealousy took her breath away.

"About a year after we arrived," Louise replied, "and Béa hoped I wouldn't notice. Instead, almost immediately, it was clear to everyone. He is really charming, and I must tell you that I would like a love like that, too." She giggled as she looked at the ceiling as if she were dreaming. "Then he decided to stop." Louise's contrite tone contrasted with her almost amused, or at least pleased, expression. "Rumor has it that he preferred a maid from the Hotel Majestic in Sankt Moritz to Béa, but can you believe it?" she then continued in a whisper. Cecilia listened without replying but suddenly felt greedy for details and hoped Louise would go on. "For Béa, it was really a great pain; she never wanted to confide in anyone, not even me, but she was completely prostrated by that abandonment. She closed in on herself and allowed herself to be consumed first by grief and then by anger for months on end, without ever mentioning it to anyone. Since then, she has often told me to beware of men because they only want to play games. Suddenly, she decided to feign indifference, but I think she hasn't given up even now that so much time has passed..." She stared at the ceiling again momentarily and then asked, "Do you think I, too, will experience such a passion, sooner or later?"

Cecilia looked at her condescendingly. "Sure, Louise, but now, no more gossip about your sister. I must reply to this letter. " She cut it short not show how much the idea of Béa and James together had unexpectedly hurt her. That image was before her eyes all the following night as she tossed and turned in bed under the suddenly too heavy comforter.

Every evening, most of the hotel guests, but often Marco and Franciszka as well, would gather in the library, where Lapo would tinker with the radio until he tuned in to Radio London, which broadcast war news in several languages. Cecilia, too, had started going there, but not out of genuine interest, since the war seemed far away. She hated hearing about bombings, destroyed cities and massacres anyway, but she joined since she did not want James, who never missed it, to think her superficial. She leaned against the windowsill, standing next to Lapo, who, with a concentrated expression, listened to the sizzle of static, trying to intercept a few words. Then, when something was finally picked up, he waved for everyone to be quiet.

If he heard even a word, he would look up at the sky as if he could see the sound coming through the air and into the device.

Everyone had their own station during that ritual. Louise would sometimes stand next to Cecilia, but then Lapo would look up at her nervously and she would return to her sister at the back of the room. "Why does he do that?" Cecilia had asked her once. Louise had moved her hands up and down as if bored and then had whispered to her, "Franciszka says he is bothered by smells that are too strong, and when I go too far with my sister's perfume, he doesn't want me near him," and, rolling her eyes, had sat down in her usual chair, some distance away. Indeed, the perfume on Béa was a delicate fragrance; on Louise, who sprayed an exaggerated amount of it, it was cloying even to noses less sensitive than Lapo's. Still, Cecilia did not say so as not to mortify the girl.

Some evenings, despite long attempts, nothing could be heard. Lapo would not flinch; he would try and try again, he would turn the knobs, and he would be there hours at a time. Cecilia, on the other hand, would get nervous. Once, after half an hour of futile attempts, she proposed going into the living room. "There won't be any fundamental news today either," she had suggested, bored by all that trying and straining of ears. Everyone gave her a disapproving look.

Lapo would not allow anyone to approach the radio, not even James, who had offered to try to tune the signal and then returned to sit next to Béa. Suddenly, the usual electrical sizzle also ceased; no more noise could be heard. Lapo then began to fiddle with the small screwdriver he always had. Cecilia looked around, caught a glimpse of James and Béa in the half-light, and then, seized by a moment of irritation, struck the radio violently with her hand. Lapo trembled slightly, stiffened, and stood up. For a moment, Cecilia was afraid he would hit her, but instead, he left, walking with wide strides out of the library. Franciszka, who had entered just before, barely held back her anger, then turned to Cecilia without looking straight at her, striving to maintain a respectful tone: "He can't stand rough gestures; he doesn't want to be touched or have anyone touch the radio." "All we need is the one with his foibles," Frau Klimo said dismissively. Cecilia, at that point, perhaps not to feel on the side of the sullen German, turned to Franciszka, "I'm sorry, I didn't mean to."

Reading was not an occupation that could fill all of Cecilia's days. Within two months of arriving in Sils, she realized that she had become somewhat deluded concerning what her life could have been there. Sure, she was far from the war, but, after all, boredom often threatened to creep into her days.

Fortunately, there was Anna, with whom she spent a lot of time chatting and studying German, Louise, who, though tedious, was still a company, and then, above all, there was James. She felt how much he longed for her, despite her state, and she delighted in the wit, intelligence, and vivacity of the man she could not have described in any other way than "dangerous." As soon as time permitted, they would spend long hours on Lake Sils, walking the road through the prairie and the paths leading to the dark fir peninsula jutting out over the lake. They would wander inside the peninsula and often sit on a log that stood at its end. They listened to the lapping of the water and the light wind in the branches. Occasionally, they would see some deer, and then they would abruptly interrupt their conversation to observe the animal. The contact with that wonderful nature, the cold air of that autumn that would soon give way to the whiteness of winter, were the backdrop to their longing for each other.

Some mornings, they would take refuge in the pool, whose windows looked out onto the woods behind. Then Cecilia would remove her silk stockings, raise her skirt slightly and sit on the edge swinging her feet in the warm water. On the other hand, James wore swimming shorts that she found ridiculous and swam long, broad strokes. Then he approached her, rested his head on his folded arms on the pool's edge and watched her.

The time spent with James fulfilled her completely, but Cecilia did not shy away from meeting with someone else occasionally. In particular, Louise Beauvent had become very attached to her.

With an anticipation she found absurd and ridiculous, Cecilia had spent some mornings helping her decorate the hotel for Christmas. Not that she cared much, but it passed the time. James often slept late, while Cecilia would come down early and, with a bored air, take out a few stained-glass balls from the wooden boxes and hang them on the huge tree placed in the middle of the room, or tie red ribbons to the small, braided pine wreaths that her friend would then hang in the windows. Louise was enthusiastic about that activity, and Frau Monika Brunne and Franciszka gladly let her do it.

Cecilia inwardly pitied Louise and resented Béa. However, she often dined with the two sisters or accompanied Louise on long walks. She wanted nothing more than to spend her time with James, but she did not want to be more conspicuous than she already was. She realized that in the small community that had been created, everyone was aware of what was going on between them, and, certainly, the fact that she was pregnant aroused even more criticism. Marco, the doorman, often spoke of Emilio, Cecilia's husband, whom he had known since childhood. Much to Cecilia's embarrassment, he mentioned him at every opportunity with the other guests, calling him "a good man," as if to emphasize, she thought, that such a husband did not deserve a wife like her, one who, while expecting a child with him, spent too much time with another. Cecilia considered Mark to be of disarming goodness: he lived in the memory of his dead wife. He did everything he could to make the strange child she had given him happy. She, therefore, understood that he felt close to Emilio. For yes, Emilio was undoubtedly a good man, a decent man, much more than James. Still, he was utterly incapable of arousing the slightest emotion in her.

However, maintaining good relations with everyone

seemed essential to her. Besides, she would need help when the baby was born.

Louise loved walking along the lake, and Cecilia, despite her burgeoning belly, did not mind accompanying her. They would walk along the road that led to a small village. There, they would stop; Louise would get some milk, some cheese, and some vegetables from the farmers to donate to a centre run by a dozen nuns, a large home that took in children whose families wanted to keep them away from the war. Louise, with her eagerness to do good and her good heart, often went there to help the sisters with the little ones. She made dozens of beds daily and busied herself in preparing meals, mixing dishes, slicing, cleaning and serving them to the children. Cecilia, with the excuse of pregnancy, although Louise had repeatedly invited her to help, gladly kept away.

Occasionally, Anna Zeller would join their walks, with one or both of her children. During one of those afternoons spent strolling on the peninsula, on the rare days when the pale sun was peeping through the clouds, Anna and Cecilia, sitting on rocks, watched Louise and Anna's youngest son playing on the little beach bouncing flat pebbles on the water.

"How are you doing here, Cecilia? It's been a couple of months now, if I'm not mistaken... time to take stock," Anna had asked her in a gentle, almost maternal tone, leaning her face against her arms on her gathered legs and turning toward her with the wind tousling her long black hair. Cecilia had smiled at her, feeling at ease. "Well, Anna, for the first time, I feel close to something that, perhaps, could be called happiness." Cecilia herself marvelled at the confidence she had wrung from her.

"Is it James or the coming baby that makes you happy?"

Cecilia was surprised by such a direct question. Still, she

did not feel like lying as she would have done with others, partly because it was clear that Anna had guessed a lot and that there was a lot of gossip about them.

She had thus lowered her gaze and opted for an indirect response.

"I did not want this child, Anna. It just happened that way, and it was not supposed to happen. I think I don't want children, I never wanted them."

"What about James?"

Anna continued, sensing that she had broken through the young woman's armour.

"James... is James. I wouldn't know what to tell you about him."

"I see passion among you. An unexpressed passion that, sooner or later, when it can, will inevitably make its way. And I'm worried about you, Cecilia."

Cecilia tucked a lock of hair behind her ear and with a sarcastic smile replied, "You don't have to worry, I can fend for myself. On my own. As I always have."

"Be careful, dear; James is a dangerous man who can reach any woman, even the smartest or strongest. He will go beyond your defences and hurt you. If you were honest with yourself, you would admit that something like that is already happening: in front of him, you feel fragile, even you, a woman of extraordinary strength."

Cecilia felt stung and did not respond. But Anna continued, "Before you came, he deeply hurt Béa, the beautiful Béa. They had an affair, then he got fed up, and she was very, very hurt."

Cecilia felt a pang of fierce jealousy overtake her. She still imagined Béa's beautiful body in James' arms and thought of her own body, deformed by an unwanted pregnancy.

She rose up, searching for the right words to silence Anna,

"I already know, Anna; Louise told me everything." That sentence came out more vehemently than she would have liked. Then Anna gently but firmly took her arm and smiled:

"Forget it, Cecilia; maybe I exaggerated; maybe I'm just envious. I have never had such passion. I loved David very much, and I still love him. But it often weighs on me to always be the strong one in the couple, the one who carries everything through without ever giving in for a moment. Maybe having a passion that can make me fragile would be great." She smiled again with a hint of bitterness. And then she gestured with her hand as if to chase away a harassing or unseemly thought, "But there are the boys, my children; I adore them, don't get me wrong, but of course, I could never have anything you have. And when I see David is a good father to them, and they grow up happily with us despite the terrible time they are in, their teenage years… I tell myself that I couldn't wish for more and that maybe it's impossible to have everything in life, and it's not even fair to wish for it. Passion and stability, family and a great love, children and freedom."

Cecilia sighed, filling her lungs with the cold mountain air as if to retort, but Anna's son reached them running, followed by Louise to show his mother a strange insect that had landed right on the back of his hand.

One day, returning from one of the walks, Cecilia found Lapo instead of Marco sitting at the counter, intent as usual on dismantling the little radio that he and his father kept in their small office. When she walked in, Lapo did not look up. She approached and was about to ask him for the key, but he pulled himself up, grabbed a key, and placed it on the counter without taking his eyes off the radio mechanisms. After that, he went back to work without ever looking at her. Cecilia was stunned and wrinkled her forehead as she looked at the key to ensure it was hers. Then, she looked at Lapo but dared not say anything and turned away, amused, wondering how he had realized it was her. At that moment, she saw Marco walking toward her, smiling, "Don't be surprised, ma'am. Lapo does not need to see to understand who has entered the hotel. He can tell by the step, maybe even by the scent. He is like that. That's his charm." Cecilia smiled even though this freaky guy, who might look like a fool to the superficial eye but actually had surprising features, was disturbing her. He never made eye contact with her, yet he seemed to be able to peer deep inside her and find out who she was more than anyone else.

One evening, news of a conference in Tehran came over the waves broadcast by the library radio. Cecilia stood with her arms folded, leaning against the windowsill and staring at the toes of her own shoes: she could hardly declare that for most of those there, it was good news, but for her, the thought that peace was being discussed was cause for relief, yes, but also for concern. It was wrong, selfish, aberrant, and unmentionable, but there it was. Only the continuation of the war would allow her to stay up there, in that little world, in that bubble where she could breathe, be herself and be with James. She wanted a little more time; she did not want to return to her former life. She looked up and saw Danielle and Walter Klimo livid with anger: they would not tolerate Hitler's enemies taking their victory for granted. Louise and Béa were commenting on the news under their breath, whispering to each other as they sat on the tips of their armchairs in the back of the room. Then she looked at James; he was a few steps away from her, standing behind Lapo, who seemed lost in the waves the radio picked up, a thousand miles away from the hopes and thoughts of them all.

For the first time, she thought she might leave Emilio when she returned to Milan; maybe she could hold onto this new reality. She could not imagine what that would be like. As she pursued these thoughts, the others were arguing animatedly; hopes had been raised that Hitler could be defeated. After casting a contemptuous glance at all the onlookers, the Klimo strutted out of the library as if to say that Germany would not lose, and that the three presidents gathered in Iran were deluding themselves.

6

Engadine, 2010

Sitting on the soft cashmere blankets of the bed, her back leaning against the blue silk backboard, Cecilia was restless and tired that evening. She had spent the whole day between bed and sofa, never venturing to the living room. She wondered if she had done well to go to Sils so early that year. Her nephew Matteo would be arriving soon, thanks to a break between exams.

It was still cold, and the snow made her walk around the lake complex. She had breakfast, lunch, and dinner brought to her room by a young boy who must have been about Lapo's age in the war years.

In fact, even though she insisted on returning every summer, the guests from '43 had all but disappeared, apart from Franciszka – they had become friends over time – and Lapo, whom she had married a few years after the end of the war to stay by his side and care for him, as she had always done. She knew that life in the hotel, with its routine and set hours for everything, was the only possible one for him. Of course, after the war, the bustle of customers made the hotel a more hostile place in the eyes of Lapo, who did not like meeting new people. But during peak season, he could limit himself to spending time between their little apartment, the library and the garden when no one was around.

Franciszka, brought to Switzerland by her mother as a little more than a child in 1939, immediately after the German occupation of Poland, had soon started working as a waitress and, more importantly, helping Monika Brunne with her ever-growing offspring. She then remained there and became personnel manager. Even now that she was old, she continued to care for many things, closely followed the hiring of waiters and janitors, and nothing ever escaped her notice. At the same time, since she was considered an institution there, even by the recent owners of the hotel and the grandchildren of the Brunne family at the time, she was allowed to move around almost as if she were a customer.

Lapo, now as then, stayed away from Cecilia and did not love her. She understood: she had never thought him worthy of much attention, and then, since that day so many years earlier when she had hit the radio with violence, he had always stayed away from her. However, Franciszka often sat next to Cecilia in the yellow library, where a modern computer now ensured that clients could connect to the Internet. They talked about the old days, and Cecilia hoped she would live much longer because her friend was proof of what she had experienced.

"Why did a girl like you marry Lapo?" she suddenly asked her that day. Indeed, Franciszka had been a beautiful girl with long red hair, a sharp, freckle-filled face and big teal eyes. And even that year, she had to answer Cecilia's usual question.

"Because I didn't want to leave him when Marco died, I was afraid the Brunne family would kick me out, and Lapo would be left without any protection. And I lived like that, tied to a man to care for. I love him very much. But I understand it is hard to understand. Lapo is not as stupid as many believed then; Lapo is just closed in on himself, in his own world, he has some problems communicating with the outside world, but he also notices things that we completely miss."

"I know, but it took me a long time to realize it too. Sure, we all saw that he had a way with the radio. I still remember how he kept the library books or room keys perfectly organized. Still, otherwise, he seemed absent, detached from what was happening around him and simultaneously so tied to his habits, his schedule, the regular rhythm of the days and terrified of change... However, that night, when I had lost the ring, I realized how much his ability to remember any small detail was his way of interpreting reality, of reading it, of connecting with what was around him. At one point, I realized I no longer had the lapis lazuli vera on my finger. Do you remember?"

Franciszka nodded, "Of course I remember! It was a ring I really liked."

"Lapo had begun to accurately describe the rings we all had on our fingers that evening. And he remembered accurately not only what mine looked like but also how far I had worn it and at what point in the evening he had not seen it on me. And indeed, we found it tucked between the cushions of the armchair on which I had sat for a few moments and which Lapo had pointed to..."

"Of course, he cares about details, and rest assured that if something is suddenly amiss, he will not miss it. Even today it is so." After uttering that sentence, Franciszka fell silent and lowered her eyes: she thought she had said something too much. Cecilia shook her head as if to say not to worry. They had often talked about why Lapo's incredible powers of observation had failed when he could have changed the course of things on the terrible night so long ago.

The friendship between the two women was born many years after the war, when Cecilia realized that Franciszka did not condemn her for what had happened but suffered for her, though without pitying her. At the time of the events, she stood defiladed, like a shadow behind Lapo and the Brunne children. She spoke little, and to Cecilia, she seemed utterly insignificant: she was much too focused on herself to consider a mere maid, younger than herself.

Then, ever since she started going to Sils Maria every year again with her son Manfredi, summer after summer, they had grown closer. Indeed, Franciszka seemed the only one who understood why, with a small child, Cecilia insisted on going there and not elsewhere – to atone, to catch up, to pretend she could go back.

That evening, Cecilia walked with her cane toward the elevator to go down to the lobby. During the war, there was no elevator, but later, given the affluent clientele that frequented it, the Brunne children decided to install one.

Cecilia pressed the button with her bony index finger and waited. Then, as if seized by a sudden desire, just as the doors had opened, and a young couple with two blond children from the upper floors were greeting her politely and inviting her to come in, she turned to head for the wide staircase.

Leaning against the wrought-iron balustrade with one hand and clutching his cane in the other, she descended those white marble steps covered with a red carpet, perhaps slightly cheaper than what had been there at the time, but very similar.

She wondered if it would not have been a better idea to spend those months on the French Riviera, in the Cap Ferrat villa, where she had not been for some time. That was the right place for a lady of her age and with a bad heart; at least, that's what Dr. Albert Charlier had told her, delicately, as only he knew how to do. Indeed, if she had been there, she could have already taken some lovely walks in the pine forest and felt the warm sun on her skin. Yet, stubbornly, she continued to go to Sils every summer, except from 1946 to 1952. During that time, her husband Emilio Alesini had managed to prevent her from doing so, fearing that going back there would exacerbate her grief and her sense of loss. Then, tired and apathetic, she had not found within herself, for once, the strength to impose herself. She had spent months and months on the terrace of Cap Ferrat, staring at a distant point in the sea. But since '52, when her son Manfredi was just two years old, she had decided to return there, alone, and had been adamant to do so.

And so she had done, from year to year, even after her husband Emilio had died and even after Manfredi, in 2000, at the age of only fifty, had crashed in a car accident while drunk, racing along the roads of the French Riviera in his Porsche. Indeed, Cecilia reflected, she had not been able to keep any of the people she had loved and none of those who had managed to love her with her. And now there was no more time to love someone without losing them. She had no one left in the world but her nephew Matteo and the memories of so many years prior, of love during the months of war.

After all, her husband had loved her to the last day, but she had never reciprocated, had not experienced a single day of passion with him, nor had she ever felt any genuine impulse. Indeed, perhaps his reaction after the events of 1944, too composed and measured, had made her lose any real chance of loving him. Tenderness, for a woman like Cecilia, was not enough; she did not know it, and she did not care. Emilio had not wanted to know how things had gone in his absence or the real reasons for the tragedy that had befallen them. He did not want to listen to the voices of his friends, first and foremost Marco, the doorman, who was telling him the truth. He loved Cecilia too much to attribute such blame to her. Therefore, he had merely welcomed her back without a word, returned with her to Milan, and let her give birth to another child, another boy. And he had hardly ever spoken of the incident again. Not feeling sufficiently punished by Emilio, Cecilia's self-inflicted punishment was that of a life without love. Since then, her soul has become like a thin, hard and cold glass sheet. And she was still waiting for someone to break it, ridding her of all that pain and anger at herself that had made her cold and impenetrable.

Perhaps that was why she had failed to truly love her son Manfredi. She had been there for him, but more obsessively than lovingly. She was tormented by the thought that he might fall, get hurt, that someone might hurt him. She had always indulged him, spoiled him beyond measure, and while her husband Emilio watched her smugly and surprised by what appeared to him as immense maternal love, she felt within herself that all that attention, all that anguish, was dictated not so much by love as by a desire to atone, to punish herself, to never feel free again.

While the responsibility of never having truly loved her husband did not oppress her because she, in fact, attributed it to his frailties and did not really deal with it, the fact that she had never been a good mother, that she had never been able to put even her own children before herself, frightened her. In that case, it was impossible to blame it on them, innocent children.

She admitted, without discounting herself, that she had never had a moment of genuine maternal love, and she carried this knowledge on her shoulders along with the anguish that she could not now make up for it. She had been what she had been; her life was gone, and there was no return, only remorse and regret.

Cecilia also entirely attributed herself to Manfredi's death. He had found himself managing an immense estate, crushed by the weight of a responsibility too great for him. Manfredi was the man she, his mother, had moulded, suffocating him in a bubble of excessive attention, of exaggerated protection, aimed, in fact, at compensating for the lack of genuine love. And so, he had become a man devoted to alcohol, perhaps even cocaine, luxury cars and beautiful women. Women, however, who did not love him and whom he did not love until one of them had managed to get married.

This spiral of unlove, this inability to feel genuine feelings, now seemed to Cecilia a condemnation that had started with her and was in danger of perpetuating itself. She hoped that her grandson Matteo would not carry on this heavy legacy.

Lost in her terrible thoughts, Cecilia went to dinner every night in elegant clothes. She resented that people now attached so little importance to style. She often saw women flamboyantly dressed as expensively as they were vulgar, flaunting designer garments by this or that haute couture designer and not accepting that they were growing old out of foolish and superficial vanity. Cecilia, too, had been and still was vain. Still, she knew that that beauty, which as a girl she had masterfully used to her own ends, had made way for a different, more subtle charm that never left others indifferent, attracted them, for better or worse. None of the tourists who now frequented the hotel in Sils could, in fact, fail to notice the elegant lady who always sat at the same table in the dining room and then spent the evening reading books in the same corner of the lounge, the one where the bow-window overlooking the forest was.

Cecilia read a lot, although she had become slow. Occasionally, she had to go over the same line several times. In the library, she was often with Franciszka. Sometimes, they spent long hours in silence, and occasionally, they talked instead.

Everything was the same there, too, except in the corner where the radio used to be towered the large flat computer screen connected to the Internet. Cecilia found it horrible; if it had been up to her, it would have disappeared. Still, Franciszka had explained to her how important it was to offer customers access to the net, especially since cell phones didn't get great reception on bad weather days.

The library parlor was somewhat secluded and sparsely frequented by the other guests, so the two friends felt free to give vent to all their thoughts and let memories roam freely through that place that had contained their lives in the distant years of their youth when facts, happenings, acquaintances, and emotions happened and circumstances were changeable and not immovable as they were today.

"I have never loved my children, never fully, never really. I am a horrible woman," Cecilia said one afternoon in the yellow library. Lately, she would start speeches like that, from nothing, as if she was in a hurry to say all the important things before she ran out of time. Franciszka, looking up, brushed a strand of white hair from her face and removed her glasses.

"I don't have children, Cecilia, so I don't know how they should be loved. You did what you could, dear. You loved them as well as you could, that's all. Unhappiness has not left much free space in your heart to love." Franciszka had become accustomed to entering directly into the subject as if an eternal conversation that needed no recapitulation was always open between them. Cecilia let herself fall into an armchair, "Tonight, as I wore my black dress, I was telling myself that, perhaps, I was doing this for one of the last times. The end is near, I know."

Franciszka smiled, "You've been saying that every year for years. We are almost the same age, so I suppose the end is near for both of us. But you don't have to worry. Our life has been long, very long."

Cecilia sighed, "No, it was like drawing a breath. I always believed I had time, you know? Now, there is no time for anything."

Franciszka reached out her hand to take her friend's, "Don't torment yourself any more. You have atoned enough, you have suffered enough. You did what you could to understand what happened then. We would have liked to know, but life didn't let us."

"No, not all of us, Franciszka. Someone knew and wouldn't, even years after, give me the answers I sought. Someone hurt the child, someone knew exactly what happened."

Franciszka did not add anything; she just closed the book and placed it on the coffee table. Then, after a few minutes, she said to her, "Go to dinner, Cecilia; it's late."

Cecilia nodded and, with difficulty, got up from the chair. Before leaving, she approached the bookcase and looked up. She reached out a hand and grabbed one of the volumes placed on the second-to-last shelf. She stared at it without a word, opened it, and a few fragments of yellowed paper fell to the floor. Then, she closed it, put it back, and walked out, waving to her old friend.

"Today, I saw your nephew Matteo. He is a handsome boy; he looks like Emilio," Franciszka exclaimed one day, breaking the silence they had been standing in for hours. In uttering those words, she closed the book she was reading and, taking off her reading glasses, shifted her teal eyes to her friend's face.

Cecilia did not like to hear her husband mentioned. Matteo looked handsome and more like his paternal grandfather than his father, Manfredi, who had taken Cecilia's colours instead. "The important thing is that he does not have his mother's soul. She is beautiful; there is nothing to say about that, but she is a woman of incredible dryness, frivolousness, and superficiality. I believe Matteo is not like that, although sometimes I worry about him. His mother has neglected him a lot... I know that coming from me..." She lowered her gaze, and her friend shook her hand briefly but firmly. "She never loved him; maybe that's part of why she allowed me to be with him a lot when he was little. I bet she is still on an exotic beach today, as she was then, with a handsome, penniless boy. His father, my son Manfredi, was not bad but too fragile."

"Matteo has you," Franciszka said.

"Do you think it is a coincidence that even now, at the age of twenty-five, he does not give up spending a few days of his summer with you here in Sils when he could be anywhere in the world?" Cecilia had never thought about it, but it was true: she and her grandson had spent countless vacations up there. He had been a cheerful, good-natured child, a bit bossy perhaps, but he had always been loved, and very much so.

She first saw him when he was already a month old: her daughter-in-law had prevented her hated mother-in-law from visiting until then. Then, she must have thought that a willing grandmother would help manage the baby. Cecilia had thus gone to the lovely house in Porta Venezia clutching a small package that contained a handmade cashmere blanket purchased at a nice store downtown. Her daughter-in-law was at the gym because the extra pounds and fine stretch marks marking her belly were upsetting her like the worst of catastrophes. Manfredi was out working, or, perhaps, screwing up, through inability and, above all, indifference, the estate that had been in the Alesini family for decades. She had found the little one with a maid. She had nodded to the woman, who had immediately disappeared into the spacious kitchen. Then, she looked at him. He had dark, slightly curly hair, big brown eyes, and chubby cheeks. Cecilia felt something inside her creak as if the cold sheet of glass that had kept her from love for so many years was about to shatter. The baby had stretched his arms out in her direction, and she had cautiously taken pressed him gently to herself, almost like someone doing something uncomfortable. That child somehow felt like her last chance.

As soon as she was allowed, she had taken Matteo to Sils: with him, she had spent beautiful summers, of walks and stops by the lake, of stories and games. At times, it seemed to her that those vacations could, at least in part, give her back something of what she had lost. When they walked together, Cecilia marvelled at the pleasure of feeling her grandson's tiny hand in hers. Whenever they approached a fork in the road, she let him choose where to go, "Right or left, Matteo?"

The child looked at her with big eyes, shook her hand, and replied, "You decide, grandma! I don't know which path is the most beautiful, where we will find the most animals, the most fountains, or the most colorful flowers!"

"No, Matteo, you have to choose. In life, you must choose, and you can rarely predict what will happen one way or the other. But you have to know how to seize the right moment, the instant when you still have, perhaps briefly, the most possibilities. Seize the right moment, the one that leaves you with multiple paths, just before fate is fixed by circumstances, which our choice inevitably helps to create."

"But Grandma, this is just a walk; let's go wherever you prefer!"

Cecilia forced him to choose the path: "Then, tomorrow we can try the other way; you can choose again. Think of it as an advantage! In life, it will not always be like that!"

At that point, Matteo, exhausted, would choose. And then, in the evening, he would tell her, "I did good, didn't I? That was a good walk today, the right one." And Cecilia would nod by covering him with the soft, puffy comforter and turning off the abat-jour. "What walk are we going to take tomorrow?"

"Tomorrow, you will choose again, Matteo," she smiled at him in the darkness, finding some relief from her pain in those nights. Sometimes, she scolded him, but Matteo did not resent that. He sensed Grandma's strong character and liked it; he loved having someone who could stand up to him, not bend to his whims. From a very young age, he considered this the manifestation of attention and interest to which he was not used to receive from either his mother or his father, who always gave him everything, one out of indifference and the other out of weakness.

Then Matteo had grown up. He had undoubtedly remained attached to her. Perhaps, Cecilia sometimes told herself, precisely thanks to those beautiful summers they had spent together. Although in Milan, as was only right, he spent most of his time with friends or current girlfriend, he never gave up spending at least a few weekends in Sils.

Emilio had never wanted to accompany her to Switzerland. He detested that place and found his wife's obstinacy in wanting to return there repeatedly, as if in an endless torment, incomprehensible. Over the years their relationship had become non-existent. If at one time he found himself having to put up with Cecilia's restlessness and whims, only to always give her up willingly, simply because he adored her, since, after the dramatic events that had befallen them, he had found himself with an apathetic and tired woman, dulled like a fire without oxygen. It seemed that some vitality was only found away from him, in the only place in the world where Emilio could not follow that beautiful, once beloved, tough and tormented woman. He had spent long summers away from her for years, first in Milan, alone in the heat and mugginess and then, in the last years of his life, in Cap Ferrat, where he joined his son and daughter-in-law, who spent their vacations there in luxury. At the same time, their child, Matteo, stayed with his grandmother in the mountains.

Franciszka redeemed her from her thoughts by lightly tugging on her arm, "Cecilia, it's late. Let's go to sleep."

"You know what I've been thinking all these years?" Franciszka signalled for her to continue. "If you married Lapo, there can only be one reason in the world."

She stiffened. "This again? I told you, I married him because I was sure he wouldn't be alone, and I promised his father I would stand by him. Monika Brunne was fond of him, but Marco feared that his children might kick him out... while I was considered a pillar of strength here, the reference point for the most valuable clients, like you, for example, dear Mrs. Cecilia Alesini," she added with a mixture of pride and irony.

"You loved Marco very much, didn't you?"

She hesitated to respond, sighing.

"Did you love him?"

Franciszka looked her straight in the eye without saying a word. Then, she stood up and said, "I'm going to my husband, Lapo, Cecilia."

"I did not mean to be intrusive, my friend, but this is perhaps the last year I have to understand why a woman like you, beautiful and intelligent, chose to live without love, without passion, without children." Franciszka threw back her head and shook her hands, like someone sick and tired of hearing such talk, but Cecilia continued, determined to get to the bottom of it. "And I told myself, a few years ago now, that beautiful and intelligent women have only one reason to vow to unhappiness: true love, the great love of their lives."

"Forget Cecilia, I am not unhappy. I am serene, and that is enough for me."

Having said this, she walked away slowly, under the weight of her past. At the glass door leading to the hallway, she stopped and addressed her again, "Marco could have been my father and still lived in the memory of the great love for his wife, Lapo's mother. He was attached to me like a daughter, and I think he greatly loved me. But my feelings were different. Every time he stroked my hair in a fatherly way or gently scolded me because I had done something wrong at work, I prayed that suddenly his attitude would change, that he would realize that, over the years, I had become a woman, a woman who loved him and who always loved him." Her voice cracked slightly, and she made a great effort to push back the tears about to surface. Then, returning to herself, she opened the door with a firm gesture and disappeared into the hallway.

Cecilia took this time, yes, the elevator to the second floor. Her thoughts were boulders that evening; she felt tired, exhausted, and without strength. She promised herself that she would be examined by Dr. Charlier the next day.

It was already noon, but Cecilia was still in bed. She felt particularly fatigued, occasionally drawing in a deeper breath than the others, but it seemed she could not inflate her lungs as she would have liked. She could not tolerate her mind, still so lucid, being harnessed to that increasingly frail body. Even though old age was like that for everyone lucky enough to make it to over ninety, she felt that weakness should be a punishment for her and her alone. A few years earlier, she had broken her femur as she was locking the door to the room. She had heard the very crack of the bone breaking and found herself on the floor. Since then, after the operation, she had begun to use a cane, but that morning, she suspected that soon she would no longer be able to move freely, even with it. It was now undoubtedly her last year to walk the path through the peninsula woods to the bench where Nietzsche sat and where a large stone bore the inscription of some of his verses.

She was reminded of when her friend Anna had translated the inscription for her on one of the afternoons spent chatting and trying to learn the language that seemed as fascinating as it was difficult. At the same time, Anna's children searched the woods for deer and squirrels.

"*Alle Lust will Ewigkeit*," she repeated those words she had read many times in that far-off time: "Every pleasure wants eternity."

At that moment, she heard a knock at the door. It was Dr. Charlier, who had been trying to travele to Sils from Zurich as much as possible since spring and then during the summer.

"Good morning, dear doctor", Cecilia greeted him, adjusting herself on the cushions to compose herself.

"Don't worry, madam. How are you doing?"

"Not well, unfortunately. I'm very fatigued."

"You should not be here. This altitude, for a lady of your age and with your heart...."

Cecilia looked at the ceiling like a disobedient child who had no desire to be scolded.

"I know you won't listen to me, so let's at least see about adjusting the dose of your medication," the doctor replied, pulling the stethoscope out of his frayed leather bag.

"You know, doctor, I've always hated doctor visits – and now, here I am. Luckily, I found you up here!"

"Yes, but I'm not always here. If I shouldn't be there when you need me, don't wait for me; let them take you to the first available doctor."

"I have to die, on the other hand, don't I? One of these days...."

"We try to delay this inescapable issue for as long as possible."

"How are your daughters? Do you have a picture?"

Charlier took his cell phone from his jeans pocket and showed her a picture of two beautiful girls. "They are already fourteen and sixteen years old; they are really grown up," he said.

The doctor was a handsome man. He wore his fifties well, was sporty, and loved windsurfing on the lakes of the Engadine and walking in the high mountains. He was not very tall, but he still had a lean physique. When he was in Sils for weekends or vacations, he did not shave every day, and his beard, more grizzled year to year, set off his unique light hazel, almost amber eyes. He wore his salt-and-pepper hair slightly longer and dishevelled than a doctor of his prestige, who aspired to become the head of the important Zurich cardiology centre where he worked, should have been able to afford. But Cecilia appreciated this concession to vanity.

He had divorced the previous year. As he had told Cecilia past summer, his wife had been cheating on him for two years, and he had not noticed. And then, one day, she had simply left, blaming him for the failure of their marriage. According to her, the proof of guilt was precisely demonstrated by the fact that he had not noticed her affair for months – "You live in that hospital. You don't care about me or anyone else except your patients. So, you know what? I'm leaving so you can stay in the hospital even longer. By only thinking of your patients' hearts, yours has hardened..." She almost started crying as Albert's world collapsed. He did not understand. Of course, he had had his own affairs, like everyone else in the hospital. He had long been in a relationship with Agnes, his colleague. But it had never meant anything; it had never crossed his mind to leave his wife for the beautiful doctor. Agnes was his refuge in the long nights in the hospital, in the failures and successes of the job that gave him no respite and always kept him on edge. But Laura, his wife, was his family; she was his private life and the mother of his beautiful daughters. She was, in short, something else entirely. He had loved her and, perhaps, still loved her. He had remained silent as he watched her take the door of their home and go who knows where into the arms of who knows who. And then he had ended up with Agnes, who had waited for him for a long time, begging for him to leave his wife, something he would never have dreamt of doing. He had found himself in a stable relationship with her. He would never admit that it weighed a little on him at times; however, he could not let another woman down, making even more problems at the hospital. Even if his private life had sunk so miserably, the same fate, at least, would not befall his career.

"It seems like yesterday that I gave birth right here in this room," Cecilia suddenly sighed, changing the subject.

"Don't think about it, madam."

"Oh, yes, I think about it. They told me it hadn't been a complicated birth, but to me, it had felt like dying." She smiled bitterly and then whispered, "And maybe it would have been better to die."

Albert had heard the birth story many times from Cecilia and, more importantly, what had happened afterwards.

"Childbirth was a big event; all the guests at the time thought their say worthy. Monika Brunne, the owner of the hotel, was amazed, with her eight children, that I was in such pain; Anna helped me a lot, shaking my hand and telling me when to push; Louise played it cool but was scared, while Béatrice Beauvent and Danielle Klimo were horrified by the screaming. That witch Frau Klimo complained about the noise..."

Meanwhile, he had finished his examination and was listening with his stethoscope slung around his neck and his arms behind his back, like a doctor making a tour of the ward. As soon as Cecilia paused briefly, looking at a distant point toward the lake, Albert said, "Things aren't great, Cecilia, but you know that, of course. Tormenting yourself with painful memories is not good for you."

"I have been tormenting myself all my life, doctor; I am a prisoner of these memories, but, as you see, I have survived so far. In fact, it is these memories that keep me alive. Before going, I had hoped to understand what really happened then, who hated me to that extent..."

Charlier placed his prescription pad on Cecilia's bedside table and, after removing his glasses, merely squeezing her shoulder with his hand as a sign of understanding and closeness, scribbled prescription on a sheet of paper. "Get them from the pharmacy – they can order them; it will take a few days to get them; in the meantime, get some rest, dear lady."

Cecilia paid little attention to the doctor's words and continued to chase her memories: "With Manfredi, it was a whole different thing. Much quicker. I felt nothing, or at least I don't remember anything. I was in a nice clinic in Milan. Everything was easy, quick, and painless. I think at that time, my ability to perceive and feel was limited. I simply let myself live."

Albert looked at her, almost intimidated, not knowing what to say. He knew her story and sincerely felt sorry for his elderly patient. He had been following her for years now and detected suffering and passion behind that leathery exterior. He remembered vividly the day, some fifteen years earlier, when the hotel owners had asked if there was a doctor among the guests because a lady had fallen ill. Albert, then a promising young doctor from Zurich who was there on vacation, had rushed to the lady, who had had a heart attack in progress.

Once out of danger and back in Milan, Mrs. Alesini had given him a generous check. He had since become her cardiologist during their stays in Sils.

He had met her that she was already elderly, but he had never doubted that she must have been a beautiful woman. She was still very charming. As the doctor put away his instruments and handed the prescription to Cecilia, he thought that the aura of suffering and mystery surrounding her still made her one of the most magnetic women he had ever known.

"Try to rest, now, Mrs. Alesini; eat lightly, and you will soon regain some strength with the medicines I have prescribed, but don't do anything to fatigue yourself. No long walks and overall, stay calm," he spoke slowly to give emphasis to the last word: he doubted that the patient would follow that advice.

Cecilia nodded absentmindedly as her mind once again returned to unforgettable, distant days.

7

Engadine, 1944

It was an evening in January 1944 when the news of a major bombing raid on Berlin by the British Royal Air Force came from the Yellow Library radio. The BBC was broadcasting on the continent in several languages. Usually, Italian or French was picked up at the Maria, and sometimes English. That evening, from Radio London, accompanied by some background rustling, the singularly British-accented Italian mixed with a Neapolitan inflexion of Colonel Harold Stevens, known as Colonel Buonasera resounded, and it fell to Cecilia to translate the terrible news. Seven hundred planes had been deployed, over two thousand three hundred tons of bombs. Cecilia strained her ear as she stood next to Lapo. It was a thankless task. Anna looked at her with wide eyes and saw, in her eyes, the dissolution of the hope that her life might return to what it had been, and that anti-Semitism and persecution would only remain a bad memory. The truth was that the Germany she had lived in no longer existed, that Berlin and other cities would change their faces forever. Even if it was good news that Germany was tired, even if she was looking forward to nothing more than Hitler's defeat, that had also been her country, the place where they had married, where their friends had lived, where their children had been born. Anna looked around: the boys and David had gone out. The Klimos stood petrified, Danielle sitting on the tip of the chair, Walter sunk against the backrest, supporting his chin with his clasped hands and glassy eyes. James stroked his beard absorbedly while Marco stood by the door, hands behind his back. Louise and Béa chatted under their breath, probably wishing of news proclaiming the war's end was approaching. Joseph Brunne, sitting on a stool, stared at Louise's back without taking too much interest in what Cecilia was translating, while Monika and Franciszka, with their index fingers on their lips in a sign of silence, took two of the younger Brunne children, who were in the library playing checkers, out.

When the broadcasts ended to make way for a music program, everyone was silent for a few long seconds. Then Lapo suddenly turned the ignition knob and stood up, leading the others like a wave to do the same.

Those months in Sils had flown by. Cecilia's belly had grown, and she was finding it harder and harder to carry herself around, but that did not mean she gave up walking. It had snowed a lot in the last period, and now that it was March and the snow had slowly begun to melt, walking had become a little easier. The long months spent in the hotel, the routine of the days always being the same, and the strain of walking so far with snowshoes had made the winter long and monotonous. Christmas had passed almost like any other day for everyone, except for Louise and the Brunne children. Cecilia was simply relieved that her husband could not join her. He had written to her that business, the war, and the grave situation that had arisen in the last months of '43 did not make possible for him to enter Switzerland; he would surely succeed when the child was born. He would find a way at all costs.

All that whiteness had fed her up, although she liked it

when she and James were left alone in the living room late at night, as when chatter with other guests was replaced by an intense silence laden with unspoken words. They just stood there, watching the glistening snow on which the light from the two small street lamps in the garden reflected: dim lights in the black darkness of winter nights. Even the large fireplace could not warm that space after the Brunnes turned off the modern heating system they had installed a few years earlier.

Now, on the way out, there was an endless, continuous sound of water. It seemed that the world was slowly melting under the faint rays of a still uncertain sun. Soon, there would be no more snow. The night was still freezing, however, and Louise, Monika, and Anna had all advised, to no avail, for Cecilia not to go out: she might slip and fall, just as had happened to Louise sometime before, and hurt herself, which, in her condition, was absolutely to be avoided.

Cecilia would still go out as soon as she could. She would walk for a long time, not thinking about the baby she was carrying, who would soon decide when to come into the world.

That day, she had just returned with Louise and Anna from a walk along the lake despite the cold, overcast day. It was drizzling, and low clouds shrouded the mountains and the whole landscape in a thick greyish blanket.

As soon as she had finished climbing the stairs, just as she was about to push open the revolving door, she felt a stabbing pain in his lower abdomen. She could not hold back a small cry. "This is it," she said, wide-eyed and suddenly frightened.

Anna approached her and encircled her shoulders. "Don't worry dear, I'm going to call Monika Brunne. We will help you. In the meantime, you, Louise, try to contact a doctor; we will need him, especially when the baby is born, to check Cecilia's and the baby's condition."

Louise ran to find Marco so that he could call the doctor, while Cecilia clung to Anna and asked her to take her to the room.

"It will not be easy to climb two floors of stairs."

"Better than giving birth in the hotel lounge," smiled Cecilia, who then contracted her face in a grimace of pain.

Slowly, stopping with each contraction, the two women reached room 225. There, Cecilia lay down while Anna removed her skirt and panties.

"Breathe, dear; take long, deep, slow breaths."

At that moment, Monika entered with the neutral expression of someone used to this situation. "How are we doing?"

Cecilia squeezed Anna's hand: another contraction.

Cecilia's labour lasted several hours until suddenly, she felt it was time to push.

It was then that Louise, half curious and half frightened, stopped in front of the door, trepidant to approach her friend.

A few moments later, Cecilia's piercing scream was accompanied by the stentorian cry of a newborn: "It's a boy," smiled Anna, "he's beautiful." Only then did the doctor cut the cord. He quickly examined the mother and baby, and left. Cecilia was exhausted and dazed, and when Monika handed her the baby, wrapped in a little white sheet, she asked her to hold him a moment longer. "But look at him; he's your baby." For some reason, Cecilia almost couldn't look at him; she was upset by the tiny little being who had begun to cry again.

"Attach it to your breast, Cecilia," Louise told her, finally entering the room, almost stymied. "That's the way to do it, isn't it?" she said, turning to Monika and Anna.

"Sure!" said Monika, also bewildered by Cecilia's cold attitude.

Then Anna gently took the infant from Monika's arms and

laid it gently on Cecilia's chest. She pulled her nightgown from one breast aside without giving her a chance to object and rested the little head next to her nipple. Cecilia remained motionless, but the little one grasped the nipple with his lips and instantly calmed down. Anna's eyes moistened slightly. Cecilia, on the other hand, stood there, rigid, her arm still in an unnatural position in supporting her baby. It seemed as if she had just witnessed a scene from a black-and-white movie, the kind she had occasionally seen at the cinematograph in Milan, images of a tale she did not want to be the protagonist of.

After a few minutes, when the commotion of those around her began to jar with her own absence, Cecilia asked her friends to let her rest and put the newborn in the wicker cradle that Franciszka had brought into the room earlier, at Monika's invitation.

As soon as the baby fell asleep and Cecilia's bed was changed, everyone left the room except Anna.

Seeing that Anna had stopped, Louise went back, not to be outdone. She left only when Béa called to her, "So it's born? Is it a boy or a girl?"

"It's a boy," Louise replied.

"Cecilia's screams could be heard all the way down the hall," Béa said, "I took refuge on the second floor, in Danielle Klimo's room, but even there, she could be heard. We couldn't take it anymore."

Louise dared not retort: she had liked the idea of assisting her friend at such a critical moment, of being the one who had been responsible for getting the doctor called. She hoped she had become Cecilia's best friend that day, a closer friend than Anna. However, she did not dare answer her annoyed sister: she would not contradict her beloved Béa, not for anything in the world.

Locked in that room with that screaming little bundle complete of needs, despite the attentions of Anna, Louise, Monika and the help of the diligent Franciszka, she felt like she was going crazy. She felt like a prisoner with the tiny jailer, Leonardo, for that was what she had decided to name the baby.

Emilio, of course, had been immediately notified of the birth by Marco, and as soon as he could, he travelled, excitedly and happily, to her. It was the first time he had been able to reach her, and Cecilia had the feeling of a stranger's intrusion into her own world, into a dimension that belonged to her and her alone, where, for her husband Emilio, there would never be room. He had managed to take with him most of the clothes Cecilia had left in Milan and had personally arranged them in the suite's closet. He liked being there, making himself useful, so much so that he cared for things typically foreign to a man of his rank.

He had arrived with his open and sunny gaze, his friendly and kind ways toward everyone, shaking hands and dispensing smiles. He had lingered with Marco for a long time, talking about the beautiful summers when he, still a boy, spent long days playing alone. Emilio had met all the regular guests except James, who had gone to photograph some of the most beautiful Swiss peaks. He had said that he had been planning that report for some time and that the weather made those days perfect, but Cecilia was sure he simply wanted to avoid meeting her husband.

As soon as he had been brought to him, Emilio had clutched the baby to him, supporting his little head gently, lullabying him when he cried, gently stroking his little face with his index finger. He had stayed several days before having to return to Milan. "I can't wait for this war to end and for us all to be together in Milan, in our home." It seemed to Cecilia that the hotel room, with her husband and the child inside, which she still struggled to consider her own, lent itself well to representing what her life in Italy would be like in the years to come. She thought of the sense of freedom James had given her in those months and how breathless she felt when her husband showed her affection, or when her child clung eagerly to her breast. As soon as Emilio announced his return to Milan, she breathed a sigh of relief and wished that her stay away from that good and boring man could last forever.

The child's dependence on her, then, did not make her proud, did not make her a "mother" in her innermost being, but sometimes took her breath away. She felt inadequate, which prevented her from feeling actual emotion, and she was ashamed of it. But then she chased those thoughts away, telling herself that, after all, Franciszka, Anna, Louise and Monika would help her and that soon, she would have every right to be freer.

After three months, she only longed to see James again. It was hard for her to admit; she kept that desire hidden in the back of her mind but always found it there, untouched. She would not talk about it with anyone, not even Anna or Louise, because they would find it indecent, unworthy, unjustifiable.

Nursing the baby had soon become too onerous a task for her; the crying of the little one, perpetually hungry and never satiated by the evidently insufficient amount of whitish liquid that, almost inexplicably for her, gushed from her nipples, drove her mad, stirred things inside her that she had never imagined possible, and that she hated could be plucked by that little being.

Moreover, Monika had decreed that he was too small for his age and that Cecilia's milk was not enough or not nutritious enough. She suggested using goat's milk, readily available up there, light and digestible by infants. She had used it herself when breastfeeding the twins; having to take care of all the other young children at the same time had proved impossible even for her, who knew a lot about babies, breastfeeding and motherhood. There had been no other solution; finding a wet nurse in those days was unthinkable. The women who lent themselves to breastfeed other people's children, at most, took care of the little refugees who had distant mothers or whose mothers, simply, for fear of crossing the border illegally, had lost their milk.

Cecilia had experienced the end of breastfeeding as a liberation. She told herself that if Monika advised her this way, it was undoubtedly a viable path. She then felt endless relief. She could begin to reclaim her own body.

During that time, James drifted away, disturbed perhaps by Cecilia's new condition. In fact, this had not bothered her; she knew it was only a matter of time between them, and waiting would allow her to regain her lean physique. Not that it had rounded out much with pregnancy, but for James, it had to be perfect.

Becoming a mother had not changed her love for James or her attraction to him. On the contrary, she felt that from then on, nothing more would stand in their way.

The little one was three months old when Cecilia first came down the hall, swaddled in her most elegant black gown and with the long pearl necklace knotted on her breast and stopped by the clasp of small diamonds arranged in a flower corolla.

When he had seen her coming down the stairs with her hair perfectly styled by Franciszka, James had feigned indifference, but in fact, he had winced, and she had noticed. He had walked toward her, forcing himself not to run. He took her left hand, looked at her, and she stopped on the last step so their eyes were on the same level. He began nervously twisting her hand, shaking it, unable to let go. Cecilia inwardly exulted. Being desired like that excited her like never before. The tranquillity she showed hid an impetuous turmoil. She felt an unexpected warmth pervade her lower abdomen. She longed for it. It had never happened to her. Certainly not with Emilio.

On that early summer day, on the last step of the staircase, as she felt the roughness of James' skin, she felt genuine desire for the first time.

Suddenly, both recoiled from their thoughts and, letting go of their hands, walked toward the dining room.

Marco watched them worriedly for a moment, then returned to his papers.

After dinner, Cecilia had gone up to her room. She knew that if she left the baby late at Franciszka's, she would be criticized and did not want to arouse gossip. She had noticed Marco's stern look and vowed never to forget that he and her husband were really friends despite the difference in social rank. She also knew that Danielle Klimo thought of her as a bad mother; she could see it in his face every time she met her, not to mention the looks of rancour that Béatrice gave her all the time.

Of the gossip about her and her inability to be a mother, she had spoken to Anna one afternoon as she had visited her in her room. She was pretty in simple clothes, with her long dark braid leaning on one shoulder. Whenever Anna was around, little Leo would stop crying.

"When you had your first child, were you… immediately his mother?" Cecilia asked her, watching as she cradled the little one in her arms. "I mean, did you feel like a mother right away? Did you realize that immediately?"

"I think so, I would say so. But that doesn't mean it has to be that way for everyone, Cecilia." She placed the infant in the cradle and gently approached her, "Give yourself time, Cecilia. Get to know him slowly, your baby. And one day, you will feel that you have become his mother inside you. Don't care what others think; I know there is so much good in you. Only too much loneliness, too much suffering. Love is not always immediate. Love can also be learnt with time."

She smiled at her, her teeth very white and her eyes bright.

At that moment, Cecilia wanted to be a mother like her. She looked inside herself, searching for a feeling that everyone took for granted and that she could not find. Yet, she told herself, it had to be there somewhere.

Once back in her room after dinner, still excited about seeing James again after so long, Cecilia found Franciszka gently laying little Leo down in his wicker cradle. Seeing Cecilia enter, the girl put her index finger to her lips and, moving cautiously, covered the little one with the sheet and blanket she had made for him. It was made of very soft blue wool, which she had made by unravelling a sweater that a customer had given her mother years before.

Franciszka explained that the baby had fallen asleep in her arms after drinking milk, then, excusing herself, left.

Before long, while she watched the baby sleep peacefully, Cecilia heard a soft knock at the door, as if someone had been waiting for the maid to leave the room and only then decided to make themselves heard.

She went to open it, confident that she would be confronted by James Ashton.

She saw him leaning against the doorframe, his Rolleiflex hanging around his neck, and his expression between amusement and arrogance.

"I would like to take pictures of you, Cecilia. What do you say?"

She lightly pushed the door as if to close it.

"Stop Cecilia," James said "Don't be like that, and let me in, and don't tell me you don't want to..."

Sighing, Cecilia opened the door, stood still, and watched him as he entered decisively.

When he asked her to sit in the large armchair, her vanity overrode everything. She surrendered to him, clearly sensing that they were both sliding toward each other that evening and that she was doing nothing to prevent this from happening. However, that thought did not worry her but filled her with excitement and enthusiasm.

Cecilia meekly obeyed, no longer speaking. She sat in the armchair, leaned against the backrest and relaxed completely.

At the first click of the Rolleiflex, she sensed a spark of intimacy that she felt she had never had with anyone. The attunement that had already been established between them over the previous months was now palpable in the air and heavy with desire.

James relentlessly photographed every detail of Cecilia, with the black silk dress marking her small breasts, hips, and thighs. As he shot, Cecilia relaxed until she felt completely at ease, even though James' lens was getting closer and closer until he photographed her clear, burning eyes.

After the last shot, he placed the camera on the small table next to the armchair where she was sitting without a word. Kneeling down, he slipped his fingers under the strap of her dress and slid it down her motionless white shoulder. She stood still and closed her eyes, waiting for his kiss, not caring about the baby sleeping a few steps away.

She felt his lips warm and thought they were as she had wished. She closed hers and let herself go into a long, passionate, and final kiss.

Suddenly, Leo began to cry. Cecilia got up, moved James to the side with her hand, went to the door, and opened it.

James smiled at her, walked to the threshold, went back to get his camera, and then left, stealing a kiss on her cheek. This left her flushed, confused, overwhelmed with desire, and happy.

Cecilia gladly accepted Louise's invitation to walk in the Fex Valley. That, along with the peninsula, were her favourite spots. With the summer, thousands of flowers dotted the light green meadows, while on the other side, dark forests of timber and larch stretched across the valley beneath snow-capped peaks; at the far end could be seen the glacier, a glittering goal to be reached, while in the middle ran like a silver ribbon a stream. Little Leo would stay with Franciszka and Lapo, as always. Now that she could no longer nurse him, she could care for him very little. Her breasts, fortunately, had not been affected by those three months when the baby kept pulling at her nipple as if it were made of rubber. In the service staff apartments or kitchens, Leo was pampered by everyone. The cooks gave him milk, and he, happily in the arms of now one and now the other, played at grabbing wooden spoons, pots, and pans. Of course, Monika Brunne and Danielle Klimo had harshly criticized the habit of leaving him there. "He's always alone, that child," Danielle Klimo had once said to Cecilia with bemusement, on one of the first times they spoke, months and months after living under the same roof.

"Alone? He is never alone," Cecilia had replied, annoyed. "Monika's children constitute good company for the child."

"But little Brunne babies are older, and a child of that age needs to spend time with his mom!"

"I don't know what to do with him. Franciszka and the cooks are much better than me. Perfect nannies."

"But you're not a nanny; you're his mom!" intervened Monika, who had evidently been listening to the whole conversation. Cecilia, annoyed by the alliance between the old and obnoxious Danielle Klimo and the younger Monika Brunne, who she felt should have been on her side anyway, gave the two women an annoyed look while shaking her head. She turned and walked away.

Cecilia admired the beautiful day as she walked down the long path in the valley's heart. The sun was laying its rays on the meadows, which then fell with myriad sparkles into the stream. Louise was cheerful and chirped tirelessly by her side. "You should not have an affair with James. You are married, and he is not a good man."

Cecilia shook her head and replied, "But what do you know about James and me?"

"Come on, Cecilia. We've been living with a few people in the hotel for months. Everyone knows everything about everyone, and there's no one not chatting about you!"

"There is nothing to say about us."

Louise smiled with a malice that Cecilia had never seen in her. "He is a handsome man, Cecilia, I almost envy you. I've never had anyone."

"You have time; you are younger than me." Indeed, Cecilia looked at her friend and noticed how ugly she was. The ungainly features, the shoulders and hips too big, the nose too pronounced, the small eyes. There was no comparison with her sister Béa, who had large dark green eyes, a slender figure, full lips, and shiny, straight raven-black hair. As if she had read her mind, Louise asked, "You don't like my sister, do you?"

Cecilia gave a strained smile but did not dare to deny it altogether. "I find her too serious, too haughty. She judges everyone, even you; after all, she does not treat you that well."

"What are you talking about? Since we've been here, my sister has been like a mother to me, even though we're only four years apart!"

"It seems you don't hesitate to make yourself uncomfortable, though."

Cecilia referred to an incident that occurred earlier, one evening at dinner. Béa, Cecilia, the two Klimo elders, James and the Brunne family, were all around the same table. It was the birthday of one of the owners' children, and a toast was planned at the end of the meal with one of the countless bottles from the hotel's cellar. James had arrived begrudgingly and flopped boredly onto one of the overstuffed chairs. He had cast a glance at Cecilia and brushed her knee with his hand: the only upside to those situations was for him to tease Cecilia by embarrassing her since she was persistent in wanting to keep their relationship falsely clandestine.

The table was missing only one person, and there was only one empty chair – Louise's. However, no one seemed to notice. Louise had the characteristic of always going unnoticed, despite her size, Cecilia had thought a few times.

As the festivities began in the dining room, Louise was in her room in front of the mirror. She had washed for an hour, rubbing her skin with the sponge until it was red. Then she had tried on several dresses, some of her sister's, but it was impossible to fasten them. Hers were too plain, too dark. Ultimately, however, she opted for the usual black dress; after all, Béa said that black was slimming. In fact, at that moment, Louise was observing the layer of fat running around her waist. She tried to hold her breath: better. She had to remind herself not to breathe. In front of the mirror, she wondered about her makeup. She had repeatedly watched her sister give herself powder and lipstick. She did not do it often, partly because it seemed absurd to think about such things while war rages in the rest of the world. Besides, she could not go to the nuns' centre for minor refugees with carmine-red lips. But that night would have been different. Men could like her; maybe even James would look at her and shake his eyes off Cecilia. Louise was ashamed of her thoughts; she had always considered her a friend, even if she did not appreciate certain attitudes, and she was shocked when her sister opened her eyes to Cecilia's relationship with James. But since the afternoon she had met Herr Brunne in the woods on her way home, something in her had changed. His hands had unexpectedly groped her buttocks and breasts, and she had felt, for the first time in her life, desired by a man.

And the part of her that deprecated Cecilia and her sensuality was in constant conflict with the part of her that wanted to seduce, to be loved.

She had her sister's lipstick and rubbed it on her lips, tried to hide a few pimples with powder, sprayed herself several times with Béa's expensive perfume, and headed downstairs late.

Louise had entered the dining room feigning confidence, approached the table where the others were eating, and flaunted a smile from her lipstick-stained teeth. Béa had looked at her from the bottom of her chair, observed her for a few moments and, with a sarcastic look, had said to her, "You really have no sense of the ridiculous, little sister, with that makeup you look like a clown who has just finished his show..." Béa had then laughed, seeking the complicity of the diners with her eyes. Louise had been petrified, then, with tears in her eyes, had turned to head beyond the glass door. The last thing she had heard had been Herr Brunne bobbing boisterously behind her back.

"Sometimes my sister sins insensitively, but she loves me very much…"

"If you say so," Cecilia replied, "I am certainly not the best person to judge other people's feelings and sisterly relations.

"Because you don't have sisters?"

"No, because I don't have great affection, that's all. I don't think I really love anybody, and nobody loves me."

"Why do you say that?"

"Oh, but I don't mind it, it's okay. It's just how it is; I'm incapable of arousing or feeling affection."

"What about James?"

"Again?"

"Don't you love James?"

"James is passion, Louise, passion, just that. And that's enough for me."

Louise smiled, satisfied that she had wrung confidence from Cecilia, and fell silent. Cecilia, for her part, regretted having let herself go. She certainly did not wish to arouse sympathy by talking about the emotional desert in which she lived and in which she was sure she was perfectly fine.

Perhaps it had been during one of those processions of orphan girls behind the carts of the dead that she had decided to be fine without affection, just as those deceased in their coffins.

Danielle Klimo simply found it absurd that the Brunne family had kept the tradition of dancing in the salon on the third Friday of every month.

As war raged in Europe and around the world, as Switzerland took in or turned away thousands of refugees pressing at its borders, once a month, guests prepared for the ball.

Danielle had almost always refused to participate and prevented her husband from coming down, partly because she had not missed how he looked at Cecilia Alesini.

Danielle, who had also once been beautiful, seventy years old, however well-worn, could hardly compete with Cecilia's youthfulness, freshness, and uncanny charm. Béa, too, did not go unnoticed, but she was of a more restrained, less engaging beauty.

Cecilia did not forgo nylons and fashionable dresses of the late 1930s, complete with mink or fox collars, cuffs, and fine jewelry.

For Danielle, this was intolerable. The war had imposed austerity on everyone; even in that privileged place, no one dared to flaunt riches, jewellery or textiles, which very few in Europe could now afford. Only that devil of a woman whom God had placed in her path for a still incomprehensible reason.

That evening, Walter had been strangely adamant that he would not give up the evening for any reason and had even dared to threaten to go down alone. Danielle had then thought of indulging him just this once. After all, she had been able to control him completely all her life conceding little in those rare times when he raised his voice.

Those were her thoughts as she applied lipstick while sitting at the desk mirror. Walter was already waiting for her, standing by the door.

As soon as they descended, the Klimo immediately saw Cecilia. She stood in the centre of the room, dazzling as never before. She wore a powder pink dress that wrapped her slender body and left her back bare. Her perfectly wavy blond hair fell long to her mid-back, and her white-skinned hands poked out from the tulle sleeves. She was absolutely out of place but truly beautiful. Danielle had the impulse to return to her room and take her husband with her.

James, Louise and Béa were also there.

Soon after came the Brunne family, Monika, with her large

build, and her husband Joseph, who passed with a concupiscent gaze from Cecilia to Béa to Louise, who awkwardly and clumsily as always kept her gaze downcast.

In one corner of the room were all the children: the Brunne's, dressed in white, with the little girls coiffed in long, tasselled braids, little Leonardo in Franciszka's arms, whom Lapo watched adoringly.

Marco stood behind his counter, from where the occasional croak of the radio through which he always hoped to pick up news of the war would come.

The Brunnes had equipped the salon with a gramophone and a few rifled records, which often jammed, for the times when musicians failed to show up on time.

"Come," said James, intent on tinkering with the gramophone, calling Anna and David Zeller, who had just peeped into the large room. "We were reminiscing about the great snowfalls of this winter. Fascinating, aren't they?"

Danielle found that blanket of snow simply frightening; it made her breathless to be stuck up there among those people. "Let's hope next winter will be milder; otherwise, we risk being isolated, and I don't know how many supplies the Brunnes have!" she said in a forcibly joking tone.

"Oh no, don't worry about that; we could survive for quite a while up here, a whole winter until the thaw!" laughed Monika. She no longer loved summer now that the many vacationers could not fill the hotel with cheer.

Louise intervened, pained at the thought, "If you couldn't go out, it would be a shame for the refugees at the sisters' shelter; I couldn't go and help the sisters and the children."

Béa commented, "Imagine that! No one would be able to stop Louise from reaching the nuns. Do you remember when, during the heaviest snowfall, the peasants had entrusted her with the horse-drawn sleigh cart just to reach the nuns? And she handled it brilliantly!" Béa laughed, and everyone imitated her. Louise could not understand why that episode was so comical: she wished to help the nuns and the refugee children with them despite the snow and had borrowed the sleigh. She had fared well, it was true, although she had struggled hard, while she was confident that her sister Béa would give up after a few meters. So, that hilarity had seemed stupid or even cruel to her.

"She is sturdy and strong, our Louise," smiled Herr Brunne lazily, "and she could even do without the horse." He ran the tip of his tongue over his lips in a gesture that made Louise blush.

The evening began.

James invited Béa to dance. It was his game to make Cecilia jealous. She looked at him with blazing eyes. Béa had a candor, an understated elegance, and a queenly bearing that she did not possess. She wore the usual yellow dress, as always on those occasions. It was not much, on closer inspection, but her black hair and green eyes shone in contrast to that light fabric, and the whole was simply delightful.

Herr Brunne had invited Louise, who blushingly began to dance awkwardly with him. The Klimos sat down, and the Zellers danced slowly, while David seemed, despite his height, smaller every day beside his wife, Anna.

Cecilia sat with an indifferent air, legs crossed. Occasionally, she cast her eyes toward her baby, who stood quietly in Franciszka's arms. And she waited, without giving away how much it weighed on her, for James to come to her and leave the slender waist of the beautiful Béa. Occasionally, he cast her a mischievous glance and gently ran a hand over Béa's back.

Around ten o'clock, the children were escorted to their rooms. With the excuse of following her little one in Franciszka's arms, Cecilia walked away, glancing surreptitiously at James, who was chatting softly with Béa.

Once the little one was asleep, Franciszka left, and Cecilia went to wait. Soon, James would return to his room, and she would run to him. They had met often since he had shown up at her door three months earlier.

At eleven o'clock, with her heart in turmoil, Cecilia stood up. She looked down the dark corridor. She had heard everyone returning to their rooms.

She ran into James's room and found the door open. He was sitting in the armchair by the fire, looking deep in thought.

"She is wonderful, Béa," she said, smiling at him with a teasing look. "You never danced with me tonight."

"You're the one who says we shouldn't arouse suspicion, but do you think no one knows about us? Naïve, I love you when you play naïve – exactly because you are far from it, my dear."

Cecilia sat on his lap, then, without saying a word, squatted at his feet and began to caress his inner thighs. She wanted him so badly after watching him dancing with someone else all night.

He relaxed and let her do it. Then he lifted her off the floor, lifted the long, tight skirt of her dress, and caressed her bare back with both hands. He held her standing in front of him and calmly undressed her, mastering her arousal. When she was completely naked, he pulled down her breeches and penetrated her by slowly moving her hips with his hands.

The next day, James walked confidently on an uphill path, and Cecilia tried to keep up with him frantically. They wanted to reach the small alpine lakes that, like precious pearls, lay along a path that skirted the Corvatsch massif. Cecilia had worn a thick sweater because she was not used to such a cool summer, but now she was panting, her cheeks red from fatigue. The air was even thinner and colder; the clear, glazed sky contrasted with the shimmering glow of white mountains at the summit, then grey, then light green, and finally dark with fir trees. The trail was narrow, the rounded pebbles slipping into the valley when he stepped on them. "Wait for me!" cried Cecilia to him when she felt she was too far behind. But her voice was lost in the infinite mountain, the peaks, and travelled through the crisp air without reaching him. She paused to catch her breath, her right leg outstretched and firmly planted on the ground and her left leg resting on a boulder covered with a light layer of moss. She slipped off her sweater and fastened it around her waist as a chamois stared at her from a distance. Then, she quickly escaped higher up. She looked at James further and further away, who did not stop, and then looked down at the valley and the serpentine path through the boulders they had been walking.

A few patches of snow still shone in the sun that bathed that pristine landscape, that stone desert, in light. At the far end, like a small patch of green and blue, Sils could be seen with its lake and meadows. Somewhere, there was that child Cecilia was struggling to love. She thought of him on the swing with Franciszka or sitting on the lawn next to the little Brunne children chasing each other. Perhaps he deserved better than a mother who ran away as soon as she could with her lover, but that was the only way Cecilia could endure being the mother she had never wanted to be. The feelings she had for James had given some life to her arid, dry and barren soul like the stones on which she had been walking all morning. Being desired by that man fulfilled her like nothing ever had before. At the same time, her son's outstretched arms distressed her profoundly and put her on edge because they burdened her with a responsibility she did not feel like taking on: loving a helpless being, becoming the world for him, protecting him. She simply did not know where to begin. It troubled her to sense that the little one was looking for her and somehow, perhaps, loving her despite the distance she had put between them as if to say: don't love me; I am incapable of loving you. And he, small but stubborn, looked at her with his big eyes and, although he spent most of his time with others, toddled happily when he saw her coming. It was inexplicable.

No doubt Emilio would know how to love the little one when they could one day be together. At that thought, Cecilia's heart, which had calmed down after the climb, sped up. The war would not last forever, and then, what would she do? What would become of her and James? How would she return to Milan, to the big house in Corso Venezia, with Emilio and the baby? She could not even imagine a life away from there, from Sils and James. Sometimes, it seemed to her that the world she had left behind just a few months earlier was gone forever the moment she had crossed the border that night. Instead, she now realized that, sooner or later, that world and that life would call her back.

"Cecilia!" James' powerful voice rose from a distant point to reach her.

"I'm coming!" she replied with all the breath in her throat and resumed her March.

Having reached within a few steps of the wooden cross on the far tip of the mountain, Cecilia drew in her breath and climbed up, crawling at times. Once beside James, she leaned over the mountain's crest, and her heart sank as her gaze was lost in the endless blue expanse. It was magnificent, and it came naturally to her to clasp his hand.

"What will happen when the war ends? I wish it would never end…"

"Don't say that; people are suffering because of the war; you can't always think of yourself." "This is how I feel. I don't want to go back to Milan for my wedding."

James turned to her, and she seemed to catch a glimpse deep in his clear eyes of a shadow of annoyance. "Cecilia, we never made any kind of promise to each other. We are here today, walking through the mountains and making love. Nothing more. We both know that one day, our lives will pick up where the war left off."

A few days earlier, there had been news of a large landing of American troops on the northern French coast, and the liberation of Europe seemed increasingly imminent. Cecilia looked at a distant point beyond the mountains, beyond the horizon, and said nothing. She could not cry, not in front of him. Instead, she smiled and began to descend slowly without looking back.

Franciszka brought the baby to his mother. Cecilia took him gently and looked at him. He was beautiful, growing. He had long dark eyelashes, light hair on his little round head, remarkably rosy skin, small heart-shaped lips, and a perfect little nose. Cecilia gave him a kiss and suddenly felt a disconcerting feeling of love. She began to feel that surprising emotion more and more often, as if it had been revealed to her unexpectedly that this baby was Emilio's, but it was also hers. Her baby.

She almost felt like crying. Then she held back at the thought that James was waiting for her down the hall, in her room.

Arriving in the room, Cecilia gave milk to Leo, who then fell asleep peacefully. Then she gently laid him on the soft comforters Franciszka had laid on the bottom of the crib the Brunnes had provided for her.

She hesitated a few moments, afraid it was not a good idea to leave him alone in the room again that night, as she had done so many times before. But then she thought in a flash about the war, which would end and perhaps take James away from her.

She turned and walked out, slowly closing the door behind him with a turn of the key.

The long hallway was dark and silent; no one would hear her footsteps on the soft carpet, but just in case, she took off her shoes and walked lightly.

She rested her fingers on James's door, and he opened it at the first touch. He was waiting for her. He was dishevelled, and a few wisps of blond hair fell over his eyes. He did not say a word and drew her in, holding her arms. Then he leaned her against the wall and began to kiss her, opening her lips with his moist tongue, then running down her neck after unfastening the first few buttons of her dress. Cecilia tried to pick up any noises outside and thought of her baby, across the hall, a few meters from her, but actually far away: he was not crying, or at least he did not seem to be. All was quiet.

And then she had no more time to think about anything else. With a frenzy that took her breath away, James was unbuttoning the buttons of her dress one by one. She began to respond to his kisses with increasing momentum as she felt his hardness through the velvet of his pants and his panting in her ears.

He pulled off her dress, and at that moment, the long necklace she wore around her neck snapped, causing a cascade of pearls to fall to the floor. Cecilia became bolder and unzipped his pants and held his erection in her hand. He opened her bodice and wrapped her left breast in his hand while he kissed her right nipple, running the tip of his tongue all around it.

Suddenly, he lifted her off the floor and gave her a half-turn as if in a strange waltz of those they had danced in the parlour on festive evenings. He threw her on the bed vehemently. He opened her legs, pulled off her panties and penetrated her with force. Cecilia was overwhelmed with excitement. He began to move rhythmically inside her, with quick and powerful strokes, until, moaning, they both climaxed and lay exhausted and panting, looking up at the ceiling with the crystal chandelier.

"I love you," Cecilia said. She had given herself up. He had won. She no longer cared. She was utterly dominated by James. And that made her feel fulfilled as never before. She had left all defences aside and thought he could do anything with her.

That night, he had chinked the armour she had always lived in; it was now his and would be forever. She felt overwhelmed with weakness, but she loved being that way.

Beside her, James, who had bent the will of that strong woman, felt all her fragility and, suddenly, felt a new erection coming on.

No one had ever involved him to that extent, given him such intense pleasure. And yes, he had had countless women.

"Hey, what are these big words? You've been amazing, Cecilia. Every time is beautiful."

Cecilia regretted saying she loved him and smiled, trying to posture defiantly.

"Yes, James, it was nice." She kissed him on the cheek and, trying to come to her senses, stood up and began to search for the pearls in the necklace.

The image of her naked gathering pearls on the polished parquet floor of the room would accompany James forever. That was the moment she broke through to him. She was a wonderful woman. And James knew that no one else would be like her.

Then, he was ashamed of that tender thought and told her, "Get dressed, it's getting cold, then we will look for the pearls."

Cecilia put her clothes back on, placing the pearls she had found in the ashtray.

Then, something jolted her – a wail – it was the baby; perhaps he had woken up. He needed her.

"Goodbye," she told James, and, leaving the pearls behind, she ran out, cheeks still flushed with passion.

SAMAR AND CECILIA

8

Engadine, 2010

It was already April, but a grey sky loomed over the small Swiss town, not promising anything good.

As I got off the train in Sankt Moritz, I immediately sensed an air unlike any I had ever breathed. It was fresh and light, not full of smog like that of Paris or of horns, sea, and spices like that of Algiers.

Few people got soff the train with me and then dissolved through those orderly streets among the anonymous buildings that seemed ugly, without cracks and without soul.

I had imagined it a glittering place, but instead, it had the flimsiness of an architect's model.

Following the signs to the Majestic, the first of the hotels where I had an interview, I travelled on deserted roads, which not even the beauty of the surrounding landscape could somehow make welcoming.

I dwelt on being a foreigner, which I had never felt until a few weeks before. Being so blond and pale in Algiers only made me feel different when my father told me more about his past and sent me to Europe, searching for the origin of these features I had always lived with, without giving it much thought. I had also been somewhat of a foreigner when I had begun to want, albeit vaguely, to follow a different path from my mother's, which had made me, in her eyes, a rebellious girl to be brought back into the well-defined dimension she wanted for me, regardless of how well that model fit me, or did not. I felt "foreign" to my mother, and I realized that on that first morning in Switzerland. Yet now, in the unfamiliar and vaguely hostile place in which I found myself, the image of her suddenly appeared to me as that of a safe haven.

After all, I had also been a foreigner during the weeks spent in Paris, which had failed to fulfil the many promises we had believed in as young girls when imagining France as a country where we could be happy in – even though we had never been there.

Until then, my only real home had always been my father's embrace. Until he told me he felt he belonged to our world, yes, but not quite fully. As if the uncertainty of his mutilated identity had challenged mine as well.

I snuggled into Madame Gourmand's sweater, not only because it was cold but because it made me feel welcomed. Time was running out, and it seemed increasingly difficult for me to compose the mosaic of his identity in what little remained of my father. I clutched in my hands a few pieces of different colours, puzzle pieces that did not fit together. It would do no good to force the fits, as I had done as a child, because I wanted to see the full picture as soon as possible.

Upon entering the hotel in Sankt Moritz, I found it almost gloomy. The burgundy brocade curtains, the too-large walnut tables with inlaid legs, and the heavy carpets gave the lounge a sad air. For a moment, I was breathless, and then I turned my gaze to the somewhat sullen woman coming toward me, looking perplexedly at my cheap blue dress and ballerinas. In fact, I felt a little out of context.

I had not even had time to smoke a cigarette as soon as I got off the train because I was afraid of being late, and now, out of nervousness, all I had left was to bite my nails.

The woman addressed me in German. I responded with the sentence I had prepared following Marc's advice, saying my name and explaining that I was there for an interview with the person in charge of personnel.

"I am in charge of the service staff here," she replied without extending his hand. "Come," she continued, leading the way to a small study behind the reception desk. I sketched a smile as my heart pounded in my chest and obeyed her invitation to sit in a small chair in front of the desk. She put on her glasses, searched through the papers she kept in the corner and pulled out my résumé.

"How come you speak Arabic?"

"I am Algerian," then, in the face of the woman's look of impatient anticipation, I whispered, as if everything in me was unbecoming, inadequate, out of place: "Half Arab and half French."

The woman looked at me doubtfully, glancing at the documents she was holding.

"What experience do you have as a waitress?"

"I worked for a few weeks in Paris in a restaurant..." At that moment, I saw the bistro with the colourful tables and thought that calling it a "restaurant" was too much.

"Any other experiences?" the woman asked, removing her metal-rimmed glasses and planting her small, sharp eyes in mine.

"No."

"Here, Miss..." she looked at the stack of resumes in front of him, "we're talking about a luxury hotel, a select clientele from all over the world. We are looking for people with experience in the field, not people improvising. Our staff almost becomes a travelling companion for the guests. However, we will let the agency know, but the positions we could hire you for are all already filled."

For the first time in a long time, I felt like crying for a reason unrelated to Dad's illness and the idea that the only world I knew, however imperfect, would be broken forever with his death. I wondered what I was doing there, and suddenly, I missed Algiers, the courtyard adorned by the somewhat peeling yellow and blue tiles leading to the narrow staircase that led to the apartment, my home, my father and even my mother, and it seemed to me that the purpose of that trip no longer had any meaning.

I got up, biting my lip and shivering slightly from anger, discouragement and the feeling of cold from which not even Madame Gourmand's sweater could protect me from.

The woman greeted me briefly, and I slipped through the door. Without looking at the dark hall any longer, I stepped out into the open air, heaving to keep me from crying, walked down a narrow street, and found myself in the centre of town.

I had appointments at two other hotels, but it seemed that the Majestic was the one Marc was banking on the most. I looked around for directions and for a foothold, a sign, any trace that would make me feel a piece of home, of my roots, but, I kept telling myself, it was impossible: that place was utterly foreign to me. What a stupid thought, of course, that place *was* foreign to me! Our origin does not necessarily have to be where we feel at home. Maybe home is just where we were loved, the heart space where we were loved, at least for a moment. It was that space my father was looking for: that moment in his childhood before his encounter with Nour's love. If he could find it, everything would be reassembled. But even if that love had been there, how could I find it?

None of the interviews went very differently from the first one. I was not the only one that day looking for seasonal work in the hotels in the valley. I met girls and boys my age, mostly South Americans and Asians, who converged on the Engadine every year. I exchanged a few words with some of them and realized that almost all of them had already worked there and were pretty much sure of succeeding in their search for that year.

Walking from one hotel to another, I noticed the public buses were yellow, like those used to transport students in Algiers. With my mania for seeing signs of fate everywhere, that fact seemed auspicious, but I soon realized that time was running out, and I had to hurry up and decide what to do. Perhaps I should have boarded one of those buses that travelled through the valley and let fate, intuition, take me right along. What a fool, I felt. The clock was ticking, and I dreamed everything would work out like magic when I needed a concrete idea instead. I could have taken a train and gone back to Paris, hoping to be called in the next few days by one of the hotels, which seemed difficult, or I could have tried some other avenue to find a job, stayed and tried to figure out if my father had really spent the first months of his existence up here.

I had checked online to see if there were any children's homes in the valley or any traces of an active orphanage in the past, but nothing. I should have talked to someone who had been there during the war, but how? Every option seemed like a dead-end.

I still had almost an hour to wait before I could return. It was a long journey. I would have to reach Zurich from Sankt Moritz and then go to Paris from there. Fortunately, Madame Gourmand bought me one of those expensive open return tickets. I didn't know how to tell her that her help had been for nothing. I picked up the phone and thought about calling her, but then I decided to talk to Marc first and called him. I imagined the phone ringing in the small office in Paris. He answered it almost immediately.

"I don't think the interviews went very well, Marc, I'm sorry. Let's say that the need for Arabic was, in fact, of interest only to the Majestic and, anyway, for a position where more experience was also required. Now let's see what happens. I don't dare calling Madame Gourmand; I'll talk to her when I get to Paris. Do you think there is any chance for a job?" I uttered these words all in one breath.

Marc let out a long sigh and tried to reassure me, "Don't worry about it; it's no problem. Of course..." he hesitated for a moment, displeased of having to say it aloud, "they usually give an answer straight away, so that people don't come back shortly... however, it's not necessarily the case..."

I heard the doorbell ring as someone opened the agency door, and Marc cut it short, relieved, "I have to go now, Samar." Then he added, perhaps out of fear of being too rude, "Take it easy, see what happens; maybe they'll call you back. And have a safe trip." That kindness brought me to tears, and the tears I had managed to hold back in front of the obnoxious Majestic woman suddenly slid down my cheeks. I hated disappointing the people who were trying to help me.

I stopped before a shop window to wipe my face, pretending to look at the sportswear on display. Two people were inside. One must have been the saleswoman, going back and forth from the shelves to the counter carrying some garments to a not-too-tall man who stood with his back to me, his hair ruffled. I couldn't say why I dwelt on that scene; it was so mundane, so ordinary. Nor do I know why I noticed that the gentleman was so dishevelled, who, soon after, walked toward the checkout counter holding a white sweater, disappearing from my sight.

When I pulled out my cell phone to look at the time, I suddenly realized that I was in danger of missing the last train to Zurich and then Paris. I ran like a fool, I had chased my thoughts, I had cried, I had foolishly wondered how such a dishevelled man could be in such an expensive store, and now I was in danger of spending the night in the place I was beginning to hate, with no chance of finding an affordable room to spend the night. The station was not far away, yet when I arrived, transfixed and sweaty despite the cool evening air, a dot was already flashing on the scoreboard next to my train, which was, in fact, leaving the station, moving slowly.

Missing the train by a whisker, I sat daunted in the station waiting room, clutching my yellow sweater, scared and alert. I gasped when a policeman asked me something in German. I understood that he most likely wanted my papers. I rummaged frantically through my bag, tucking my hair behind my ear. I pulled out my passport, all the papers Marc had handed me in a plastic folder, and the lost train ticket. The man scrutinized the papers sternly, wrinkled his eyebrows, squared me expressionlessly, perhaps thinking I would make no trouble, and slipped into the guardhouse without a word.

I dozed off intermittently, and dawn surprised me with the hubbub of the first passengers. Dragging my suitcase, I entered the small station bathroom.

I looked in the mirror: the dark circles under my eyes were more pronounced than usual, and that strand of makeup I had put on for the interview the day before had leaked miserably, making them very dark. I looked horrible. The neon light in the station bathroom made me even paler; my eyes seemed too light, and my lips were colourless, dry, and cracked. It seemed to me that only the freckles stood out below the now patchy blush. I quickly scrubbed my face with ice-cold tap water and the cheap soap from that public bathhouse, hoping no one would notice me. I tied my hair by tucking a pencil I had found in my purse into the bun. I went over my eyelashes with black mascara and some colour back on my cheeks. I put chapstick on my lips and tightened them by rubbing them together. I looked at myself again and found myself unexpectedly pretty, but most of all different from the girl who had left Algiers a few weeks earlier, from the girl who had taken the fear-filled passport photo. After all, I felt I had accomplished things: I had left, I had found a job in France and people who loved me, I had made it as far as Switzerland. Of course, I still hadn't accomplished anything, but could Dad consider this change of mine an accomplishment? Maybe Mom criticized me for being afraid, but could she have been, in a small part of her heart, a little proud of me? As I wiped my hands with the rough paper towel, I felt as strong as I had ever been: I would go back to Paris, call Dad, and ask him what he preferred me to do. I stay and get my mind on something else to find out his story or come back with more experience in my pocket and a new light in my eyes, but there is no answer for him. I chased away the thought of not arriving in time to say goodbye to him, an idea that was taking hold of me more and more, filling my whole mind with black, bottomless anguish, like dark walls widening inside me, leaving no room for anything else, and walked out of the station. The train was still a few hours away.

I was sorry to go back to Paris because if Isabelle and Pauline Vernet's little brother had been born there, and he was my father, that was where I should be. But without a job, I could not stay. Perhaps I could have looked in other areas; possibly Madame Gourmand would have had some other ingenious idea, like when she had searched the telephone directories for the name 'Vernet'. I decided to go back, but first, I wanted to go to a lovely patisserie I had noticed the previous day, to reconnect with the place, to like it and perhaps meet an old man who could tell me something about long ago. SINCE 1894, the pastry shop sign said. I walked in, wondering if Madame Vernet had ever passed through there or had coffee with Maurice at one of those little tables. I thought she would be a mother soon and was planning the trip to Algiers. I walked in as if those walls could speak to me.

I sat at a small table in the corner, tossing my cloth bag onto the chair before me and setting my trolley down next to it. Fortunately, no one seemed to pay attention to me or my looks.

I ordered a slice of Sacher with tea – real lady's stuff, I thought to myself. There were not so many people. In the other corner of the room sat a family, probably German, with three beautiful blond babies. At the counter, two men, one younger than the other, were chatting over two cups of coffee.

The girl at the bar placed the slice of Sacher intended for me on a beautifully decorated plate and added plenty of whipped cream. Then she brought me a tray with the cake and teapot across the room.

I looked admiringly at the slice of cake and, suddenly elated, grabbed the small fork and began to eat it with gusto. I had not touched food since the day before when I had eaten Madame Gourmand's sandwiches on the train.

Looking up, I noticed that the older of the two men at the counter must have been the same as the one I had seen in the store through the window. Yes, it was him. I didn't want to stare too much, but there was no doubt about it – he was also wearing the white sweater with braids that I had seen him buy.

I looked down and finished my cake. Then, I checked the time on the cell phone display: I had to go. I got up, approached the cashier to pay, and headed for the glass door. Just as I was gaining the exit, suddenly, voices, background music, and the clatter of dishes seemed to rumble and mix in my ears. I opened the door, which felt so heavy. I took the first of the few steps that led to street level, and the image of the small town, of houses and cars, blurred, became opaque and then splattered with dark spots. I felt weak in the knees and a sudden sharp pain in my head. I reopened my eyes a few seconds later; at least, I think so. The taste of chocolate from the cake made me nauseous; I forced myself not to vomit.

Some people were around me. It took me a while to recognize the waitress, the mother of the blond children sitting inside, and then the two men drinking coffee at the counter. Everyone talked to me in German, and I couldn't understand anything. I touched my head where it hurt and felt wet. Blood. It must have been a nasty cut. I sat back down. The older of the two men motioned me not to move. "Keep still," he said in German. "I have to catch the train," I answered him in French, suddenly lucid. I did not want to miss it. Then the man, dabbing at me with a napkin the maid had brought him, said to me in heavily accented German French, "I'm a doctor; you need stitches here, you hit against the edge of the step. Did you trip or faint?"

"I think I fainted," I replied, composing myself.

The younger man handed me a glass of water.

"Look, I would like to take you to the hospital in Samedan to get stitches, and since you hit your head so hard, I would have you kept for observation until tomorrow," the doctor said.

I got up from the floor, holding the napkin over the wound and trying to hide that I was still dizzy. "I have a train to catch. I have to go, and I have no money to stay here or to pay for any kind of treatment. I'll get stitches in Paris." I moved the hand that held the napkin and looked at it: it was soaked.

With professional flair, the doctor folded another one meticulously, wrinkling his forehead. "We're taking you to Samedan now; we can't let you go like this."

Meanwhile, the bakery owner had gone out and offered to drive me to the emergency room in her car. I gave up, not feeling up to travelling to Paris; the wound hurt, and my whole head was throbbing. In great embarrassment, I got into the car, keeping my napkin compressed over the wound so as not to soil the seat. The doctor and his friend followed us on the motorcycle.

When I came down in front of a large white building a few minutes later, I was definitely feeling better, but still losing blood. Maybe there really was a need for stitches. I walked in next to the bakery lady, still holding my napkin pressed to my temple. The doctor caught up with us, passed us, and approached the admitting desk. I noticed that the nurses knew him. When I was led to the outpatient clinic, the bakery owner said goodbye and returned to Sankt Moritz. The doctor spoke briefly with the doctor who had greeted me and, then, to reassure me, told me that he would come by the next day. He greeted me cordially, and his friend, who was waiting outside, waved at me.

When they were gone, I felt like crying. I wanted to go back to Paris, or rather, to Algiers. They sat me down on the crib to medicate me, and after the anaesthesia injection, they sewed some stitches. I would be left with a scar on my left temple. A little later, I was taken to an all-white room, where they gave me broth I did not touch.

I didn't feel like calling my parents, who would be overly frightened, so I just sent a message to Madame Gourmand telling her that I would be back the next day and that I was fine, without adding any other details.

Soon after, I didn't know how, I fell asleep exhausted.

I must have slept an incredible number of hours since the next memory I have is the nurse who, at dawn, was measuring my fever. The doctor who had stitched me up also came in momentarily, took one look at the suture, and, satisfied, told me I could go. They left some papers to sign on the bedside table and told me I could pay the bill later since Dr. Charlier was vouching for me. I guessed that Dr. Charlier must have been the doctor who had rescued me outside the bakery, and I wondered how I could thank him if he did not come by.

I let go of the pillow to gather strength and got dressed, unsure how to reach the station. Someone knocked softly. The door slowly opened, and the doctor's curly head popped out.

"Good morning; how are we doing?"

"Good," I replied, pulling myself up and composing myself. He sat at the end of the bed and looked at the folder. I was uncomfortable with that stranger and adjusted the blanket to completely cover the white T-shirt they had made me wear the night before.

"As soon as I get back to Paris, I will ask my parents to give me the money for the hospital."

"Don't worry now; you can take your time. Do you need anything? Would you like me to accompany you to the station?"

I didn't want to take advantage of him again, so I said no, I would make it by myself.

He must have noticed the uncertainty in my eyes that contradicted my words. He remained suspended momentarily as if about to leave, then reconsidered. At that moment, our gazes met, and I seemed to catch a glimpse, beyond the lenses, in his lively hazel eyes, of a drop of amber.

"What are you doing here all alone, Mademoiselle?" I glimpsed embarrassment in the man and was amused. The tension soon melted away; I felt unexpectedly at ease. Besides, it sounded strange to me to be called "Mademoiselle." He must have been in his fifties, maybe a few years younger. He hadn't shaved in a few days and had a great mass of dishevelled hair and a nice smile that made him likeable.

"What is a foreign girl doing here in St. Moritz, all alone, out of season?" he continued.

"Unsuccessfully looking for work," I replied, increasingly relaxed as I looked at the sad geometric decoration on the bedspread.

"Where are you from? You speak French perfectly, but I can't frame your accent."

I hesitated. "I am Algerian," I replied, suddenly deciding to trust him.

"You joke. Are you perhaps a Frenchwoman from Algeria?"

I smiled. "My origins are complicated; we don't have time to discuss it now. I have a train to catch; I'm returning to Paris without a job, and from there, I'll probably fly to Algiers."

The man extended his hand to me, and I shook it without hesitation.

"I am, however, Albert. I'm here on vacation. I'm originally from Geneva but a resident of Zurich. Nothing too complicated."

"I am Samar."

"Look, if you need a ride to the station, it's no problem. From Samedan to Sankt Moritz, it's only a few kilometres. Below is my friend Matteo waiting for me in the car."

I hesitated but then decided to trust. I would be able to catch the train by noon.

"All right, thank you. I'll get ready quickly and be there."

He left. He would wait for me in the hallway.

I dressed in a hurry, glancing at the bathroom mirror to look at the scar with its black dots. I tried to hide it a little with my hair, tied my shoes, threw my T-shirt in the suitcase, unplugged my cell phone, put it in my purse, and went downstairs.

Albert was waiting for me and smiled as if outside the hospital; he was more relaxed. The boy beside him extended his hand to me cordially, "How do you do? I'm Matteo, Albert's fraternal friend." He looked like a cheerful boy, supposedly about my age, and his lively expression immediately reminded me of Mehdi, although he was much taller.

We got into the car.

"Samar was looking for work here," Albert broke the silence.

"What kind of work?" asked Matteo.

"I interviewed at the Majestic and other hotels, but it was a bit of a disaster. I'm going home shortly. I have a train in a couple of hours."

"At the Majestic as a receptionist?"

"No, no, as a waitress. They are looking for people who speak Arabic but apparently also much better German than I do."

Matteo seemed to have a sudden idea, "Albert, we know very well where mademoiselle could be hired, *n'est-ce-pas?*"

Albert brightened up.

"Forget about the train, Sara," Matteo continued, suddenly on a roll.

"My name is Samar," I corrected him.

"Okay, Samar, forget the train and come with us."

I don't know why they took my situation to heart, but maybe that was my last chance to try to stay at least a little while. Besides, Switzerland seemed so hostile that I almost regretted it would be only a bad memory.

"If you want, we'll take you to the hotel in Sils Maria, a charming place not far from here. You'll see, they'll hire you."

At the name of Sils Maria, I jolted and immediately visualized the notebook in which I had written that name at the Vernet sisters' house: it was the location where their mother had not allowed them to go skiing because the place reminded her too much of the child who had died of pneumonia in Algeria. "We have good contacts." She continued, turning slightly as she drove. "We will convince my grandmother to put in a good word for you. Albert is the only one in the world who manage her." When the lanky, distinguished boy mentioned Grandma, I thought I discerned a note of sincere affection in him. "She's had a heart condition for years, but she doesn't give up and keeps coming to the mountains at two thousand meters and, when she's here, she gets treatment from our good Albert. We don't know how he has kept her from a heart attack for years." He gave a big, expansive smile.

I looked at the clock on my cell phone: I would have to go to the station shortly thereafter to catch the train. Then I thought that if I returned to Paris, it would be difficult, no, impossible, to unravel the mystery that had led me there. I would have no choice but to return to Algiers. Tormenting my thumb's cuticles with my forefinger and thinking longingly about the pack of cigarettes lying somewhere in my bag, I told myself that a hair-thin thread had led me to Switzerland. Perhaps it would be a mistake to let it go.

"All right," I said resolutely. "I'll follow you."

I sank into the leather seat and felt that something was happening. I still didn't know what, but I sensed clearly that the impulse to cross the threshold of the bakery to indulge in a slice of Sacher before leaving had brought me to some kind of turning point.

Matteo drove confidently along the lakes of Sankt Moritz and Silvaplana, then, having arrived at another lake, climbed up some hairpin bends and parked next to a building that looked like the fairy-tale castle I had dreamed of as a child. "Here we are," Albert said very softly.

I got out of Matteo's car and observed the entrance to the hotel. A few steps led to a revolving door. Matteo and Albert joined me, and we started to go up. I walked in squeezing myself in my pullover. For a moment, I was dazzled by the large hall that opened before me, with the chandelier composed of dozens and dozens of lights hanging from the centre of the ceiling. I did not immediately notice that Matteo had headed for the reception desk to my right, just below a beautiful staircase with a wrought-iron railing. Suddenly, he called me, and I approached him, extending my hand to the strange man looking at me blankly.

"Lapo! What's going on?" asked Matteo to the older man, and then, turning back to me, in a lower tone, "Excuse him, Samar, Lapo has been here forever; he was born here. He is the son of the historical concierge of this hotel, a friend of my father and grandmother. He lives in a world of his own, but he has exceptional abilities..." The man had already looked away, but the moment he had looked at me, I seemed to catch a glimpse of astonishment and perhaps almost fright. I would have liked to know more about him, but Matteo had already entered the hall, and Albert and I followed him.

"Grandma!" he exclaimed as he leaned toward an elderly woman sitting at one of the many walnut tables in the living room to hug her. "Good evening, Cecilia," the doctor smiled at her once beside Matteo. Then, she noticed me and raised her eyes to a blue that must have been more intense in the past.

She then turned to his nephew with a mischievous smile, "Matteo, don't tell me you came to introduce me to your girlfriend!"

I lowered my gaze, intimidated.

"No, she is a girl we met yesterday in Sankt Moritz; we gave her a hand because she had a bad fall. She would like to work as a waitress. She speaks French and Arabic perfectly."

Cecilia squared me, frowning a little. With my yellow sweater a little untucked, the big green bag and the mascara that had perhaps started to run again, I knew I didn't look like a maid of a five stars hotel. I felt awkward, but Matteo's grandmother, after a few moments, opened up in a warmer smile than I would have expected and held out her white, somewhat gnarled hand to me. "Too bad, you are the prettiest of all the girls Matteo has ever introduced me to." I shook her hand while sketching a smile and said my name quickly, feeling entirely out of place. Then my scar, which now hurt a little, came to mind, and I brushed it off.

"Mrs. Alesini, I would be grateful if you would give her a hand," Dr. Charlier intervened, with an enthusiasm that amazed me. Then he turned to me, "For the stitches, don't worry; I can take them out in a couple of weeks if you're still here."

Cecilia looked at the doctor and gave a mischievous smile. "If you ask me, doctor, I can only beg Franciszka to hire her. I still have some power here, you know."

"We have no doubt, Grandma," Matteo added.

"Follow me", Cecilia suddenly said, leaning on her cane to get up from the chair.

I was dazed; too much was happening so fast. Striving to put aside my instincts to turn on my heels and slip through the door, trying to master the panic I felt rising within me, I followed that elderly lady who, despite her polite manner, was a bit awe-inspiring, and left Albert and Matteo there, with an air of complicity.

Cecilia led me to the reception desk and asked the boy to call her Franciszka, the person she had mentioned earlier.

She spoke briefly on the phone with what must have been a friend and hung up.

"Franciszka is waiting for you downstairs in the offices on the basement floor," she winked at me. "Go down the staircase at the end of the hallway, and you will see the office door."

Nodding to say thank you, I started, panicked, down the hallway. I had already been interviewed in a fancy hotel and did not want to be humiliated again.

I descended the stairs, fearing my legs would not hold me up. When I arrived at the bottom, I saw a door with an OFFICE sign. I paused for a few seconds, rolling a lock of hair around my finger. Just as I was about to knock, the same older man I had just met opened the door from inside. He looked at me as if surprised for a few seconds, then left, shuffling his feet.

I went in a few steps and asked permission.

At a desk sat a very old woman, much older than the hag I had interviewed with at the Majestic in Sankt Moritz.

The woman stood up and held her hand to me, "Good morning, I'm Franciszka. Tell me a little about yourself," she began directly, with what must have been her standard ice-breaker phrase.

I felt strangely at ease as my breathing became regular again, and I told her I wanted to get a job there to improve my German. I immediately bit my tongue, thinking about how the woman at the Majestic would respond. Still, things turned out differently: "Actually, it would be better to know it well enough already to work here, but Cecilia told me that her nephew Matteo and Dr. Albert Charlier accompanied you here." I merely nodded, not mentioning that I had met them by chance just the day before.

"You can start tomorrow for me. First, you will have to interview with my younger colleague, who, alas, will replace me when I am gone or unable to work. But don't worry. I will tell her that hiring people who know Arabic is important at this time. Then I will give you some tips to make a good impression on her and our guests when you are a maid at the Grand Hotel Maria."

I felt a flicker of joy inside me, and it was not lost on me that she had put me on a first name basis, as if I were already part of the staff.

I was assigned one of the small rooms reserved for staff in the basement, near Franciszka's office and apartment.

Perhaps reading the weariness of that incredible day on my face, Franciszka pointed me to the bathroom I would share with my colleagues and immediately left me alone. I realized I should call my mother, but I did not have the energy to listen to her voice, which was thick with disapproval, and instead put it off until the next day. Instead, I called Madame Gourmand, sure she would be pleased with the latest developments. She answered immediately, and I thought I had heard the beads of the curtain of what she called the "cabin" jingle slightly. As expected, she enthusiastically welcomed the tale of my adventure and cheered me on. Her words, full of warmth, went straight to my heart and almost succeeded in bringing her round face, intelligent and wry eyes, good humour, and strength beside me.

That night, though overwrought, I did not close my eyes. The trolley with the few things I had with me was left open on the floor; I had stored nothing in the light-coloured wooden closet. The uniform I was to wear the next day was hanging on a hanger on the closet door. I couldn't imagine how I would manage and how any of this would help my research.

Early the next day, Franciszka knocked on my door, but I was already up and had just finished dressing. She explained that for the first few days, I would have to work alongside some colleagues and learn how to prepare and serve breakfast and move around the kitchen and then the dining room. I would have a few hours off each day and then one day a week, to be agreed with the other girls, entirely off. I sighed, thinking that every minute of my free time, I would use to seek the truth. Finally, Franciszka led me down the hall, where there was a back door that I was to use to enter and leave the hotel. Beyond the door, an outside ladder led to the level of the main entrance, but on the side of the building.

After giving me all the instructions, Franciszka gave me a few more minutes to finish getting ready. I didn't have much time to phone home. Still, I couldn't put it off any longer, even though I was sure Mother would not appreciate it, would tell me to come back as soon as possible, would get nervous and worried, as if Switzerland was on the other side of the world, a place full of danger. The phone rang for a long time, and then my mother answered in a tired voice. Unexpectedly, when I told her where I was, his voice resounded, alongside the usual concern, a melancholy note: I felt her sense of genuine lack this time. Perhaps it was because Switzerland seemed to her much, much further away from Algeria than France, and somehow it was so unfamiliar, so different from what we had ever known and imagined. I, too, felt a wave of affection for her and realized how much she must have suffered from seeing Dad lose his strength day after day. She did not refrain from greeting me with the usual "be careful," and then, almost in a whisper, as if it were something to be ashamed of, before passing Dad to me, she said, "I love you." Dad saw in my having gone to Switzerland a sign of some progress, a jolt in a situation that had been too long immobile. He said he felt pretty good, but something in his voice made me not believe him. That doubt accompanied me throughout the day, along with anxiety about what awaited me in the new reality in which I found myself.

***

On the evening of the interview, Franciszka had brought Lapo dinner to his room as usual. He was confused, more than expected.

"I saw Cecilia today," the man had slurred.

"Sure, me too. She's been here for a while, Lapo…"

"No, not the old woman, not the old Cecilia, not the old Cecilia." He had repeated this sentence, muttering, almost to himself.

"And which Cecilia did you see, then?" Franciszka said condescendingly.

"The young, young, young Cecilia."

She had smiled. "What are you talking about, Lapo?"

"The young one."

At that moment, Franciszka had had a flash: "Are you perhaps referring to the blond girl who came into my office today?"

Lapo had nodded: "She was the young Cecilia, the young Cecilia, the young Cecilia."

"You're right; she does look a bit like her," Franciszka had softly stated, twitching her lips in nostalgia for the times when Cecilia, like her, was a young girl with her life ahead.

"She doesn't just look like *she* was the young Cecilia. She was her. It was her," Lapo had continued, gradually losing himself in his world.

"Now rest, Lapo," Franciszka had said, adjusting the pillow behind his back. "Now rest." She had kissed him on the forehead, as she had every night for sixty years, and had gone to the living room where Cecilia was waiting for her.

Usually, she did not like to mingle with guests, and that was why, to enter and leave the hotel, she always used the small door dedicated to staff that led directly into the basement where her office and small apartment were located. When she went for walks with Cecilia, they would meet in front of the hotel's main entrance. Still, she would get there by climbing the narrow stairs that led from the back door to a small clearing on the right side of the Maria, just where the library faced, bordered by the woods. They were often in the library, which was much less crowded. Still, even knowing this, Cecilia would occasionally ask her to join her in the large hall.

When she joined her at the small table near the bow window, Cecilia ran her gaze across the entire hall. "Every time I walk into this hall, I feel like I still see the people from back then... remember?" she said with a sigh. "We were all standing here, locked in an absurd community in a luxury hotel. It was a somewhat unreal situation, a peculiar condition." "Yeah," Franciszka nodded.

"It's almost like I can see Marco," Cecilia continued, "watching the guests in the hall from his counter at the reception desk, Lapo intent on adjusting the radio in the office, Anna with David and the children, the Brunne's who were hardly visible, their eight children..." She gave a short laugh as if she still didn't believe it. "And then – and then the obnoxious Klimo, how evil that woman was! A real devil! And then Louise and Béa and... of course, James..."

"All you do is torment yourself, Cecilia, let it go! Every year, the same things happen endlessly, endlessly, endlessly."

"But no, I'm quiet today – don't they say that all old people do is think back to the past, that all they talk about is war times? Here I am, a typical old woman." Cecilia felt sarcastic and slightly elated that afternoon.

Franciszka left her alone, and she picked up her cup lying on the coffee table and brought it to her lips, blowing lightly and rippling the surface of the golden liquid.

She was about to get up and return to her room when she saw Dr. Charlier and his nephew Matteo coming toward her.

Cecilia was glad that Matteo had bonded with Dr. Charlier despite their age difference. Both mountain enthusiasts, they would often go on long hikes together or surf the lake on their windsurfs.

She felt her heart open as she saw what a handsome, dark-haired, charming boy her grandson had become. Matteo and Albert sat with her to tell her about their day until around twenty-three; tired, Cecilia left them alone.

The next morning, she and Franciszka had the driver drop them off at the lake. After walking the first part of the road, they sat on a bench right on the shore, just before the beginning of the path leading to the peninsula.

"Every pleasure wants eternity," Cecilia said, quoting Nietzsche's inscription carved on the boulder at the far tip of the peninsula as she let her back go against the bench and gently rested her cane beside her.

"Anna and I had started from that sentence in our German lessons. I wonder what happened to my good teacher, my friend Anna, and her beautiful family. I think after the war, they all went to Israel… She never looked for me again; perhaps she was too good a person for me, for the Cecilia I was then, a lost woman who asked for nothing but atonement." She sighed and arranged behind her ear a silvery lock that had escaped her bun. "I never got to a good level of German, but in those months, I had begun to understand it and say a few words. I always wondered what exactly that inscription meant. Pleasure and suffering. Pleasure even deeper than suffering." She whispered the last words, staring at a point on a distant horizon, beyond the lake, beyond mountains. "I have also often wondered if those months of passion were worth all the suffering that came after. I don't know; I can't give myself an answer, but I know perfectly well that if I went back, I wouldn't have the strength to give up that love. Am I crazy?" Without giving Franciszka time to respond, Cecilia continued as if unable to stop that wave of memories sweeping over her. "My suffering is irrelevant, but that of the other people involved is not. I should have suffered only myself, denying myself the love of my life."

"You have paid a very high price, Cecilia. Now, you should forgive yourself. It's time," Franciszka said, interrupting the violent and tumultuous flow of her friend's thoughts.

"How can I forgive myself if I don't know exactly what happened that night?"

"Forgive yourself because you suffered again and again; life did not spare you pain, either before or after that period. You allowed yourself a few months of genuine happiness."

Cecilia squinted her eyes, which were suddenly glazed with tears.

"Do you remember 1955? I was thirty-seven years old, and Manfredi just five."

Franciszka nodded, "I remember the day in 1955 when you arrived here, like every year." She lowered her gaze, then raised it again and looked around as if looking for a foothold, a cue to change the subject. But Cecilia continued.

"I will never forget that moment, the first night of that summer. I had gone down the stairs with Manfredi, but he had asked me to see the hotel's new elevator to push the buttons. We stood there in front and waited because it was busy. When the doors opened, the world collapsed on top of me: James and Béa were there, facing me, laughing, holding their hands and talking under their breath like two lovers. I was speechless and immediately noticed, because Béa wanted me to notice the wedding ring they wore on their finger. They had gotten married. Can you believe it? James married Béa. There, out of my unhappiness, came her happiness."

"Do you think they were happy? James and Béa, I mean."

Cecilia sighed, carefully weighing her words. "She was; he was the man she wanted all along. I don't know about him. I'm still so selfish that part of me hopes he was unhappy, at least a little, next to that woman." At that moment, a flash of exultation caught Cecilia, illuminating for a few seconds the gloomy night where those memories had led her. "Of course, that day in front of the elevator, he was speechless, too. He looked straight in my eyes for a few seconds, as only he knew how to do. He dug once again into my suffering, my torment, my passion, my love. He went through me in those moments as he stepped out of the elevator, and his wife, Béa, greeted me, flaunting an unnatural cheerfulness. He still loved me, Franciszka; he still loved me." Cecilia repeated this a couple of times to demonstrate her statement's absolute conviction. "He looked for me in those days when I called in sick and stayed locked in my room waiting for Mr. and Mrs. Ashton to leave again; he looked for me several times. But I did not let him find me. I never wanted to talk to him. Because I did not deserve it. Béa, on the other hand, clearly deserved that happiness. I had little Manfredi and my husband, who had stood by me despite everything, and he had Béa." Again, the weight of that past seemed to crush the elderly woman, forcing her to take a break. "I assure you that to this day when I can't make it up on foot because of this damned heart, and I'm forced to call the elevator, I think that when the doors will open, I'll be shown that scene of James and Béa together again, married, registered at the front desk as James and Béatrice Ashton. And I want to die."

Franciszka nodded, "I know. That day I knew you were coming; I had seen it in the register and was distressed. I was sure that Béa had arranged her vacation right here on purpose to let you know that she was in the place that should have been yours. I hoped you had postponed your arrival until the last minute. I didn't want you to spend a moment like that. You and I weren't great friends then, but I knew how bad you had felt in '44, and it seemed to me it was bad enough, more than any woman has to endure."

"You are very nice for saying that. But I was not just any woman; I was the worst of mothers, as Danielle Klimo called me."

Franciszka snorted, "That was just a witch, a sour witch. She hated you because you were the most beautiful of all, and her husband dreamed of you every night for sure." She laughed like a little girl. And Cecilia also roused herself for a moment from her gloomy thoughts. She laughed, "Walter Klimo was really an insulting man, a victim of the witch he married." She thought back momentarily to Emilio, who had always loved her unconditionally.

Then she resumed the thread she had momentarily abandoned: "On the day of their departure, he came to my room to say goodbye. He knocked for a long time, begging me to open for him, but I did not. I stood there, behind that door, in silence. Suddenly, he stopped knocking and talking, but I felt his presence. We remained motionless, divided by that layer of wood, breathing lightly, each trapped in the hiding place where we would never find ourselves again. I sensed the strength of our love passing like a thin thread through that door and uniting us inextricably. After a few minutes, I heard his slow and heavy footsteps start down the hallway. I opened the door without a sound and saw him for a moment just before he turned the corner. I heard Béa's voice asking him where he was, telling him to hurry, that the driver was waiting for them. I have lived off that moment, Franciszka, I got by with the knowledge of our love of, all these years. *Alle Lust will Ewigkeit.*" Cecilia's gaze was lost far away, toward the end of the peninsula, among the shady pines and the faint lapping of the lake's tiny waves.

"The following year, I asked the Brunne's eldest son, who was then in charge of the hotel, if the Ashtons would be coming, but he replied that no, they had not booked and had moved to Canada, so at least they had written to him in a note. And so, despite the unparalleled beauty of the Engadine mountains, he didn't think they would cross the ocean to come to the Maria."

Franciszka listened in silence. "I know, these unlived loves keep you for life in a cage from which it is impossible to get out. I understand you, and you know it. That was the same year that Marco died. And, probably, also the year when our friendship was really born, Cecilia, the friendship of two women held captive by memories."

Then, seized by a sudden thought, she got up, grabbed her cell phone, and called the driver of the hotel bus: "Mrs Alesini wants to be taken back to the hotel. " Then, turning to Cecilia, she said, "I have to go back to Lapo's. I have to make him some food!"

"Of course, dear. I'll have that young lady I hired for you bring my lunch to my room today. She's good, isn't she?"

"Yes, very smart."

"I think Dr. Charlier was bewitched by her," Cecilia smiled, moving her hands as if to cast a spell. "When he came with Matteo and the girl, I noticed a new light in his gaze. He seemed suddenly happier as if he had found an unexpected surprise."

"But Charlier is twice his age, and by the way, I know he is in a relationship with a colleague. Samar would, if anything, be a better match for your nephew Matteo; I suppose they are the same age."

"Yes," Cecilia replied, "but only Albert has eyes for her, Matteo doesn't."

Franciszka shook her head in disapproval.

Cecilia continued, in German and alluding to the notorious racism of the terrible and bigoted Danielle Klimo, imitating her, "Is it ever possible that the upstanding Dr. Charlier, forty-nine years old and of pure Aryan race, fell hopelessly in love with an Algerian maid far younger than himself?" She then threw back her head, laughing and momentarily becoming the carefree, cheerful girl she had never been.

Franciszka always laughed when her friend spoke in German, imitating Mrs Klimo: "Stop it, Cecilia, stop it. I am still over ninety years old, a little respect! You will not compare me again to the terrible Danielle Klimo for my disapproval of Albert. I will be offended to death! And anyway, I would say that Anna Keller taught you German very well, my dear!" she concluded, climbing into the bus.

* * *

I had only been in service for a week, but it felt like I had been there for a lifetime and had made no progress with my research, and this kept me awake at night, until I fell asleep just before dawn. I had checked again on the internet to see if there was any record of any orphanages in the valley during World War II, and I had come across the history of refugees from other countries, mainly from France, but not only. Among them were many children: one could find black-and-white photos showing them on arrival at the Geneva station, then they were sorted into families who kept them with them, while, according to the articles, their parents were sent to labor camps. What if my father had been one of those children? A child fleeing the war, taking refuge in neutral Switzerland who had then been unable to join his parents or had lost them to a bombing? References to the Engadine, or at least to the canton of Graubünden in which it is located, were not there. What if, instead, he was a child who had been a refugee in Switzerland illegally? In that case, reconstructing his history and tracing his birth parents would have been truly impossible. While these thoughts did not leave me, I went about my work willingly. I was in charge of service in the dining room, but not only that. In the mornings Franciszka would ask me to run a few errands, such as going to the village at dawn to order everything that would be needed for that day – from milk to bread. At other times, the elderly Mrs. Alesini would ask me to bring her tea to her room or assign me other small tasks, and I was happy about it, both because I was grateful to the woman who had personally intervened to get me hired and because

I found her charming and in her own way sympathetic. Franciszka, on the other hand, had almost immediately become a kind of grandmother to me. Indeed, despite her completely different appearance, with her white-skinned face covered with freckles, she reminded me of the warm and sweet ways of Grandma Nour. One day I had called Madame Gourmand from the hotel phone meant for staff and told her about Franciszka. I had imagined her smiling behind the beaded curtain, happy to know that I was in good hands again. It had been a short call, the small phone monitor indicating that my credit card was being drained quickly. In those few moments Madame, thrilled to know that her help had not been in vain and genuinely passionate about my story, had encouraged me to jump in, to ask for information without shyness from those who were there during the war. Perhaps Franciszka was already in Switzerland during those year. I counted on finding the right moment to soon have a chat with her.

The other maids in the hall and those on the floors, who were in charge of tidying up the rooms and keeping the hotel clean, were nice and welcoming, almost all of them were foreigners, like me.

We exchanged a few words, mostly in English as they were mainly South American and spoke Italian, a little German, but not French. I understood, however, that they all had hard and complicated stories of distant men and children whom they hoped to someday re-embrace. They shared adventures in breaks from work, when we would sit together on the stairs at the back of the hotel, thinking about our lives. And what life did I have, what was my life now? *Where* was my life now? Paris, Algiers? Switzerland? All the places in the world, even Sankt Moritz, seemed to me endless miles away from Sils, as if I were on another planet, and yet, at the same time, that place seemed to me the only one able, at that moment, to contain my anguish a little bit, to give me some hope of being able to bring my father his answers.

At night, in the bed of the small room in the basement, I was going over the information I had about the Vernets, my father's adoptive parents: Françoise and Maurice Vernet having failed to have children, had gone to Switzerland, and had told everyone that they had had a baby boy, Gérard, with the help of a Swiss doctor. In reality, however, although the twins knew nothing about it, Maurice Vernet had confessed to Nour before he died that this child was not theirs, but that they had adopted him. A few years later, unexpectedly, Françoise had become pregnant and had given birth, in France, to two twin girls. At that point, she had probably not felt like keeping a child that was not her's and had stayed in Paris with her husband, telling everyone that little Gérard had died in Algiers from bronchopneumonia. That child, then, had been adopted in Engadine, and so, I had to start by finding out by how a child could be adopted in Engadine during the war's years.

After much hesitation, I gathered all my courage and, out of the blue, asked Franciszka, who had come through the kitchen just before the evening service to check that the girls' uniforms were perfectly ironed: "Were you by any chance already here during the war?".

"Of course!" she replied pleased with that question, as if it made her happy to think about those years. "Not only was I already here in Switzerland, I was already in this very hotel! My mother started working here when I was a child, and I have stayed here since."

"Did you meet any wealthy French people named Vernet in the past?".

Franciszka wrinkled her forehead. "Vernet? No, I don't think I've ever met any Vernet at all, if they had been here I would remember. I don't think I've ever forgotten about any hotel guests, least of all those from those years. Why do you ask? Who are they?"

I was sorry to lie to the woman who was helping me, so I answered her half-honestly: "I know that my grandmother used to work for them in Algeria, because they were in the French colonial administration, and she told me that they often used to go on vacation around here...."

Franciszka, who in the meantime had been distracted fixing the uniform of one of the girls, added, "Perhaps if you get a chance ask Cecilia Alesini. If they were wealthy Parisians, I might not have known them, maybe they were in Sankt Moritz. Then, I was just a very young waitress, Cecilia Alesini was much more socially active than me and had spent a few years here just during the war."

For a moment, I saw a nostalgic smile appear on old Franciszka's face, then, in a peremptory tone, the chief chef gave orders to the whole kitchen to begin serving.

***

Cecilia Alesini had asked for room service that morning. Carefully, I stowed sandwiches and croissants in the basket, filled small glass jars with homemade raspberry, apricot, and peach jam, and folded the napkin neatly. I should have been the one to bring Mrs. Alesini her breakfast, and I found it a little uncomfortable. The woman attracted and intimidated me at the same time. I would have loved to go outside and smoke a cigarette or even just play with a strand of hair for a few minutes. The problem with the role of a maid in a luxury hotel was that I could not afford little outbursts due to my anxiety. I certainly could not serve meals with my nails damaged or wrap my hair around my fingers as I worked, even less so since I always had to have it pulled back into a tightly pulled bun.

Algeria, from Switzerland, seemed a world away.

I phoned home often, but did not always talk to my father, who was frequently asleep. Conversations with my mother were no longer as distant as they had been a few weeks earlier. She seemed to have abandoned her coldness to give way to the resignation of someone who feels she is on the verge of losing everything she holds dear. She spoke in whispers and repeated only that my father's condition was getting worse. I could see now that she was telling me the truth and that this was no longer just an argument used to convince me to return. And yet, the very worsening of Father's condition was prompting me to stay a little longer. I felt I was on the right track and understood, contrary to Mom, how important it was for him to leave this world having found his origins. Mom said there would be no point in doing so now, since Dad would soon pass away. On the contrary, it was clear to me that the very last stretch of life required closing the circle and having a brief moment knowing who one is now and who one has been, all in order to die in peace.

I understood this clearly because I myself felt disoriented by the precariousness in which I was living, I almost felt as if I had neither a life to return to nor one to which to go to, or at least a life that was truly mine, a dimension of my own, a world made up of people, streets, references, habits, to which I really belonged. This feeling of not belonging to a place and not having an identity at times became more difficult to deal with and oppressed me, amplifying my anxiety in a sometimes-unbearable way.

Having finished preparing the tray, I quickly headed to room 225. I knocked softly, biting my lower lip nervously, and Cecilia Alesini's voice invited me in.

"Good morning, Madam," I greeted her in French. "Here is your breakfast."

Cecilia answered me with a brief smile, closing the book she held in her lap and settling the pillow behind her back.

I placed the tray on the coffee table and began to set everything up. Inside I knew that this was an opportunity to ask the old lady, as Franciszka had advised me, if she had ever met the Vernets. But I couldn't speak; I felt my tongue was numb.

"How do you fit in here?"

"Good," I replied, without looking up.

Then, emboldened by the fact that I didn't have to break the ice, with my heart in turmoil, I quickly said, "I know that during the war you were here, in this hotel. Did you ever meet Françoise and Maurice Vernet?" And then I quickly added, as if to justify myself, "My mother worked for the Vernets, when they were in Algeria."

Cecilia concentrated for a few moments, "No, I don't remember that name. I knew some rich French people who were here during the war, but maybe these Vernets were not really in Sils. Maybe they were in Sankt Moritz, or some other location. Of French people I knew only the sisters Louise and Béatrice Beauvent. They were daughters of a wealthy Parisian antique dealer, so it is likely that they knew the Vernets you are looking for, but I know for a fact that Louise, after the war, shut herself up in a convent and died years ago, and I have no idea what happened to her sister"

Cecilia sighed, seemed to get lost in memories for a moment. I dared not answer anything, although I would have liked to bring back the conversation about the Vernets and their possible residence during the time they had been in Switzerland.

I noticed that Mrs. Alesini had left that room and that conversation with her mind, to go to a distant place, that of memories. I clearly perceived that I had entered for a moment the private area of that elderly woman with elegant manners and intense gaze.

I no longer knew what to say, and quietly left, leaving her alone with her thoughts.

Before returning to the kitchen, I decided to take a break on the small balcony in the hallway. It was a beautiful day. I pulled out a cigarette from the pocket of my starched apron and lit it, lost in my thoughts. No one knew the Vernets who had been in the Engadine during the war. On the other hand, the best-known locations were not many. So, if they had adopted a child, they must have gone to some institution that cared for abandoned children or orphans. I was going around in circles, not finding any solutions. It was then that I heard a movement behind me. It was Dr. Albert Charlier. I sighed, as if I had been caught doing something improper, and quickly extinguished the cigarette that was still half burned against the balcony railing, then held the cigarette butt in my hand. "Good morning, doctor."

After our first meeting in the bakery, I had adopted more formal ways with him — he was Mrs. Alesini's doctor as well as a client.

"Good morning, Samar, take it easy. Go ahead and smoke your cigarette, even though you shouldn't. I'm a cardiologist, I can't avoid telling you." He smiled warmly, hugging me with his gaze.

"We Arabs are fatalists by nature," I smiled. "There is nothing to be done, we wait for life to take care of us, if and when it wants to."

Albert looked at me for a moment without speaking, and I, suddenly embarrassed, lowered my eyes.

"Now you are in Switzerland, we are not fatalists here. You should stop smoking. I'll stay in Sils for a while, then go back to Zurich." He looked at my wound, squinting slightly. "Before I leave, I'll remove your stitches, a few more days and we're all set. How was our dear Mrs. Alesini today?"

"Good, lost in memories, but good."

"Sometimes memories are terrible. It happens to me too: those small details fixed in memory become the torment of my days. I got divorced last year, and it was not easy."

I suddenly gained affection for him and felt an absurdly ridiculous and unjustifiable rush of jealousy for the woman who evidently still managed to hold on to him with the memory of the past.

Uncomfortably, I snapped the cigarette butt I held in my hand, dropping the tobacco it contained into a thousand crumbs.

"Now I have to get back to work," I hastily stated, biting my lower lip.

"Goodbye Samar, sorry for keeping you busy."

"Don't worry, it was a pleasure, doctor."

"Let's ignore the formalities. Call me Albert, okay?"

I only wished to disappear into the kitchen, to escape from the wave that had swept over me the moment that man had offered me again, after the first meeting in the bakery, the intimacy of his first name.

Without answering, I nodded goodbye to him, re-entered the hallway, and quickly descended by the back stairs. I seemed to feel his gaze on my back until the very last moment. The beating of my heart returned to normal only once I reached the entrance to the kitchen.

My colleagues, when they had a day off, often went to St. Moritz by bus to hang out by the many shops. Or, if they only had a few hours off, they would sit at the little wooden tables that were scattered around the stretch of woods accessed by our staircase. Occasionally I would join them, but I did not want to force them into English. And then I had to search for my truth, and even though I still had nothing concrete to do, no real leads to follow, I wanted to keep myself focused on my purpose. Often I would sit on the steps and smoke or think or take a walk in the woods around the hotel, pondering over my goal. I had never gone as far as the peninsula, in part because I had no proper shoes for long stretches. I was constantly thinking about the child who had arrived in Switzerland who knows how and then was never claimed by anyone until he had been adopted. It could also have been a Swiss child orphaned for reasons other than the war. Strangely though, he had been given up for adoption to two Frenchmen.

One day, as I was sitting on the last step of the staircase, with my eyes closed and my face turned toward the sun, I heard my name being called. It was Matteo. Seen like this, from below, he looked even taller and thinner than I remembered him. He was wearing large hiking boots, a huge backpack on his shoulders, clutching a water bottle in his hand.

"How are you doing?", he asked.

His friendly face and his gentle manner made me feel good, "Yes, very good. I haven't seen you in a while."

"I've been in a mountain lodge. Now I'm staying here a few more days, and I wanted to ask you if you would like, when you're free, to take a walk with Albert and me. I don't know how far you've walked until now, but I don't think much, based on what Grandma has told me."

Perhaps because I instinctively looked at my shoes, he added, "If we ask Franciszka, she will certainly find us a pair of boots," he smiled and made me think a little about Mehdi, and about those like him, for whom everything was always simple.

"I'd love to," I replied, really thinking about it, "although I don't know how much stamina I have in hiking. I'm not particularly athletic, I'm not used to heights, and I'm not used to such cool temperatures even in summer." And then I felt a little guilty diverting attention from my research, although the truth was, unfortunately, that I had no concrete trail to follow.

"I would say you should not worry about potential problems but enjoy a nice walk with us. Then if you are tired, we will go home. Everything will be fine, you'll see." He closed the sentence like that, with "you'll see," just as Mehdi used to. That convinced me.

A few days later, I was still sleeping when Franciszka knocked on my room door and left me a pair of boots of my size: "They were mine many years ago, they are not fashionable, but the quality of the past was evidently better than today's, since they are still like they were originally. Use them. But if you want to go with Matteo and the doctor hurry up, they are ready and waiting for you at the main entrance."

My heart skipped a beat. I washed my face, lost a few moments in deciding whether to tie up my hair or not, then with some flirtatiousness, thought of leaving it loose for once in its full length. As I got ready, feeling a little ridiculous in those boots, a cotton sweater I got in Algeria, the usual yellow sweater and a pair of jeans, I was thinking not of dear Matteo, but of Albert. I had not seen him since the day on that little balcony the week before, but I had looked for him often with my eyes, in the dining room, in the living room or in the hallways. I had hoped that he would ask for room-served breakfast, wondered where he was, if he had returned to Zurich, and was saddened by the thought that I might never see him again, and instead ... now he was waiting for me, of all people.

I ran up the stairs in my boots, which were the heaviest shoes I had ever worn. I saw them. Matteo waved cheerfully at me, Albert stood a step behind him and gave me a polite nod. We walked on, initially only Matteo breaking the silence with some jokes. He told us about his grandmother, how much he loved her and how she had a difficult character, how his mother and grandmother always detested each other and then added with a note of sadness that his father had died many years ago, which had been a great sorrow for him and his grandmother, less so for his mother, he added sarcastically. Thus I realized that Matteo, in his outbursts, in his optimism, in his being positive, so much that he reminded me of Mehdi, actually had a deep sorrow with him, which made him feel as close to me as an old friend.

When Matteo stopped talking, I knew it would be my turn, after all, I had told very little about myself. I caught my breath after a short climb and talked about Algiers, Paris, mentioned that I, too, did not get along very well with my mother, to then fall quiet.

From up there, the landscape was so beautiful, so still, covered in green and blue. So cool the air, so clear the sky and so bright the sunbeams filtering through the trees. All this beauty reminded me, with a melancholy feeling, of my father. Maybe he was born right there, but never got an opportunity to enjoy that beauty or to breathe the fresh air that now swelled my lungs and filled my eyes with tears. "My father is sick, very sick, I doubt he'll have much longer." Albert reached for me and laid his hand firmly on my shoulder. They did not ask me what I was doing here, why I was not beside my father. I was grateful for this. I did not want to be judged, even to me it sometimes seemed absurd to be so far from home in such a beautiful place and to even be happy at times. And I had to tell myself the reasons again to dissolve the guilt away.

When we arrived to a small lake of an incredibly bright blue, we sat on a large boulder. I confessed to being exhausted and relaxed my back against the smooth, cold surface. I looked up at the sky and I remained startled when Albert sat down beside me. He was looking at the still surface of the water. I raised my head to see where Matteo was, and he waved at us from across the lake. "That boy can't sit still," said Albert, returning the greeting to his friend.

Then, lowering his hand, he inadvertently brushed against me, "Sorry," he said, suddenly embarrassed. I shook my head. Matteo had disappeared from our sight.

"Do you like it here?"

"I really like it; it's a new landscape for me." I replied without removing my gaze from the sky.

"I love this place, as soon as I have a minute available, I run here. I feel free. My wife did not like the mountains."

I remained silent, I would have liked to further discuss his marriage, but did not want to give it away.

After a while he continued, "I made many, many mistakes. She is one of those women who needs to always have her partner with her, before any decision she would call me, but I was always very busy with my work and as soon as I had free time I would come here. She says I'm immature, I think I'm just independent and having a woman next to me who wasn't was suffocating me, I admit it."

I did not know what to say and was grateful when he broke the silence again. "You are free, independent, so young and so brave."

I laughed and lifted myself up on my elbows.

"Me?!" I threw back my head, shaking my hair slightly. "Without my father and my friend Mehdi I would never have had the courage to make this trip, and then without Madame Gourmand in France and the two of you and Franciszka here ... I would have probably been back in Algiers long ago"

"I beg to differ, I do not see you the way you see yourself. Maybe you underestimate yourself."

I still scoffed, signaling no with my hand, but stopped when I realized that Albert had first seen in me the Samar I dreamed of becoming. And that flattered me. What if he had been right? What if I had had more strength, more independence than I had believed? What if he, just he, had seen in me things that were there, an unexpressed promise that I had never dared to look at?

I felt like ruffling his hair with my hand, but I did not. I restrained myself and, looking toward the lake, beckoned to Matteo who had just reappeared and I called to him, "Matteo come, I want to go back!"

When we returned to the hotel, Albert told me that he would join me in my room to remove my stitches. Then he followed me to my room, washed his hands in the small sink, and put on some gloves he had in his bag. He took small scissors and hinted at the bed and invited me to sit there. He leaned toward me, supporting my face with his left hand to see better. That unusual closeness pleased me. He then popped the stitches one by one with a steady hand and quick, precise gestures. It took a brief moment, too brief.

"Did your father push you to come to Europe? Why did you say that without him you would not have come here?", he asked as if he had been thinking about it the whole time we were descending, and I was amazed at the attention with which he had listened to me. Perhaps it was that gentle interest, that desire to understand more about me and my journey that prompted me to tell him the truth. I realized that on my own I would get nowhere. As I told him my father's story, or rather, those scraps of history that I had in my hand at the time, he seemed focused and serious.

"I have no idea if during the war here in Engadine, refugee children were taken in families or if there were institutions to do that. You said the people who adopted him were French, maybe it could have been a French child, maybe a French Jew..." He was absorbed, then recollected himself and admitted, "I don't know anything about Swiss history, however, I might hear from an old friend, now retired, who lives in Geneva. He worked with the Red Cross for a long time and then went on to research the history of the institution, which I believe played a role in the handling of refugees during the war."

He wrote down his friend's number on a note intended for prescriptions, titled with his name, address, and phone. He told me that he would alert him about my phone call and explain my story.

I called the professor the next evening from my room, holding in front of me the notebook on which I had taken notes at the time of the visit to the Vernet twins. I noticed the date of that day: more than a month had already passed.

The phone rang briefly, and a rough but gentle voice answered in French. "I was expecting your call, Albert told me about you! I am not a historian, but regarding the Red Cross during the war I know quite a bit; let's go in order."

"Thank you," I was only able to say to him, without him stopping talking.

He asked me in what year my father was adopted, and he repeated to himself, "Forty-four..." and then resumed, "So in my opinion there are three hypotheses. Either this child was a Swiss orphan, in which case he should have been adopted through official channels. Strange that the adoptive parents were foreigners, but who knows, in those years there was a lot of confusion, anything could have happened. I think you can check this quite easily in Chur. It's been so many years, but it should be possible to check if an adoption was registered with that name – what were they called again?"

"Vernet."

"Vernet..." he repeated the name a couple of times, so much so that I almost hoped he would say something, but instead he continued fiercely.

I meanwhile marked "Chur" in my notes.

"As for children from other European countries who were refugees here, I can tell you that Switzerland took many of them in, almost sixty thousand, but most of them were only here for a temporary stay, usually placed with families here, for only three months. Just enough time to breathe some good air, begin to forget about the war and the horrors they had experienced in their countries, and then return. These were mainly French children, I think they were mostly housed in other parts of the country, in French Switzerland, in fact. But I can check in the records of the Red Cross, which organized these stays together with other institutions, to see if the name Vernet comes up somewhere."

"Thank you," I repeated, overwhelmed by that flood of information.

"Wait," he resumed, "this is just the beginning of the story. Keep in mind that since 1942 the number of foreign children housed in Switzerland, even for long periods, increased greatly. This paradoxically happened precisely to coincide with the government's decision to close the borders: that decision caused a wave of protests, prompting the government to moderate its decree." I heard him flipping through a book or perhaps the pages of a document: "Many orphans, homeless and children of prisoners of war, traumatized and abandoned, undernourished or with health problems, such as scabies or tuberculosis, came in. At that time, in Geneva, the old Carlton Hotel was converted into a shelter. Your father may have been part of this wave. These children were taken care of by Red Cross Child Rescue, but not only. Many religious humanitarian organisations were also involved."

"But did children enter Switzerland on their own?" I managed to ask as I slipped into a very brief pause of his, wondering if my father had been born in Switzerland to a woman who had taken refuge there already pregnant.

"No, not always. Very often they came in with their families, but then the families were divided: the women were assigned to boarding houses and the husbands to labour camps, the children given to local families, so yes, your father may have been taken in by a family and then for some reason stayed here and given up for adoption. However, I think information about these children is recorded, and if families in the valley took them in, it shouldn't be impossible to identify them. I don't think there were that many in Engadine. An alternative to placement with families consisted of homes run by welfare organizations, usually linked to religious communities."

I had taken many disorderly notes; looking at the clock, I noticed I would soon have to go down for dinner. It became clear to me that time was passing quickly and made completing that research before my father's disappearance impossible. I could have gone to Chur to see if there was any record of any official adoption, even disregarding war-related events. Then, I would have had to look for families or some institution in the valley that had hosted refugees, which shouldn't have been too difficult. Those who, like Franciszka or Cecilia Alesini, were already in Switzerland must have had some knowledge of which families had taken care of other people's children and then perhaps adopted them as their sons. Also, if there were any religious institutions that took care of runaway children, they would have known...

"The most difficult hypothesis to verify is that the child you are looking for entered Switzerland illegally. Then it would be difficult to find his traces." The professor was continuing. "If he went through the Red Cross I can check him, I'll let you know as soon as I find anything out. You should drop by the municipality of Chur, then, try and find any traces of families who have taken in children in the valley or religious institutions. Such families may have also taken in illegal immigrants...." I was grateful to him for pointing out specific ways forward, although when I hung up the phone I was more confused than before, but at least I had something practical and tangible to do, some paths to follow.

I then went to Chur the next morning, before lunch. I took the yellow bus and it was not long before I arrived. There, I found a kind lady who was busy checking the records from during the war. She did not show them to me, but she told me that only three children had been adopted at that time in the valley, and that there was no Vernet listed among the adoptive parents; they were all local families, from the valley.

I asked her if she knew of any religious institutions that took in children in the area. She was not very cultured in the subject, but merely pointed me to a convent still active in the valley, in Sankt Moritz, which I had already identified. I guessed I could try that solution.

I arrived at the hotel, rushing just in time for lunch, wanting to call the religious institute in Sankt Moritz that very evening.

That same afternoon, Albert asked me if I wanted to go with

him to the lake. I wasn't sure if he meant the two of us alone, but as I slipped on Franciszka's worn boots I hoped so. Once we reached the shore, we sat down on the grass. We sat side by side, hugging our knees and listening to the sound of gentle ripples from the water. For the two of us to discuss the calming sound of the waves would have been really excessive. Albert stood up and took to throwing flat stones into the water, bouncing them around. I attempted to do the same without success. He took my hand to show me the movement. We were close together. I threw the tiny stone. I tried again and again. Until a flat pebble, shiny from the water, jumped on the surface once, twice, three times.

As we walked back up to the hotel a deer suddenly appeared from the woods a few steps away from us. The animal stopped and looked at us as we remained motionless. In that silence, inches from Albert, in the presence of that wild, shy creature, I had never felt so close to anyone.

When the deer disappeared into the trees, I told him about the phone call with the professor. He laughed to hear that I had not been able to talk because, yes, he expected it; he was a lonely man and loved to chat. I told him about the discouraging results at the Chur municipality and the convent I had yet to call.

"And when you find everything out, what will you do?" he asked, assuming that I was close to the truth.

"In the meantime, I don't know if I will ever find out everything, whether I do or not, I will soon return to Algiers and resume my life. Without my father."

He looked at me bewildered. "I'm going to Zurich for a while in a few weeks, so I hope to find you again when I return, although of course I wish you well with finding what you're looking for."

I shrugged, "I don't know, Albert, it all depends on my research and my father's health."

That very evening, the professor called me. He had no news: the

Vernets' name did not appear in the Red Cross records. I sighed. By now I had been in Europe for almost two months.

I called the nuns in Sankt Moritz and they replied that the person in charge would be available the next morning.

The nun who greeted me was elderly and quite friendly. She was not there during the war, but she told me that yes, there had been some children in the convent during those years. She was certain of this because, when she had arrived in the summer of '45, the nuns were still busy finding the families of some of them. These had mostly been Italian children, because those entering Graubünden usually came from Italy. "It could be possible that the nuns gave some children up for adoption, but certainly not a majority of cases," she had said, spreading her arms wide in discouragement. Perhaps having read the disappointment on my face she had nevertheless decided to take a look at the old records. These were dusty little books, but the lists of children who had been there were not long. They were Italian or French names who stayed with them for a few months, usually, waiting to be assigned to volunteer Swiss families. In many cases, the date of their reunion with their families at the end of the war was also indicated: evidently the nuns had followed their affairs even after saying goodbye to them. In all cases, however, these were children who were already at least five years old in '45. If my father had been adopted as a very young child, most probably, nothing had been recorded of his short stay. "I'm sorry," said the nun. "I can't help you."

"But weren't there other convents close to here?" I asked her, hoping I still had a chance to hold on to. "There was another one in Silvaplana, but it had been closed back in the '70s. There were very few nuns left, a couple of very old ones came here, others went to the parish of Silvaplana, but they all died in the years shortly after."

"Maybe there are records like these, related to that convent?" I asked, pointing to the dusty books.

The nun shrugged briefly to say she had no idea. I thanked her and walked out the convent feeling not only exhausted but also disappointed.

Just a couple of days later, Albert told me (shyly, not looking me in the eyes) that he would very much like, before he left, to go on another walk with me. I told him that I had no days off before his departure, but only a few hours available the next day's afternoon, between the lunch and dinner services. He seemed enthusiastic anyway, and I felt amazingly flattered. Was it possible that he still wanted to spend time with me? On the other hand, I was also sure that I had not been mistaken about what I had felt arising between us, that feeling of continuity and fulfilment.

As I set up the dining room I was on my toes, not wanting to waste a single minute of the little time I had.

As soon as I finished, I rushed to my room, threw my uniform on the bed being careful not to wrinkle it too much, and stepped into my usual pair of jeans and boots. It was a beautiful sunny day; the white cotton T-shirt would have sufficed. I ran outside and, as I reached the top of the back stairs, I saw him waiting for me, looking out towards the woods. When he heard my footsteps on the stairs he turned and his whole face broke into a smile. I knew that my colleagues had probably started chattering about me seeing a hotel guest, not to mention way so much older than me, but for the first time in my life I passed over the gossip I felt hovering around me without caring too much.

We shook hands with ludicrous formality, perhaps even Albert realized that our dating might give rise to gossip, and I found funny the contrast between the intimacy that had developed between us in a short time and the distance we sometimes maintained in our behaviour.

We walked in silence toward the lake, treading the downhill trails at a brisk pace. The reeds on the shore were lightly moved by a fresh wind, like a soft green sea. The path that bordered the lake, of gravel and white earth, was almost dazzling. We reached the other coast and arrived at the beginning of the peninsula. We had just enough time to go around the lake, without stopping for too long. We slipped into the woods, being careful not to trip over any roots. The blue colour of the lake filtered through the dense forest's leaves. "So, are you leaving?", I asked, straining not to give too much thought to that question.

"Yes, I'm going back to work tomorrow for a while." I lowered my gaze. "I'll try to come back soon, though," he added as if to reassure me.

Then, we came to a spot from which you could see a small beach, "Here, this is the starting point for my windsurfing, my sail is the yellow and blue one." I already knew this, I had once seen him standing on his board gliding fast on the lake. I had never mentioned it, though. He started talking about windsurfing with childlike enthusiasm, and I found myself thinking how his role as a prominent doctor contrasted with his being a bit of a child. And yes, he was over 20 years older than me. I had unexpectedly found in him a fragility to embrace, something to protect that he had wanted to show me, something I considered precious.

As we were discussing surfing and I was again telling him that no, I didn't want to try, we realized that the sky had completely overcast, and that it was already raining. First a few heavy drops, as if slowly they were slowly dripping from the clouds, then, suddenly, a thick, icy rain. Had I arrived to serve dinner with soaked hair, Franciszka would have killed me. Albert began fumbling with his backpack and pulled out two wrappings, opened them: they were two large black ponchos, I slipped one over my head and he did the same. Then he took my hand as if it were the most natural thing in the world and, walking fast, he led me out of the peninsula woods. When we reached the lake, he stopped for a moment, looked at me and asked, "Shall we run?" It was similar to when as children, we improvise a race. I nodded and in a flicker of mad happiness, which I would later look back on with some guilt, I started running, holding my hood with my hands, making big splashes with my feet in the many puddles that had already formed. We stopped only before the start of the climb, our hearts pounding from running and from having found each other. At least that's what I thought in that instant. We were soaked, despite our ponchos, cold and even sweaty. I was out of breath and it seemed impossible to have the strength to make it all the way up to the hotel. Albert was suddenly closer to me and then placed his lips on mine. It was an instant, not even time to decide with the movement of my head whether to respond to that kiss and he had already withdrawn. "Sorry," he said. I was a little upset that he felt he had to apologize, that he had not let go, that the moment, our moment, had already passed. I wondered what had stopped him: the age difference, his role, my position. And over the next few weeks I would dream of that moment a thousand times. I shook my head, as if to say, "never mind, never mind." We walked toward the hotel without speaking another word.

That evening, alone in my small basement room, I admitted to myself that I regretted Albert's departure. On the other hand, I certainly could not afford to ask Mrs. Alesini for news.

I feared that I would suddenly have to return to Algiers, due to Father's worsening condition, and never see the doctor again. I repeated to myself that he was twice my age, struggling to convince myself. I didn't care; I just wanted to see him. One last time. One more time. Maybe to talk to him like that day on the service balcony.

The days passed and I struggled more and more to fall asleep, thoughts of my father in Algiers, sick and suffering in the present, merged with those of the child that he was in the past, abandoned in Algiers after being adopted in Switzerland; then peeping in, as if from a hidden corner of my thoughts, were Dr. Charlier and, with him, Cecilia Alesini, the war, Franciszka and her strange husband Lapo.

These were vivid, brightly colored images that merged together in my mind, as if they had a connection, elusive, inaccessible, but certain.

One morning, having slept only a few hours, sleepy and still in pursuit of the thoughts that had tormented me the night before, I got ready to go to the village. It was shaping up to be a beautiful day.

As I walked, alone with my thoughts, along the path downhill through the woods, leading from the hotel toward the village of Sils, I glimpsed from time to time, through the trees, toward the sparkle of the blue-enameled lake. At that very moment, the large white cloud that rested over it every night was rising upward, fading into the blue sky, which grew more vibrant by the minute.

The undergrowth was a triumph of tall daisies swaying lightly in the morning breeze, alongside tiny purple bluebells and heavenly forget-me-nots. I was still not used to that lush nature. I was accustomed to the barren land, the rocks, the dryness of the desert, the endless expanse of the sea, the small houses with dusty earthen floors in the countryside, or the large buildings in the gray city streets. The scent of resin, the brightly colored flowers on the balconies, the lake and its tall grasses, the paths always damp with dew or rain, the air always cool and pungent, the outline of the mountains, majestic and with whitewashed peaks, amazed me every day. It was perhaps for this reason that I had eagerly accepted the assignment to walk every morning up to the village with the long list of what had to be ordered there: from fragrant bread to delicious cheeses and creamy milk, which the local farmers brought in at dawn, to flowers to decorate the salons and the most luxurious suites, including Cecilia Alesini's, of course, who often asked for a basket of the most beautiful, most velvety, most intense wallflowers. I did not mind that walk, not even on the way back, when the climb made me gasp slightly, I felt my lungs fill with that coolness and perceived, clear, the disconcerting sensation of being in my place, albeit miles away from Algiers. Thoughts of home always brought me back to the reasons that had led me up there: I knew I had to hurry. Soon, Cecilia would return to Milan, the hotel would no longer need me, and I myself would join my father in Algeria. And I could not go back there without a result. Time was pressing, my father's health would not allow him to live much longer, I knew I had to get a move on. But the truth that was stirring inside me, and that, from time to time, like a flicker, allowed itself to be glimpsed, amidst a thousand feelings of guilt, was that I did not want to leave Sils. I wanted to keep walking that path every morning and then return to the hotel, to work in that glittering world that seemed to have stood still in time, where not even the most absurd of requests was considered a whim, to chat with Cecilia Alesini, that magnetic and fascinating woman. I wished that summer would have lasted forever. Because I loved everything about that place. Usually, when I pursued that thought, I would pause for a moment, let myself be distracted by a deer that, like me, was descending toward the lake, or by a squirrel running in a spiral to the top of a dark, towering fir tree. And I was trying not to focus on the most unmentionable thought, the reason that bound me to Sils: Albert. When, like that morning, that thought became irrepressible, I tried to deal with it, repeating to myself that he could have been my father, that he was nearing fifty years old and that, after all, I didn't really know him. But actually, the very moment I was trying to convince myself of that, I didn't believe it, I knew I was lying to myself. Or, rather, the fact that I didn't know that much about him and his life seemed completely irrelevant. It wasn't what *I knew*, it was what *I felt*. And I sensed a kind of continuity between Albert and myself, and no matter how much I called myself a fool, a deluded little girl, I was convinced deep down that it was the same for him. It didn't matter how much we had talked, how distant and different our lives were, as well as our histories and ages, it only mattered, I was sure, our perfect correspondence, being two surprisingly kindred souls. Here, it was the fact that I sensed a soul that could converse with mine, that held me back, that wouldn't let me go. It was the desire to merge with him, with him and no one else, that kept me anchored in that reality so distant from my own and yet already intimately belonging to me. Perhaps I should have convinced myself that for him I was nothing more than the pretty young maid at the hotel where his wealthy and eccentric patient was staying for the summer, a maid with whom perhaps to flirt with.

In the last few days, I had the impression that he was carefully avoiding me, making appointments with Cecilia only at times when I was busy in the dining room. As I walked through the last stretch of woods before reaching the lakeshore, I wondered if it was not instead me, and me alone, who thought he was avoiding me, and if it was instead pure coincidence. And in any case, if he really was avoiding me, was he doing so because being around me was making him uneasy, leading him to desire me beyond what seemed to be allowed, or was he simply noticing how much I wanted him and trying not to hurt me, like a high school teacher when a student, naive, falls in love with him?

It was then, that I saw him. Stopping right at the point where the path coming down from the woods joined the wider, white road that runs along the lake. It was seven in the morning and there he was, on his bicycle, talking on his cell phone. I hesitated for a moment, then decided to stop. He noticed me immediately and ended the conversation after briefly apologizing. Then, he greeted me by looking straight into my face and took my left hand with unexpected naturalness. "How are you?". "Fine", I murmured, focusing on the roughness of his hand and wondering if it depended on the disinfectant he had to use in the hospital. "I was going around the lake." I smiled, trying to dispel the idea that he was there to wait for me. "I'm glad I met you, I'm going back to Zurich for a few weeks this afternoon, the hospital is calling me," he said, smiling and twisting my hand as if he couldn't let it go. "If there are any problems with Mrs Alesini, you'll call me, right?"

"Of course, doctor, good work then and have a safe journey back to Zurich," I replied in a ridiculously formal way, smiling at him still excited. "I have to run to the village, it's late today, I have to do all the orders and then go back to the hotel for the start of breakfasts." He shook my hand one last time. I pulled away from him with my heart pounding in my chest. I felt his gaze caressing my back for a while, then, the wheels of the bike rubbing against the dirt road. I turned for a few moments and saw him pedaling fast in the opposite direction of mine, toward the lake. I reached the baker's white house with the beautiful wrought-iron sign in a few minutes. There was no more time to waste, I had to place my orders and then rush back to serve croissants and coffee to the guests. I entered the store, still closed to the public, from the back. The warmth of the oven and the aroma of bread baking there, for some strange reason, made a quick thought flash through my mind that was as illogical as it was intense: "He was there for me, he waited for me. I know."

"Good morning," the baker smiled at me, "give me the bread list for today's lunch, the guy with the breakfast necessities is loading the van, do you want a ride to the hotel?" "No thanks," I replied, reeling from the excitement that had been clutching my throat for a few seconds, "I have to stop by and order a few more things and then I'll gladly take a walk."

Back at the hotel, Franciszka asked me to go to Mrs. Alesini's with the basket of violets. I knocked with my left hand holding the flowers with my right arm. "Come in," I heard her cheerful voice inviting me in. "Thank you!" Then after a few seconds she added, "So Samar, how are you doing? Are you always comfortable here?"

"Yes, of course," I replied as I set the basket on the table. "Franciszka welcomed me ... she made me feel so good ... she's great."

Cecilia nodded, "When we were your age, we were not friends, I was too snobbish, she was too wrapped up in her role. We became friends later. In those days my friends were Anna, a German Jewess who was here with her husband and two children, and Louise, the Frenchwoman I told you about. By the way, have you heard any more from those French people you were looking for?"

"No," I hesitated for a moment, wondering how to keep the conversation on that topic. "Was Louise the friend who had locked herself in a convent?" I ventured. Cecilia nodded, "Was she in a convent in France?"

"Not for the first few years! She went to Silvaplana, she knew those nuns because she helped the children who were housed there."

For some reason the fact that Cecilia Alesini's friend had been in that convent, the one that was no longer there, seemed like a sign. "Orphaned children?", I asked, trying to control the tone of my voice, keeping it between firm and indifferent.

"Not only that, also refugees, usually foreigners fleeing the war in Switzerland, like me." She smiled as she looked at the ceiling.

By then I had finished arranging the flowers and was standing by the door. On the one hand I was in a hurry to get back to the kitchens for lunch, and on the other I wondered if it was worth being honest, but I didn't want her to think I had been making a fool of her, playing the part of the poor girl looking for work. It was also clear that she couldn't possibly know anything about my father:

what could a war orphan from who-knows-where have to do with a rich lady from Milan? Still she seemed unwilling to let me go, clinging to her memories.

"She was not smart, Louise, or maybe she was, but she was completely influenced by her sister. When I started coming here again, I learned that she had returned to France. I completely lost track of her sister Béa. She had gone to live in Canada and since then I had no contact with her or her husband, James Ashton."

Only some time later, thinking back on that last sentence, would I notice a brittle, uncertain note; not in the moment, focused as I was on memorizing all that information and then trying to make sense of it for something useful. "And after the war, did the children Louise cared for with the nuns return to their families?" I asked.

"Yes of course, I think so, but I don't know much about it, I then left."

I was tying my perfect white apron in an impeccable bow and meanwhile looking at myself in the mirror. My figure in the maid's uniform looked even more slender, my face even paler, my hair pulled up in a bun, made my features look a little harsh. I took mascara from the small table in front of the bathroom I shared with two other girls and applied it to my eyelashes.

Albert would be there that evening; he had returned to spend the weekend and was invited to Cecilia Alesini's table. I was excited to see him, although I had to admit, though ashamed in my heart, that I would rather have been sitting next to him than serving him dinner. I had been wondering for a while what Albert felt about me, wondering from when I found myself thinking about him too often, remembering the details of his face, his gestures and every single word he had said to me. I would go on convincing myself that, probably, after the last period, always lonely, I saw in Albert the man who would save me. I repeated to myself that he, for me, felt nothing more than big brother affection and that the kiss in the rain had been only the stumble of a moment.

I realized that the thought of him was in danger of distracting me from my real goal, which was to discover my father's origins. And that made me feel guilty.

I washed my hands and walked up the back stairs. As soon as I entered the hotel kitchen, I felt overwhelmed for a few moments by the chaos that reigned there: it always seemed impossible to me that the hotel's delicious dinners originated in that mess.

"Hey Samar, take this tray to table three and this one to table two!" said a young cook handing me two large trays full of steaming dishes. "Come on, come on, quick!"

I splashed out of the kitchen, careful not to drop the dishes.

Upon entering the room, I could not resist the temptation to cast a glance at the small table in the corner, where Cecilia was waiting, alone, for her guest, fiddling with her napkin.

Only on the third exit from the kitchen did I see him, framed by the door. He was entering the hall at that moment, at a fast pace, glancing nervously at his watch. He was late, evidently.

As I poured red wine into the glasses of some German customers, I occasionally peeked in the direction of Cecilia and Albert, who were saying goodbye.

At one point, he saw me and gave me a polite nod, leaving me with the impression that his eyes, from behind his glasses, had lingered a few moments longer than necessary in mine.

I took the dishes to the kitchen and then ran to their table, trying to mask the sudden emotion that had overwhelmed me, and smiled at both. Albert stood up and shook my hand. That formal gesture seemed to be once again counterintuitive with the intimacy that had been created between us on the lake not even a couple of weeks earlier, but at the same time, I found the strangely familiar feeling of his hand again. And as I pulled out the order booklet, I told myself that I never wanted to let go of that hand ever again.

That evening, I was busy for a long time in another room: a colleague was missing and I was running like crazy from the kitchen to the tables but I kept thinking, with my heart in turmoil, about the moment when Albert had looked me straight in the eye: I was sure that that look expressed the same words that I, too, had been holding inside of me from the moment I had met him, in the pastry shop in Sankt Moritz. Just as I was running from table to table chasing thoughts of love with him, even daring to imagine a life together, someone told me to go to Cecilia's very table. I flew, happy to be able to talk to him and feel that he wanted me too, that he was thinking about me, surrendering to the unexpected idea that I had fallen in love for the first time in my life. There he was, that feeling I had read so much about, without ever really understanding it, there was the man who made me feel recognized, perfectly myself, as if he could read and understand the whole world that I had been carrying inside me all along.

It was on that very thought that I focused on the scene before my eyes. Next to Albert, to the right of Cecilia Alesini, was a woman. A beautiful woman, I thought, a blond woman with long wave hair, brown eyes and a big smile. "Excuse me," was indeed the woman speaking, and she turned to me, resting her manicured hand on Albert's. "I have just arrived from Zurich, straight form the hospital. Am I still in time to order something?" The voice came to me from afar, as muffled, inaudible.

I tried to come to my senses and replied, "Of course, ma'am."

Albert, moving his hand slightly from hers, said, "You see, this is Samar, the girl I told you about, Matteo and I brought her here."

The woman smiled at me, she must have been in her 40s. "I am Agnes, nice to meet you. Albert told me he helped a nice girl get a job here at the hotel. Could you bring me a bottle of sparkling water in the meantime, please?"

I stood there, as if suspended. As I nodded and quickly left for the kitchen, I felt ridiculous. Evidently I had misunderstood the kindness of a famous Swiss doctor who was twice my age and would never even consider me, since he was engaged to a wonderful, refined doctor and spoke of me as an inanimate object delivered to the hotel.

I pulled a bottle out of the refrigerator and asked a colleague to take it herself to Mrs. Alesini's table. Then I allowed myself a few minutes in the back yard.

Laughing bitterly in my heart at myself, I thought it was for the best: I would only be wasting time, while I had to return as soon as possible to Algiers having solved the mystery. Albert was with Agnes, a wonderful, charming, and better suited woman. I tried to control the beating of my heart and felt it decelerate slowly. I went back to work, repeating to myself that I should not waste any more time, hoping that he would come forward by his own will. Entering the kitchen, I let out a deep sigh and felt that my lungs could not hold all the air I really needed to breathe.

QUI I felt boundless selfishness. While my father was dying, I had risked taking time and energy away from my research, perhaps at times I had wished, there it was the unmentionable thought, to add days to my being there, because I was struggling with the idea of getting away from that place, or rather, from that kind and open, tender and perhaps a little immature man. Intelligent and good. I had fallen in love with him, Algiers seemed far to me at times, and I shuddered at the idea of finding a husband there as my mother wished.

I had also disappeared with Mehdi, I had not asked him anything more about his documentary, about his life in Paris. I had proposed again and again to email him or at least text him, but I had never done so. It is true that he, too, had not sought me out again, but after all, if I was in Switzerland at that moment, perhaps a little closer to my goal, it was also thanks to him, who gotten me my visa for France quickly, then hosted me at his relatives', and finally, made the appointment with the Vernet sisters for me. Mehdi represented the world to which I belonged and I had been unfair to forget that, to wish for different things. I suddenly felt ashamed of my ingratitude and looked up his number in the phone book. Mehdi answered after endless rings, when I was about to give up. He seemed pleased to hear from me, "Samar, long time no see." I did not miss a note of reproach in his voice.

"I've been very busy, now I'm in Switzerland, I'll tell you, but what about you, how is it going with the documentary?"

"In Switzerland? And what are you doing there?"

"I work in a hotel ... now I don't have much time, tell me about yourself."

Mehdi was looking forward to telling me about his successes, and I smiled about it: he loved to talk about himself. He told me that his work was coming along well and, once it was ready, it would be presented at an independent film festival. I didn't dare ask him how things were going with the French girl, but I was genuinely pleased with the good news and hoped that I, too, would soon reach the goal of my trip.

In those days I would have tried to find out if there were any documents somewhere related to the convent in Silvaplana. Having made that last attempt I would return home, to the one place where fate evidently wanted me.

***

An hour later, as she was pouring a drop of cream into her coffee, Cecilia smiled at her cardiologist and returned to talk to him about Samar., "She's very pretty, and I think you really like her, dear doctor!"

Albert shielded himself between annoyed and amused, "She's so young! Besides, haven't you seen how beautiful Agnes is?"

"Very beautiful, and nice too, for that matter." Cecilia looked at him dubiously and went on, "Anyway, the age factor is irrelevant. You like her, and very much, I would say." A flicker of irony passed through the old woman's gaze.

"Cecilia, please."

"We've known each other for so many years, doctor, why don't you let go for once? You are making a mistake, yet another mistake. You don't love the beautiful doctor, and, after breaking up your marriage, you are stubbornly locking yourself into a story you don't actually want. Especially since when you met Samar. I saw the two of you, a few weeks ago, arriving all wet from a walk. You looked like two big black bats but you were two happy bats. I was in the library, at the window overlooking the staff entrance. You can't imagine how much anger it makes me to know that two people love each other, have a chance to be together and waste it like this. Someday maybe the conditions will no longer be there, and then you will regret this magical, perfect moment just for the two of you. It's so hard to have days of genuine happiness in life, it's never worth letting them slip away. Tell me, doctor, what's holding you back?"

Agnes returned from the toilet smiling and sat at the bar counter on a high stool drinking a coffee, taking Albert's hand. "I am glad to be here, Albert has always told me about Sils, about the hotel and also about you, Mrs. Alesini, but he has never before wanted to let me into this world that is so dear to him."

Cecilia smiled at her and stood up, leaning on her cane. "I'm tired, I'm going to sleep, good night, guys," and, casting a meaningful glance at Albert, she left the room.

Cecilia let herself down on the pillows. As she hoped to catch some sleep, she thought back to the most beautiful evenings of the war years, when, on the third Friday of the month, the Brunne family honored the tradition of the dance party by having a pianist, a cellist and a violinist arrive from Sankt Moritz.

There was no dancing now, Cecilia thought, looking around from the corner of the room next to the bow window. Still, during the war, there was always dancing, even in Milan there would be dancing in the rubble at the end of April 1945: small improvised orchestras were springing up everywhere. Now every evening, guests would sit in the little armchairs chatting with each other about the day gone by, the excursions they had made, the dinner they had just enjoyed. From some loudspeakers hanging in the corners of the spacious hall, the sound of a piano, perhaps Chopin, emanated, but Cecilia, who had now lost the finesse of her former hearing, could not distinguish it clearly.

Meanwhile, Albert, while Agnes was in the shower happily talking about the evening they had just spent, thought back to the last question Cecilia had asked him, "What is holding you back?" Many answers crowded into his mind: respect for a girl in trouble, who might think that he helped her to get something in return, or that he wanted to take advantage of his role, his position; Agnes, who had waited a long time for him, and didn't deserve to be treated this way; his complicated life, his daughters who are almost Samar's age. His career, which is at a delicate moment....

And while all these motivations swirled in his mind, part of him still thought of that sweet, wonderful girl. He imagined holding her close to him. And for a second a lump almost came to his throat. He wanted her with all of himself, but he was going to defend himself from that passion, he was going to do the right thing, what a man of his age and in his position should do when faced with a much younger girl, alone, in a foreign country.

**

That morning I was preparing breakfast when Franciszka came into the kitchen. She did this often: despite her age, she liked to make herself as useful as in the old days. She would arrange fresh flowers on trays intended for room service or arrange bows on aprons. Now that the hotel was run on a "more managerial basis," as the Brunne's nephew called it, it was in danger of losing the imprint that Monika's parents had wanted to give it, and, something that seemed inconceivable to Franciszka, customers had no idea who the owner was, because he remained locked in his office. She felt she was the sole custodian of the authenticity of the place that had been her home.

Filling a basket with sandwiches, I greeted her and then, without waiting, asked, "Do you know if around here during the war there were orphanages where it was possible to adopt children? Mrs. Alesini was telling me about a friend of yours who was helping nuns in Silvaplana, do you know if any children were given up for adoption?"

Franciszka furrowed her brow as she raised her head suddenly. She pondered for a second, as if an elusive thought had crossed her mind. "Yes, there were actually nuns there, a friend of ours was very active in helping. More or less in the late 1960s it was closed. One of the nuns had stayed in Silvaplana to help the pastor of the church that was built in those very years. Why do you ask?" "Because those Vernets, those friends of my grandmother's, apparently had adopted a child," I answered uneasily, wondering meanwhile how to justify such an insistent interest.

She looked at me intently, then, she shook her head, as if to chase away a ludicrous idea.

"When did they adopt the child?"

"In '44, I think in the fall of that year," I replied feigning indifference as poured a long honey drip into a small glass bowl.

"Why do you care so much?"

I thought about it for a moment and wished I hadn't kept what I was looking for hidden; I knew I hadn't been honest all the way with that sweet, welcoming woman, and suddenly it seemed silly. After holding my breath for a few seconds, I uttered the truth all at once: "Because that child, adopted by the Vernets in 1944, later became my father."

Franciszka grew more and more pensive, wrinkled her forehead once more, bending her head to the side, her expression absorbed as if the small silver flower vase she was polishing did not entirely convince her.

Even though my heart was beating wildly, I was determined to hold on to that thin thread that I suddenly seemed to have grasped. That was the last chance for me.

"I have no idea, but it may be that the pastor knows something about it," Franciszka murmured in an almost inaudible voice. "There is a lady who is in charge of keeping the priest's house and the church clean, I'll give her a call if you want and tell her you would like to meet with her."

"Do you know her?"

"Samar, I've lived here all my life, we all know each other in this mountain valley. She goes early every morning to open the church and I imagine she will be glad to get into this story of yours."

I took the tray with a firm gesture, "Thank you Franciszka, I have the morning free tomorrow, I will try to drop by the parish. It is very important to me."

Franciszka nodded, silent, as if absorbed, in pursuit of an elusive idea.

Then, once again, the din of the kitchens swept over us, taking our thoughts with it.

I was glad that I could reach the parish in Silvaplana directly, without having to be the one to call first. The telephone, for some reason, made me even more anxious than the direct meeting. Perhaps it was because it gave me too many possibilities for escape: on the phone one could even decide to hang up, press the little red button and escape with no effort. Escaping from a live person was more difficult. And now I couldn't afford it. Time was running out.

I had called home the night before, and my mother's tone had seemed more heartbroken than usual, while I had caught in my father's voice, in addition to an endless weariness, a bitter and painful note. He had reassured me, telling me that the state of melancholy in which he was, did not depend on me and the uncertainty of the outcome of my search or my absence, but solely on his own illness. But I had not believed him all the way. I had been in Europe for almost three months and had not yet been able to give him any of the answers he sought.

I reached Silvaplana in a few minutes on the yellow postal bus that traveled back and forth through the valley and showed up early in the morning in front of the small white church with its dark, pointed roof silhouetted against the sky like a long blade. I did not have to wait long for a middle-aged woman to show up, who, pulling a key from a pocket hidden in her dark dress, opened the door. I wished I had worn Madame Gourmand's sweater, which made me feel protected. Instead, I wore only a light blue cotton sweater over jeans. I pulled up to the door and, forcing myself not to waste any more time, introduced myself. She cracked a smile, saying that Francizka had alerted her to my arrival. "How can I help you? I don't quite understand what you are looking for."

"I am trying to find out who adopted my father in 1944. I'm not aware that there were any orphanages here, and so I was wondering if by any chance it would be possible to consult somewhere the records of the convent in Silvaplana in which little refugees were housed. Perhaps my father, who was orphaned, was later given up for adoption."

The woman sighed doubtfully, but at the same time I glimpsed a flicker of poorly disguised curiosity lighting up in her eyes. She invited me in, showing a certain pride in flaunting the small power represented by the keys she held in her hand. "I have always seen registers in the sacristy that I believe belonged to the convent, maybe, who knows, we can find some useful information there. The nuns were then very precise, they wrote down everything. I know because there is not much to do here and I happened to leaf through them, even if I never found anything particularly interesting." She smiled amusedly, and I realized that I represented for her a nice diversion from her boring days

I followed her down the short aisle, then slipped behind her into a small door at the side of the altar. "Many refugees used to come to Switzerland, sisters would take in children while their parents were perhaps in some labor camp; other children were instead taken in by available families. However, the children without parents or family, were likely to be put up for adoption. Here it is," she said after scrolling through the ribs of a dozen volumes, one for each year starting in 1940. She grabbed from a shelf halfway up the wall a voluminous register. "Here were listed all the children who passed through the convent, where they came from and when their parents took them back, almost always at the end of the war."

As she flipped through the pages to find those referring to the fall of 1944, I listened to the rustling of them holding my breath.

"Here you see: September 1944, October 1944," she scrolled the index from the left page to the right, showing me the indication of dates noted at the top.

A series of names followed. "On the left there is the arrival date, on the right, the exit date. As you can see, in those months there were no particular movements, they were probably full."

The German term for "adopted" caught my eye; I had looked it up in the small dictionary Franciszka had given me. It was, however, about a little girl, orphaned at the age of five and then adopted by a Swiss family. I felt disappointment tightening in my throat.

I lowered my gaze. "I'm sorry," she said disappointedly, "there is no sign of Vernet here. However," she brightened up, as if caught by a brilliant idea, "maybe these Vernets, if they were rich, made a donation to the nuns, at least you could be sure that they passed through here."

She climbed the short library ladder and grabbed another volume, on the spine of which was written in faded ink: DONATIONS TO THE CONVENT.

She looked for the months that interested me. Our gazes were focused on the oval of light cast on the register by the table lamp.

And, suddenly, I saw what I was looking for: "Donation of Maurice and Françoise Vernet, November 5, 1944: 10,000 Swiss francs."

"Wow!" she exclaimed cheerfully, "they really were rich! For 1944 it must have been a huge amount!"

I stood motionless staring at that line written in impeccable handwriting.

My father always celebrates his birthday on November 6, the day after that huge donation. My brain had giddily set into motion, processing a thousand questions and throwing out some answers that I still could not fully grasp.

After that moment of daze, due to the excitement of finding the name Vernet, just when I was losing hope, I said, "Why would they make such a donation? Maybe they took a baby?"

She dilated her eyes, as if she had heard the greatest of aberrations, but at the same time triumphant, for that might well have been juicy gossip to talk about with her friends in the village. "I rule out that the sisters were running adoptions illicitly! You don't mean they were selling (she stressed with particular vehemence and horror the verb *sell*) children? Impossible." And as she uttered that last word, I seemed to read in her face, "Or did they?"

"But if they made such a donation, there must be a reason."

She looked at me thoughtfully. "Yes, but the reason will never be known from these records, I'm afraid that more than this here you cannot find. However, if you find anything, will you let me know?"

"May I photograph this page?" She contracted her lips in doubt, "Go ahead, it's confidential stuff, but it's been more than sixty years...." I laughed at that scruple of confidentiality when it was clear that she was eager to shout from the rooftops about the events of that morning. I pulled my cell phone out of my jeans pocket and snapped a picture. Then, as if reminding myself that I had an engagement, I quickly went to the exit and, waving cordially, headed for the bus stop.

I was eager to return to the hotel and share with Franciszka the results of my research. I had no concrete answers, but I carried with me the clear and unmistakable feeling that that information, a donation of as much as 10,000 Swiss francs on November 5, 1944, was decisive and could be a turning point, even if for now it was only a vague hunch, still lacking form and substance.

Arriving at the hotel, I slipped in the back door and, hastily greeting colleagues, asked if they knew where Franciszka was. Someone suggested I go to her room, because she had yet to be seen that morning.

I descended the stairs leading to the staff quarters and reached Franciszka and Lapo's small apartment. I knocked lightly on the door, trying to contain the strange excitement that had pervaded me from the moment I had spotted the name Vernet in the list of the convent's benefactors.

Franciszka opened the door, and I, abandoning all discretion, entered quickly and excitedly.

"You are not going to believe this. I couldn't find any trace of my father's adoption, but on the register where the nuns recorded donations, I found Maurice and Françoise Vernet's name and a donation of 10,000 Swiss francs. But what really struck me, the detail I can't stop thinking about, is that the donation was made on November 5, the day before my father celebrates his birthday."

After speaking hastily, I kept silent and stood waiting for her reaction. She was looking at me almost incredulous, amazed, astonished.

"So? What did you think? I thought it would seem like a big deal to you."

Franciszka sighed and rested her fingertips on the table beside her, as if to support herself. Then, she said only one word: "Cecilia."

"Do you think I should talk to her about it? Do you think she could give me some pointers? But she didn't know any Vernet."

She shut me down with an abrupt gesture of his hand, out of tune with his usual manner.

"I'll talk to her, don't tell her anything yet."

Then, as if redeemed from thoughts that had led her too far away, "Now go get ready for the lunch shift, it's already very late."

As I turned to leave, I noticed Franciszka and Lapo, who had been standing in the corner the whole time of the conversation, looking intensely at each other, with a flash of awareness that struck me. But perhaps it had only been an impression, because in the short time it took me to reach the door, Lapo was back there again, where no one, not even Franciszka, could reach him.

Cecilia had specifically asked that afternoon for me to bring tea to her room. After knocking, I lowered the handle with my elbow and opened the door with my back, holding the large tray. I entered, set down the teapot and tea box in front of Mrs. Alesini feeling slightly uncomfortable: I had the impression that the old lady's arctic blue eyes were watching me with more intensity than usual, scrutinizing me deeply. "Would you like some tea cookies?", I asked in French, flashing a smile to dissolve the strange tension that had suddenly enveloped the room.

Cecilia Alesini looked up and shook her head, "No thanks, sit here, though."

"I can't, ma'am, I have to finish my tea shift." I wanted to run through the door and escape, but I merely inhaled as much air as I could, as the ceiling of the room seemed to loom.

"Of course you can, if I ask you," Cecilia insisted.

Hesitating for a moment, I sat on the tip of the chair Cecilia had indicated, as if ready to leave. She continued to watch me for endless minutes, without saying a word. Her blue eyes seemed clearer than usual.

"Now tell me in no uncertain terms the real reason for your presence here," she said finally, in a peremptory, cold, controlled tone, but with a fragile, light, trembling note that I did not miss.

I drew in a long breath, nervously smoothed my apron with quick movements and then, gathering courage, spoke without stopping, looking insistently at the legs of the small table at which we sat: "I am on the trail of a baby born here sixty-six years ago, during the war, and then adopted by a French family who later took him to Algeria and abandoned him there while still a child." Saying that sentence had taken an inordinate amount of energy out of me, as if I had jumped into the void and then saved myself by a whisker. Forgetting my role, I felt the overwhelming urge to continue, to tell her about my father, about my journey, as if I had known that woman forever. I looked up then, at the same time slipping a long lock out of my bun and beginning to twist it, relentlessly. At that moment, I dwelled on Cecilia's reaction and I was again out of breath. She was watching me in astonishment, her eyes wide, her mouth contracted, her hands clasped to each other so tightly that her knuckles turned white. I didn't know how to interpret that silence, so I resumed speaking to dissipate the embarrassment I had sunk into, "I'm asking you because I know that in those years you were here, in Switzerland, sheltered from the war and … I thought maybe you could also give me some more pointers."

Cecilia made to get up, leaning on the stick, but she dropped it and herself fell back into the armchair with a slight thud. She seemed to tremble for a moment, gasping for oxygen, then, regaining some color, said in a whisper, "Why are you looking for that child, why?"

"Because that child is now a man and he is my father. He is very sick and he wanted, before he died, to make one last attempt to find out his origins, his history."

"Do you have a picture of him?" Cecilia now looked increasingly tired, struggling to utter every single word.

"Ma'am are you okay? Do you want me to get a doctor? Or may I call Dr. Charlier in Zurich?"

Cecilia extended her hand over mine, as if to hold me back, then moved forward, looking at me closely, brushing my face with her other hand. "I don't have any pictures of my father, by the way," I said almost under my breath, as if sensing that this was a solemn moment for her, though I didn't understand why.

"You are enough," Cecilia whispered, "these light blue eyes, this diaphanous skin, this smooth blond hair are enough." Her eyes filled with tears, her voice trembled slightly. "What's wrong with her, Cecilia?"

The elderly woman took the worn copy of The *Great Gatsby* that she kept on her bedside table and opened it, pulled out a picture of a blond girl looking at the camera lens with big clear eyes and a mischievous smile, her cheeks lit with irresistible passion, a black, shiny dress, probably silk, with the strap falling over her arm. The resemblance to me was striking.

The old woman at that point abandoned herself again on the back of the chair, closed her eyes and began to narrate.

"When I arrived here, I was pregnant. In fact, my husband sent me here to escape the war and its dangers for me and the baby that was to be born soon." She reflected for a few moments. "The very day I arrived I noticed James, an English journalist who had come to Switzerland from Germany after doing a series of reports on Nazism. I fell hopelessly in love with him. And so did he."

I didn't dare open my mouth: although I didn't understand where that story could go, I sensed its importance, as if my path, my life of the last few months only began to make sense there, at that very moment.

"The passion for James destroyed my life, and yet, without that passion, I would have no life. You know what I mean?"

I merely shook my head slightly, although, by a strange trick of the mind, which I soon regretted, I saw Albert Charlier's amber-coloured, spectacle-circled eyes.

"After the baby was born, James and I began to spend many nights together." I blushed.

"I used to leave the baby in my room: he was small, sleeping peacefully for several hours at a time. During one of these nights, returning to the room, I could not find him. I looked for him everywhere, first in the room, although he certainly could not have moved on his own, then through the corridors, through the halls of the hotel. But there was no sign of him. No one had heard anything, no one had seen anything that night. We called the police, but nothing was ever found. The owners of the hotel, Monika and Joseph Brunne, Marco the concierge and his son, and all the guests were questioned: Anna and David Zeller and their children, the Klimo elders, the Beauvent sisters... There were no leads to follow, no ideas. In those years a lost child was not so much news, or at least not *my* child; everyone here hated me, or almost. They thought I was a bad mother. So, I think for many, the loss of the child was a fair and just punishment for my behavior. Hypocrites! Joseph Brunne did everything in his power to try to cover up the affair, for fear that his hotel would get a reputation as a place from which children mysteriously disappeared. Undoubtedly for his business it would not have been very convenient." Cecilia cracked a bitter smile.

I listened without a word as I felt a knot in my stomach, a chill in my back. I was beginning to understand but it seemed so impossible....

"At some point in the spring of 1945, my husband, who had joined me after the disappearance of Leo, that was the name of my first son, decided to take me back with him to Milan. I don't know if he ever knew where and with whom I was that night as his son disappeared forever, however he loved me too much and was not a strong man: he kept me with him, and we returned together to Italy. Dark months of total apathy passed for me. The celebrations at the end of the war found me completely detached from everything, from life itself."

Cecilia touched my hair with her fingertips, as if in an impalpable caress. She seemed to be having difficulty breathing. "Shall I call a doctor?", I asked timidly, though I did not want her to interrupt the story.

"No, no, not again. Tell me again, one more time."

"On my father's documents it's shown that he was born on November 6, 1944. Shortly after his birth he was taken by his parents to Algeria. When the Algerian war of liberation broke out, his parents basically left him there in the hands of what I consider my grandmother: the maid who worked for them. Many years later, my grandmother Nour herself received a letter from Maurice Vernet, the man she believed to be the child's father, in which he told her about my father's true origins and clumsily attempted to justify their despicable behavior by telling them that in 1955 they had two natural daughters, unexpectedly. My father tried for a while as a child to get in touch with what he believed to be his parents, but he never got any answers. They obviously didn't want to hear from him anymore. When I was born, again he came back to think about it. My features and colors brought him back to thinking about where he came from." I swallowed. "But only now that he is dying did he ask me to come to Europe on the trail of his past."

I suddenly felt exhausted: "I left Algiers months ago and, after some research, found the Vernet daughters in Paris. From there, I came to Switzerland, following the little information they gave me, about the fact that their parents had had a son in Engadine, who, they said later, disappeared due to bronchopneumonia in Algiers. And I found the name Vernet in the register of donations received by the nuns."

Cecilia grew paler and paler but continued our conversation with an effort that seemed immense. "I have waited all my life, year after year, summer after summer, for this moment. I have waited for you, Samar, and for the truth you are giving me, with a stubbornness that, at times, had seemed meaningless, but now, no longer." She rolled his eyes to the ceiling and then along the walls, as if she wanted to impress upon her memory every detail of that longed-for day. "I did not want to see James again, I blamed him for what had happened, while it was my fault, just mine. He for a long time tried to get in touch with me, said he still loved me, wanted to build a life with me. But I had decided to inflict that punishment on myself: to deprive myself of James, the only man I had ever really loved." She sighed, half-closing her eyes. "He then made a new life for himself with Béa, a French girl who was here with us then and who had always wanted him, and I, a few years later, in 1950, had another son, Manfredi, a blond, sweet, little boy. I spoiled him in every way; he died ten years ago on the French Riviera, while racing drunk in a Porsche. Poor Manfredi, I think the shadow of his missing little brother never left him. Despite my husband Emilio's opposition, I came back here every year. Every summer, for one or two months. Always. I tried to investigate again, but, in the meantime, the policemen who had done the search then, had left; those present here then, were either dead or living far away, and in any case, they had already been questioned several times at that time. I always waited for him, my first son: though I felt like a fool, I thought that one day I would see him coming, with his dark hair, his long black eyelashes, and that day somehow came today, with you..."

"My father is dying, Cecilia." I answered her, feeling now free to call her by name, feeling the tears pressing my eyes, for my father, for that woman, old, beautiful and alone, who seemed to have been waiting for me for a lifetime. Taken by a violent and unexpected wave of courage, I surged forward, arms outstretched, as if to embrace her. Then, regaining my demeanour, I hesitated, but Cecilia drew me to herself and held me in a long, final, bewildering embrace.

"He's been happy and now he's going to die happy," I said, pulling away from her. "We must find a way to bring you together," I exclaimed, almost thinking out loud.

"Don't let him die with the knowledge that he had a horrible mother... He won't want to see me; he'll hate me. Maybe you should come up with a different story so as not to hurt him...." I shook my head, excited and, now, also happy. I would tell my father about a strong, brave, indomitable mother who had sought him out and waited for him all her life. The truth, now, seemed to me only this. The cruelty of a moment of weakness alongside a life of atonement. We shook hands for a long time, both of us thinking, I am sure, of the continuity that was being established between us, of the meaning that our existences would assume from that moment on.

Only after many minutes, Cecilia, with the fatigue of letting go of me, of letting go of what she now knew was her niece, slowly got up and lay down on the bed. With slow movements, she reached for the cell phone on the bedside table and said, "Write down Dr. Charlier's number, Samar."

"Do you want me to call him?"

"Not now, dear," she whispered, hinting at a smile, "but it's good that you have it."

"Maybe with the doctor we can find a way to get you to Algiers, Cecilia, I don't give up the idea that you might meet." It seemed difficult, perhaps impossible, with my father at the end of life and Cecilia so lacking in strength, but I did not want to give up on the idea that mother and son would never meet.

I memorized Albert's number, then arranged Cecilia's pillows, with the affection of a granddaughter, and thought of Grandma Nour with the same tenderness. Cecilia closed her eyes, exhausted, and I walked lightly out of room 225 with the knowledge that I had made it, but with the idea that I still had something left for all the pieces of that story to fall back into place.

I went to the hotel phone and slipped my credit card into the slot. I dialled the home number and waited for the answer, repeating to myself for the umpteenth time the words I had thought about telling my father. I told my mother that I finally had some answers to give Dad and sensed her relief, her excitement, and perhaps even a hint of warmth and pride. She immediately passed the phone to him, and I was sure she stood beside him, keeping her ears open. "Samar, tell me everything!" He sounded eager, Dad, and his voice was as full of energy as ever in those months.

I had thought about it a lot, but I didn't know where to start. Then, contrary to what I had imagined, I started at the end. "I found her, Dad, your mom is alive and her name is Cecilia Alesini." His silence invited me to continue, and then I went over all the steps of my research and that story: Emilio, Cecilia's husband, now gone, the war, the nuns, the Vernets. I did not tell him about James, and at that time, I still did not know who had taken the child from Room 225, but I emphasized that since then, since that day in November 1944, Cecilia had never stopped looking for him. I also told him that he had had a brother, Manfredi, who had died years before, and that Cecilia's eyes and hair were just like mine. When I had finished, I listened to his silence, and then he asked, "And what is my name?".

I realised how important it was for him to find his name, his real name, which was neither Fahdi nor Gérard, but Leonardo, Leo.

It was then that he began to weep for all that had been lost, for that life he had not lived, that had been ripped away from him.

"Dad, I would like to try to bring her to you. She is sick with heart disease, she is very old, but maybe it is possible. I have to find a way."

"Thank you, Samar. Thank you." He repeated it many times like a chant.

At that moment, my mother took the handset from him. And she, too, unexpectedly thanked me for being tenacious, for not giving up.

And then, with gentleness I did not recognise, she asked me to come back.

"I don't know if it will be possible to get Father's mother here, you have to come back now, though." She lowered her voice, as if not to be heard by him. "He's sick, and now all he has to do is wait for you to come back and hug you one last time"

I realised she was right. "I take the flight to Paris from Zurich in two days, day after tomorrow night and from there, the next day, to Algiers. I'm coming, Mom, now go to Dad, stay with him".

As soon as I closed that call I felt completely happy. And instinctively, I called Mehdi. He would maybe have an idea, any idea, he would give me courage, he would say, "You'll see."

***

The next day a beautiful day peeped through the wide-open window of Cecilia's room. With a few hours of intermittent sleep induced by a good dose of drops behind her, she went straight to Franciszka's apartment. Her Polish friend, excited and worried at the same time, had anticipated to her that the girl had found out that certain Vernets had made a large donation to the convent just the day after the night of the kidnapping and that they had adopted a child later abandoned in Algeria. Cecilia had watched her in silence and listened attentively, not wanting to delude herself, not wanting to hope, but a strange tension ran down her back and reached her fingertips.

She had decided to talk to Samar, and the very moment she had seen her come in, in light of what she had learned from Franciszka, she no longer had any doubts.

Now she felt powerless. She had finally made it. She had known that her son had lived his life, that after a difficult childhood, he had had a beautiful existence, had been loved. And just now he was going to die. She thought that perhaps she could go to Algiers, join him for a final farewell, but she realised how little energy she had left. After searching all her life, she now felt drained. Without purpose anymore. She could not make up for lost time; there was no going back. The truth she now held in her hand gave her relief, but made her feel even more how much she had lost. Her son had lived, but without her. Sixty-six years had passed. And she had never seen him again, and he would die without knowing anything about her but her name.

One piece was still missing, however.

"But who could have kidnapped my baby? How did he end up in the hands of the nuns? Maybe one of them managed to get in, but how? Even if someone had given her the keys, it would have been risky. I could have gone back to the room at any moment, and it is true that according to the reconstruction, at the time you all were in the library listening to the radio, but someone could also have come out and noticed a stranger wandering around the hotel...." Cecilia, entering Franciszka's small apartment, had begun thus, with an eagerness to know, with the anger of one who has been defrauded too much.

Franciszka sat her down on the small sofa, shook her hand, "I would have come to you this morning, we have something to do in half an hour."

"Maybe I should try to leave for Algiers, Samar says there is not much time. I have some strength. But first, I would like to figure out who could have done such a thing and how my child ended up in the hands of the nuns in Silvaplana..."

Cecilia's last words fell between them as heavy as stones in a pond and brought a thunderous silence to the room.

They looked at each other and knew they were thinking about the same thing: the nuns, Louise. Franciszka expressed that thought aloud, "The only one who had contact with the nuns was Louise."

"She was there, too, though, listening to the radio, and no one ever said they saw her leave...." As they both focused on the thought of Louise, the girl Cecilia had thought a bit silly, but still her friend, and the relationship she had with her sister, the flow of their thoughts was interrupted by Lapo's babbling voice and his monotone tone, "Louise is gone. For a little while, just a little while."

"So, that night, did Louise come out of the library and disappear for a while?" asked Franciszka, with astonishment and anticipation.

"No, I didn't see it. I was looking for the radio signal, not looking around."

"Then how do you know Louise came out of the library?" Cecilia had been using an impatient and somewhat accusatory tone, Franciszka gently approached Lapo, motioning Cecilia not to speak, knowing that her husband might clam up if he felt attacked. "Lapo, explain well, it's important."

"As I was looking for the signal, I smelled Louise's scent disappear from the room for a while."

"Just that? How can you be sure?" Cecilia looked unnerved.

"Of course he's sure, Lapo is always sure about these kinds of things," Franciszka murmured, bringing a finger to her lips to signal Cecilia to let him continue.

"I heard the squeak of the back door, the one under the library. No one paid attention, the static from the radio was sizzling, but I heard it."

"And why didn't you tell anyone, then? Why?" asked Cecilia, but without rancour, without anger in her voice, as one who already knows the answer. "The inspector asked me if I had seen any strangers, if I had seen anything, and I had seen nothing strange and no strangers," he asserted, shaking his head, as if to chase away an unpleasant thought. Having said this, the elderly man sank into his chair and lost himself in his distant and inaccessible world.

Franciszka and Cecilia looked at each other, and it was like when the shift of a single degree of the sun suddenly shows, in a blade of light, the dust suspended in the air of a room.

"Louise...," Cecilia murmured, "Louise took Leo away from me. And she gave him to the nuns who sold him to Françoise and Maurice Vernet." Then she closed her eyes, but that did not stop the hot tears from slowly trickling down her cheeks. Franciszka took her hand, and she too allowed herself to weep, for her friend, for the fate of little Leo, for the cruelty of whom Cecilia had always considered a friend. No words were needed for it to be clear what both of them were thinking of: Louise, who was probably convinced that she was doing for the child and for her sister Béa, for James, and perhaps even for Cecilia, for whom Leo had too often been a burden. There were no words to say, only tears to shed.

CECILIA

9

Engadine, 1944

That evening, Cecilia had sensed a different and unexpected tenderness in James. She had felt it from the way they had made love, more slowly, more gently than usual, with less frenzy than the first time. And, now, as they stood cuddled on the small sofa in front of the fireplace where the embers were being extinguished, she kept feeling something suspended, unspoken. She was, without meaning to be, in a state of anticipation, though she could not have said precisely of what. Yet, it was a palpable, tangible feeling.

A soft crackling came from the fireplace, and a few red sparks were lost in the air.

"Leave your husband and be with me."

Cecilia raised her head to look into his eyes to see whether he was joking. She watched him for a while, trying to get to the bottom of those blue eyes to find the man's genuine emotions.

"I mean, to be together even after the war, in London or Milan, wherever you want."

Cecilia felt her heart burst in her chest. Even afterwards, that would be the happiest moment of her life, for she still did not know that shortly thereafter, everything would change, and her and James' destinies would be marked forever.

Then, she thought of little Leo sleeping across the hall.

"What about Leo? Emilio would never let me take him away from him. I am a mother; I should think of my son."

James lowered his eyes. "I know, dear, but maybe one day Emilio might forgive you; he might understand. And we could live in Milan; you could see the child whenever you want."

Cecilia felt all the impossible in that speech, "James, I've never cared about other people's judgment, but little Leo cannot grow up like that, with a mother with a bad reputation, and Emilio too... he wouldn't let me."

Overcome with responsibility and anguish, however, Cecilia was happy about what James had told her. He kissed her on the cheek. "Don't cry, I know, it won't be easy. But promise me that we will think about it and at least look for a way... can you?"

Cecilia nodded and hugged him tightly, standing huddled against his chest. She felt small and fragile, between the possibility of the greatest happiness and boundless despair.

She began to dress slowly and then, without greeting James but merely nodding in assent, slipped out the door, holding her shoes in her hand to make less noise. She reached room 225, slipped the key into the keyhole and entered, gently closing the door behind her so as not to wake little Leo.

A moment before she approached the bed on which, between the pillows, she had placed her son, she felt overwhelmed by a sense of finality, by the overwhelming foreboding of a looming and tragic fact for which she would be torn by remorse for the rest of her days, which would hold her hostage forever.

The child was no longer there.

Cecilia shook off the puffy comforter, the pillows, the blankets. She strained her ear, praying to hear the crying she had once so hated. The silence was interrupted only by her breathing, which became increasingly laboured. Panicked, she checked under the bed and searched the entire room. But he could not have moved; it was not possible. He had been asleep; she had left him a few hours earlier, and he had been quiet, not crying. He was asleep. Cecilia looked in the bathroom, opened the door to the room, and observed the dark, deserted hallway.

She returned, looked in the wicker crib, grabbed the mattress, and lifted it with one hand, dropping the sheets to the floor. She returned to look at the bed, sure she had left him there. She threw the comforter to the floor and shook the pillows again and again. She ran into the sitting room and looked at the sofa, armchair, and floor, even though it made no sense.

She felt a trickle of icy sweat run down her back; with shortness of breath, she rushed into the hallway and knocked vehemently, relentlessly, as if to demolish it, on the door of Béa and Louise's room, but no one opened it.

Hearing that commotion, James opened the door to his room and rushed into the dimness of the hallway toward the distraught woman with whom he had made love a moment earlier. He hugged her tightly, trying to calm her down. Between sobs, she told him that the child was gone, that he was nowhere to be found, that he was gone.

"What do you mean Leo disappeared?"

"Leo is not here, he is nowhere to be found, James."

Cecilia hurled herself at him, looking at him pleadingly, as if he could make the little one appear at that moment, at that instant. "Wait, Cecilia, let's see Brunne's and Franciszka's. Maybe they heard him crying and, not finding you, opened with the passkey and brought him down…"

Cecilia shook her head despondently as if she could not give that possibility a real chance in her mind. They ran down the stairs to reach the library. That evening, they were all gathered there, listening to the radio.

Cecilia rushed inside, shocked. Everyone was there, Franciszka, the Brunne family with the little ones playing on the carpet, the Zellers and the Klimos, Lapo and Marco, Béa and Louise. When she burst into the room, everyone turned their eyes toward her. "Where is Leo? Where is he?" she shouted, distraught, as if on the edge of a precipice. James explained that Cecilia had left her room, leaving the little one asleep on the bed, and Leo was gone when she returned. He did not miss the look Danielle Klimo gave her husband and Monika Brunne. Everyone knew that Cecilia and James met almost every night in his room. They tried to be discreet, but inevitably, in that small community, prisoner of that hotel, everything was known. One only had to look at them to sense what was between them.

"I don't know; I have no idea where Leo might be," Monika said. The room was shot through with a hushed whisper, in which all hypotheses were quickly sifted through, but there were not many. Cecilia stood there, motionless, fumbling through her mind and the eyes of the onlookers in search of a solution. She imagined Leo popping out of the group of children, sitting with his plump thighs and chubby little face. But he wasn't there.

Everyone began to get up, noisily dislodging the wooden chairs. "Someone took him from me, someone took him from me," Cecilia screamed outside herself, running her eyes over everyone's faces, fast, back and forth, back and forth. "You all hate me, you did it."

Anna approached her and held her close. "Calm down, Cecilia. We will find him. He can't have gone anywhere. And none of us would ever hurt Leo – or you."

Suddenly jealous of Anna and Cecilia's friendship, Louise also approached her, "Cecilia, dear, let's look for him; we'll find him."

Cecilia looked at her with eyes blazing with anger and compassion. At the same time, she thought she was a fool: "What are you talking about, Louise? Where do you want him to be? He still doesn't walk; he barely crawls. Someone took him. I don't see any other explanation." She was out of breath as she assimilated what she was saying. At the same time, her mind could not come up with any other plausible hypothesis.

Anna and David, followed by Béa and Louise, decided not to sit idly by but to search the living room, kitchens, and dining rooms.

"But he can't have gone there alone; he can't. Who took him from me? You all hate me, and you took him from me."

"We were all here, Cecilia, all of us," Anna reiterated with an edge to her voice this time as if the fact that Leo had not magically reappeared was beginning to sound more and more sinister to her as well.

Cecilia, stunned, turned back to the Klimo family, who stared at her impassively as if she had lost a minor object. "Don't look at us," Danielle said, and her voice rang shrilly through the room like a cold, sharp blade. "We would never have done anything to that poor, innocent child, to whom you and you alone have done harm, with your bad-motherly attitude."

They all looked at Cecilia, who felt their eyes on her and felt them rummaging through her. She felt the full weight of the thought that was going through their heads, and that was that she, she of all people, could have harmed her baby. She opened her mouth slightly, in bewilderment, "I want my baby. I am his mother. What do you think? What dare you believe?"

James brushed her shoulder and, in a quiet, firm voice, resolutely addressed them all: "She was with me, you know. She would never do anything to Leo. She loves him. Let's look for the child. Everywhere. And meanwhile, you, Marco, call the police."

Cecilia, James and Herr Brunne went out into the snow. Everything seemed untouched; the snow kept falling in broad, thick flakes. The landscape was silent and shimmering in the night. And icy. They walked the perimeter of the hotel, and at the window of Cecilia's room, James stopped, looked up, and then at the snow below. No trace of the child. In the light silk dress, Cecilia was not cold; she was out of breath. She felt her body sweating, her heart pulsing in her chest. She was not breathing. She fainted and fell into the snow, and James picked her up. As soon as she regained her senses, Cecilia kicked him away, "Go away, go away, it's you, it's you."

James held her close, "Forgive me, Cecilia, forgive me, we will find him. You will find him."

"Of course, I'll find him; I'll find him should be the last thing I do. G away, go away, James, don't stay here to remind me of what I've done. Get out of me, out of my life forever. Get out."

Now, she was screaming and sobbing. She felt lonely and lost. She hated herself. For her selfishness, that senseless passion that had taken everything away from her, the one good thing she had done, the one person who had loved her unconditionally even though he had received nothing from her. Her child. Her child.

Someone picked her up and carried her inside. She let herself fall onto the soft carpet in the hall.

FRANÇOISE

10

Sils Maria, November 1944

On the night Cecilia desperately searched everywhere for little Leo, just a few miles away, Françoise Vernet, now in Switzerland for months, thought back contentedly to how she had come within a hair's breadth of realizing her plan. She had organized everything down to the smallest detail, and now, at first glance, she would finally get what she wanted.

In previous years, she had wondered a thousand times how to solve her situation. She was already almost 30 and had been trying to have a child for at least eight years. Her husband, who also loved her, suffered deeply. There had to be a solution. While the war raged outside, Françoise Vernet had begun to fight her own personal war: she wanted a child at all costs. And she would have him so that her husband's family name would continue.

One day, a friend had told her about some of her acquaintances who were unable to conceive a child and who had gone to see a Swiss doctor, a luminary who, by all accounts in high society in mid-Europe, was able to get anyone pregnant just by walking past him. Françoise had listened attentively, wondering if her friend was indirectly giving her advice or simply speaking in generalities. She had also asked, with an indifferent air, what his name was and where he received. When she got home, she jotted down what her friend had told her on paper.

In the letter, she had intended to appear as a woman ready for motherhood, born for that noble task, and eager to hold a child. She could hardly reveal to the doctor that the thought of a child h, crossing the boundaries of her heart to instill itself, insidiously, in her brain, had become a perverse obsession rather than a genuine desire, an obsessive thought that no longer allowed her any lucidity, leading her to consider not only sex but also love and life itself as a strenuous battle to conceive. She had thus come to loathe any pregnant woman she saw, but also any child. Poisonous and exhausting anguish had crept inside Françoise like an evil fluid, making her a different woman than she was only a few years prior.

Her days, her friendships, her relationships, her whole life had been overwhelmed, making that once-always cheerful and carefree girl with big dark eyes, heart-shaped lips, dimples that appeared on her cheeks when she smiled, and prosperous breasts, a nervous, selfish woman focused on one goal, a woman worse and even less beautiful than the one Maurice Vernet had married eight years earlier, defying his powerful and wealthy family.

The moment she had given the letter to a butler to send it, she had begun anxiously awaiting the doctor's reply. All that remained for her in the meantime was to seek suitable accommodation through her acquaintances for the time they were to spend in Switzerland.

When the reply she had so long awaited arrived, Françoise opened the letter from Zurich with her heart in her throat, feeling that her future as a woman depended on that light, almost transparent piece of tissue paper.

It was just a brief communication in impeccable French, inviting Mr. and Mrs. Vernet to travel to Switzerland as soon as possible, which was a possibility given the situation in Europe. The letter closed with a promise. Françoise had decided to cling with all her might and strength: "We will solve your problem, and you will return to France with a beautiful child." It was on that much hoped-for event that the consideration of her husband, her whole family and her whole world, to which she had always wanted to belong, would depend.

She had immediately spoken to Maurice, who had given in after a weak resistance, as expected. She had already arranged everything. After the visit to Zurich, the doctor would send them to Engadine and Sankt Moritz with the prescriptions and his advice, where good air would undoubtedly benefit conception. They would stay in the chalet owned by some acquaintances who were friends of the antiquarian Beauvent. Beauvent's daughters stayed at a hotel in a resort near Sankt Moritz. Still, the doctor recommended the intimacy of a home. So, they moved to Sankt Moritz: they both took the doctor's miraculous drugs regularly and hoped; they took walks and hoped; they tried to make love as often as possible and continued to hope, although, for Maurice considering relationships as a kind of therapy was beginning to weigh heavily, and his anxiety was growing. He realized that if things did not go as his wife had predicted, it would be a disaster. Life next to Françoise would become hell. A hell with no exit since he could never admit to his powerful family that he had made a massive mistake in marrying the beautiful daughter of the maid, the only act of insubordination he had done in his life.

She and Maurice had followed the doctor's instructions to the letter, day after day. After months of trying, Maurice tried convincing his wife to return to Paris and be done with it. But Françoise would have none of it: she now felt that something was going to happen.

As she thought back to the long period that had just passed

and the failure of treatment, Françoise smiled as she considered how ingenious an idea she had developed since the Beauvent sisters had told her that, perhaps, it would be possible to adopt a child from the nuns that Louise often helped. Of course, she had never listened to Maurice when he talked to her about adoption, but she had told herself that, after all, no one would have to know that child had been adopted. They would have said that, thanks to the doctor, they, too, had been successful. They would stay a long time in Switzerland and then return with a child: their own child in the eyes of everyone, including the Vernet family. She had been thinking about this for a while; of course, it was necessary to make sure that they were given the child of a good family, not some poor man, but maybe some war orphan – and the little one had to be only a few months old.

She had dropped by that very evening to the institute director, prospecting her, should a child with the perfect characteristics for her be available, for a handsome donation. With that gesture in favour of the institute, she would likely succeed in silencing the Beauvent sisters, who were the only ones who could reveal their secret to their Parisian friends. In fact, she had noticed how interested Louise was in the fortunes of the institute and thought she would not betray her: she would only be happy to do her a favour.

It was not yet dawn when Françoise and Maurice Vernet left the chalet in Sankt Moritz for the convent. Wide flakes had been snowing all night, and now the snow had given some respite. Only the main roads had been shovelled, but their car slowly managed to reach the institute. Wrapped in her mink fur coat, Françoise squeezed her husband's hand and wondered what it would feel like to become a mother.

As she rang the bell in front of the wooden gate, pulling the icy metal rope, Françoise was surprised that she did not feel the slightest emotion at the thought of meeting soon to be son. Her husband seemed more tense. "He is an orphan, dear, who wants nothing more than us... do you understand?" Maurice nodded silently.

At that moment, a young nun opened the door smilingly, signalling for them to enter. She led them into a room where Sister Geraldine was waiting for them, sitting in an armchair with a stern air. In her arms, she held a beautiful baby, about eight months old, wrapped in a blue blanket. He had big dark eyes and was quietly sucking his thumb.

Françoise remained motionless for a few moments. Then, as if suddenly reminded of the script she had to follow, she approached the nun and gently took him from her arms. She held him close and looked dreamily at her husband, Maurice. He watched the scene of his wife holding that chubby baby and felt that he had landed in a peaceful place after a long and tiring journey.

He did not feel like asking about the documents and the regularity of the adoption. He was no fool; he sensed the thrill of wrongdoing in that affair but had no heart to spoil it. After all, the nuns knew what they were doing. They would never hurt a child.

"The amount we promised will arrive in your account today," he said. Then, wrapping his arms around his wife's shoulders, he led her toward the front door.

Sister Geraldine accompanied them and handed them a bag with baby bottles and goat's milk. "Here, give him this, although he has also started eating some solid food lately."

The Vernets thanked her and left. Whether Françoise was able to handle a small child had never been in question. She would manage, and once in Algeria, she would find someone to give her a hand.

That morning, they would return to France, to the South, and, thanks in part to Maurice's direct contacts with a certain Maréchal Pétain, embark on the first ship to Algiers.

The journey did not frighten her, even during those times of war: she had achieved her goal and would soon be able to enjoy the comforts of life in the colonies.

The ship would immediately leave Marseille for Algiers, where Maurice was expected for his new post in the colonial administration.

At the time, Françoise could not have known that she would be pregnant with twins ten years later. That they were daughters by blood, her real daughters, as she had told her husband, made her think, indeed made her confident, that she would be a better mother to them than she could be to Gérard. The fact that they were not Maurice's daughters but those of the gardener who cared for the flowers and plants in the apartment on the Rue du Bac and whom she had met about nine months earlier on one of her trips to Paris remained forever a secret, despite the sometimes almost irresistible temptation to hold it against Madame Vernet that the barren one was her beloved Maurice and not her, the maid's beautiful daughter.

LOUISE

11

Engadine, 1944

Louise knew that Herr Brunne always kept a passkey in his pocket. One evening at dinner, she sat next to him and slipped her hand into the jacket hanging on the backrest. She had agreed with Sister Geraldine that she would make a first attempt a few days later. The nun would wait at the second bend in the road from the village up to the hotel for the signal, namely, the light in Cecilia's room turned on and off twice. Seeing the signal, she would go up to the hotel, meet Louise at the back door, and take the baby from her.

When that day came, Louise was on edge: it was her moment, the one she had been waiting for all her life, the one to do essential things. Béa had hugged and kissed her, then, without a word, grabbed a red apple from the riser laid on the inlaid coffee table and bitten into it voluptuously, with the air of someone who was about to get just what she wanted.

As several nights a week, from their room, the two sisters had heard the door to Cecilia's room close almost imperceptibly, the click of the lock followed by the faint rustle of her clothes and the soft tread of her bare feet on the red runner. Then, James's door handle drops and silence. Béa felt herself dying and stifled with anger each night, but not that night: it would be the last. The two sisters had looked at the wristwatch with the mother-of-pearl dial from which Béa never parted.

For the first time in her life, Louise had read pride in her sister's big green eyes, or so it seemed to her.

He was finally making himself useful, doing something for his beautiful and beloved Béa. He was helping her. He was also helping that poor child he loved. He deserved a much better mother than Cecilia, who saw him as a burden and would only be happy to no longer have to take care of him to devote herself to her passion for James.

Before heading to the library, Louise had asked her sister, "Do you really think I should go instead of you?" She had raised her tone without realizing it.

"Of course," Béa had whispered, bringing her finger to her lips, "because this time it is you who has to help me. You will be less eye-catching, and no one will mind if you run into someone by chance."

Louise nodded, missing the ill will of that last statement but rather taking it as a compliment to her ability to be invisible, suited to that dangerous and important task. She smiled and, flaunting confidence, said, walking to the door, "You'll see that in no time. I'll pick him up and hand him over to whoever is in charge, and no one will notice a thing."

"Ssshhh, be quiet from now on," Béa had scolded her less softly than she would have liked, out of nervousness.

At that moment, Anna Zeller was returning to her room, where one of her children had forgotten a sweater. Passing by the sisters' door, she had heard them whispering. It was not her habit to eavesdrop, but she had stopped for a moment, perhaps because of the unusual tone in which the two were talking, ashamed of her curiosity. "In a moment, I'll take him and hand him over to whomever, and no one will notice," Anna had furrowed her brow without understanding. She was sure of what she had heard. What on earth was Louise supposed to take and hand over?

"Ssshhh," Béa's plea for silence and warning was clear, "You have to start being quiet from now on."

Anna shook her head, thinking of how Louise always let herself be treated poorly and hurried her pace, exactly as Lousie approached the door. She wanted to get downstairs to hear the latest news about the war. Right before the sisters, she reached the library and thought no more of the conversation she had overheard – not for two more weeks.

In those last days of October, the German retreat continued, and some were beginning to hope that the war might soon end in an Allied victory. In the half-light of the room, as Lapo tried to pick up the signal and everyone stared at his hands on the knobs, anxious to perceive a few words amidst the rustling, it would not have been difficult for Louise to sneak out unnoticed: a quarter of an hour would have sufficed.

Louise, in the dim light of the library, had gotten up and slipped out while everyone was leaning toward the radio. She had climbed the stairs quickly, clutching the key in her pocket. Arriving in front of room 225, she had drawn a sigh and slipped the key into the lock. However, just a moment before turning it, she heard a strange noise, like so many pebbles falling to the floor, like a waterfall. She had not identified it but had remained still to try to understand. The child had heard it because he had begun to cry. Louise had rushed off, headed for the library.

About twenty minutes later, Sister Geraldine, who had been waiting at the second of the hairpin bends going up toward the hotel for the agreed signal but had not seen it, turned back.

Louise had feared her sister's wrath, but Béa had been satisfied with her caution.

When they tried again precisely two weeks later, everything went smoothly. Entering the library, Béa and Louise sat as usual on the two small armchairs at the end of the room, faintly lit by a lamp with a green shade placed on a small table next to the radio. Lapo was already at his station, focused on the device, his father beside him. The Klimo family sat behind him. Anna entered last, and with David, they shook hands while the two sons played checkers. On the small sofa, next door sat the Brunne family. As expected, James and Cecilia were missing.

That evening, Radio London was reporting on Anglo-American operations in Greece. Things were going badly for the Germans there, too. Danielle Klimo nervously leaned forward with a furrowed brow, focussed on listening, while her husband seemed to doze off. Anna cast occasional happy glances at David and Monika, who seemed more absorbed in her thoughts than in the words coming from London. Herr Brunne sipped a bitter from a small glass he held in his left hand on which his large gold ring stood out, and with his other hand, between sips, he smoothed his beard.

Louise looked at them individually, then glanced at her sister, who nodded. She stood up quietly and strolled on the soft carpeted floor. She walked out of the room. There was no one in the hallways or the lobby. She walked quickly, without running. She could always say she was going to the bathroom had someone noticed her. She arrived at the staircase and began to climb as fast as she could so that, once on the second floor, she realized she was panting. She drew a deep breath and, walking this time slowly, arrived in a few steps in front of Cecilia's room, rummaged in the pocket of her skirt and grabbed the passkey with a slightly trembling hand. She inserted it into the lock and opened it. Little Leo was in the middle of the bed, quiet, surrounded by soft pillows. Louise watched him for a moment: he was rosy and plump, looking serene, his little hands clasped in two fists. He was sleeping peacefully and unaware of the devil of a mother he had, that she was in his lover's room and, most of all, of the fact that, at that moment, his life, his destiny, was changing forever. Thanks to her. Thanks to the skillful, cunning, good Louise.

Louise held the child close on the night that would seal many destinies. He moved and seemed to wake up. She gave him the pacifier soaked in soothing syrup Sister Geraldine had given her. Louise stood still for a moment, breathless, then, cradling him gently, praying that he would not cry, she wrapped him in the light-yellow blanket nearby. She walked to the door and pressed the light switch four times, seconds apart. She descended the stairs quickly and, having reached the ground floor, rushed to the basement, to the back door. She opened it by removing the latch and gently ajar it so that the lock would not click. She quickly climbed the stairs, careful not to slip on the ice that had formed on the steps. Louise looked around in the cold evening air and saw a dark shadow. Sister Geraldine was waiting for her. After handing over the baby, she went back, a little sorry that she had not even been able to greet the little one, whom she was fond of. Fonder than her mother, she told herself.

Sister Geraldine was glad that just that night, the first heavy snowfall of the season had arrived: the car would leave no tracks. Fortunately, she could drive well, and for those few kilometres, she could have made it despite the road being made slippery with ice and snow. Entrusting that child to the French couple would have come in handy; she would have been able to renovate the convent and do some good, including to that child who, Louise had told her, was in dire straits because of his lousy mother.

She had driven slowly, keeping to the main road leading to Maloja and not entering the village. Both so as not to be heard and not to run the risk of getting stuck in the snow that was falling heavily. Stopping at the second hairpin bend, she stared out the window. As soon as she had seen the light go out and come back on, she had climbed up, driving slowly, skidding on the snow, trying not to lose control. Once she had reached the small square in front of the hotel, she turned the corner toward the back door and saw it open: Louise was there with the bundle in her arms. Sister Geraldine took the baby, who began to cry slightly despite the syrup. She did not say a word, just exchanged a glance of understanding with Louise and sped downstairs so that no one would hear the crying. Reaching the car, she laid the baby on the seat next to hers and started the car. By the time Leo began screaming at the top of his lungs, it was too late for anyone to hear.

Louise returned immediately after she met with the nun, cold, and walked lightly back to the library on the rugs. All were precisely where she had left them. She had not been absent for more than ten minutes. Encouraging news continued to arrive from the front for the Allies, and Lapo was focused on the radio and moved the knobs whenever the signal began to croak. No one had noticed entering from the back of the room in a few steps and returning to her seat.

Casting a glance at Béa, she tried to calm down: she had done what she had to, and everything had gone well.

Her heart resumed a regular beat only when the broadcasts ended and everyone got up to go to their rooms. No one noticed that Louise's shoes had left slight traces of wetness.

CECILIA

12

Two policemen arrived. They hastily shook hands with Marco and Herr Brunne, who led them into the living room. Next to the fireplace that Franciszka was trying to light despite the dampness of the wood, they saw a beautiful, stunned-looking woman with dilated blue eyes. They greeted her, but she continued to stare at the tiny flame Franciszka had managed to ignite.

"They took him away from me; they took him away from me."

"Where were you?" the policemen asked.

"Yes, it's my fault. I was with my lover; what a horrible mother I am."

"Did you hear him cry?"

"No, no, no," Cecilia replied in despair, shaking her head and thinking fleetingly back to that evening when she would probably hear nothing, caught up as she was in James' plans.

"No, we didn't hear anything." James intervened, and Cecilia glared at him. "Go away, James," she hissed in a low voice.

"I just want to help you, Cecilia."

"Go away," she repeated, looking back toward the fireplace.

They asked many questions Cecilia could not answer except in monosyllables: no, she had no suspicions about anyone. Everyone hated her because she did not know how to be a mother.

"This is not true, Cecilia," Louise told her softly. "No one hates you here. We may have criticized you sometimes but hated you? Never."

"Little, naïve Louise." Cecilia shook her head. "What would you know."

The police then decided to hold a series of interviews, as they called them, to avoid the term "interrogations" to see if anyone might have seen anything.

One by one, he called the hotel guests, the owners, and even the Brunne and Marco children. The police questioned everyone at the hotel. They also tried with Lapo, but amid the commotion, he remained closed on himself, with his hands over his ears. He felt a tension that was hard to bear: the excited atmosphere, all that chattering and Cecilia's tone didn't appeal to him, and then he did not like Cecilia: the thud of her hand on the radio that evening long before still rang in his head. When Franciszka entered the room, explaining to the policemen that perhaps she could talk calmly to Lapo and ask him the right questions, they looked at her with condescension and Lapo with contempt. They had merely asked him abruptly, "Have you seen anything unusual? Someone, perhaps a stranger, walking away from the library?" He had shaken his head many times. Of course, he had not seen anyone. He had to think about the radio. Then he had gotten up quickly to go lock himself in his room.

The police spoke to Herr Brunne, who had noticed that he no longer had the passkey in his pocket but had decided not to mention it to avoid explaining why he always had it with him.

Béa and Louise were also questioned, but it was more of a formality than anything else: they were girls from a perfect family who seemed frivolous and kind. What could they possibly know about such a story? Louise was a bit flustered and merely imitated her sister, who stood algid and motionless in her chair, moving her head and eyes slightly to say that she could not imagine what could have happened.

When Louise got up to leave the room immediately after Béa, she met Anna, who was walking in. Their gazes met for a long, long moment. Anna felt a chill run down her spine. She thought back to what she had heard long ago. Not long, not more than two weeks. She seemed to catch a terrible flash of awareness in Louise's eyes, usually so blank. She went past her and headed inside. She sat with a hole in her heart in front of the policemen. When one of them asked her what she thought had happened to the child, if she thought it plausible that someone had taken him away, she hesitated. Perhaps she should have said that the Beauvents were discussing a plan a few days earlier, taking away and delivering something to someone, with an air of complicity. And that Béa particularly would have had her own motives to take the child away from Cecilia. Then she thought back to all that the war had taken from her, to all that Cecilia had had because of that same war; to her family, to all those who were never heard from again, to how vital that shelter was for her, David, and her children to stay together while so many others were divided; to how little time it takes to lose everything and also to think about everything. And she chose to keep silent, shaking her head to say that no, she knew nothing. She sustained the younger policeman's gaze briefly and pointed her eyes straight into his, then repeated aloud that no, she had no idea what could have happened to the child. A policeman, notebook in hand, summarized the results of her interviews with Cecilia. Everyone was in the library, everyone except her, little Leo, and James. From what they had been told, no one had moved from there. The child could not have been far away. Having reached this point, the man lowered his gaze and remained silent. His heart was wrung; he would never be able to utter the words that were going through the minds of everyone present in a terrible, hellish vortex. No one could have taken the child far away in the space of a few minutes; someone, however, could have harmed him or killed him (that was the word no one dared utter) in an instant. Although hiding the body would have taken a long time, really. Cecilia seemed not to have heard a word. She was utterly still, wrapped in the thick woollen blanket that chafed her pale skin, flushed with frost. Suddenly, she visualized images of her dead child somewhere under the snow. Yet they had looked and looked again at the garden; he could not have been made to disappear like that, no matter how much it snowed. In the meantime, two other officers had arrived and searched the length and breadth of the hotel grounds and walked the road to the lake repeatedly. There was no trace of the child.

The night destined to mark Cecilia's existence forever had slipped into a whitish dawn. In the days that followed, Cecilia seemed plunged into a state of total passivity, without hope, without words, without more tears. James and Anna took turns in her room to be by her side. But she did not even care about them; they were like ghosts reminding her of her sin, inadequacy, and worthlessness. She had lost all vitality, all desires; she had become closed in again, emotionless, defeated. A step back again from her boarding school years, in which, at least, she had longed for riches and luxuries. The emotions she had felt in the last few months, that movement within her, that chinking of the armour that had led her, finally, not only to love James but to feel blooming day by day, now she was sure of it, she felt something incontrovertibly, a more subdued but tenacious love for her child: the emotions had all died down as if suddenly smothered. The woman she had been for the past few months seemed far away, lost in a dream. But neither did she find the one she had been before, before the war, before James. She was a woman without herself, without identity. A woman who deserved nothing but loneliness. Marco had warned Emilio who was desperately trying to reach them. The disappearance of his son had plunged him into the worst of nightmares. Still, he had endeavoured to maintain the rationality and control that had always been his own, throwing himself into the practical organization of his trip and asking his friend for a myriad of information and details about the affair. By the time Emilio, thanks to some of his contacts, managed to get into Switzerland, a week had already passed since the disappearance, and Herr Brunne had begun to press for the story to be kept quiet. He certainly could not allow the hotel to get a bad name. So, he began to pressure some of his acquaintances for the police to stop searching.

Emilio entered the hotel transfixed and rushed to Cecilia's suite without greeting his friend Marco. Arriving at the door, he opened it and embraced his wife, clutching that slender body, which now appeared even more intangible and minute.

She remained motionless, nailed to the floor of the suite, her eyes fixed in a distant spot. "We will find him, my love, we will find him."

After a time that seemed interminable to him, Cecilia answered in a feeble, muffled voice, as if from another existence: "No, we will not find him, ever. He has been searched everywhere; he is not there. It's only my fault, only mine."

Emilio embraced her with new momentum. "But no, it's not your fault. How could it be?"

Cecilia shook her head and slumped on the sofa, her eyes vacant, lost in a forest of ghosts.

Only toward the end of the year had Cecilia spoken to Emilio again. She had hardly spoken to him since her arrival at the hotel. That year, too, Louise had set up the big Christmas tree and adorned every window in the great hall with little wreaths of pine, mistletoe, and red ribbons. After a long time, Cecilia had come down that evening and sat at the small table near the bow window. The other guests had greeted her with a hushed whisper, and no one had dared to greet her.

James had merely looked at her, not daring to utter a word. She wanted nothing more to do with him and, in fact, had never even glanced at him since the night of the kidnapping.

Emilio followed her with infinite patience, a steadfastness in loving her that was incomprehensible to all.

Marco had tried to talk to him one day, drawing a wide breath as if to engage in a complex, delicate, painful discourse. But then, he had kept silent. He had told himself that there was no point in adding pain to pain. His friend's condition was painful enough as it was without him knowing where exactly his wife was that night and what relationship existed between her and James.

Another time, Danielle Klimo spoke to Emilio, telling him about his wife and James in no uncertain terms. Still, he did not really want to listen to her. He had looked at her wordlessly, without comment, and then, slightly curt, had walked away. Even Danielle had told herself that perhaps that good man, who had inexplicably married that devil of a woman, did not deserve to the full extent the rawness of a monstrous truth.

One evening, Cecilia looked at Emilio and said, "I want us to stay until the thaw. Then maybe we will find him dead, somewhere in the garden under the snow, and we can leave."

Emilio approached her, excited and sketching a smile. Hearing again the voice of the woman he still loved had overwhelmed him. "Of course, we will stay; we will stay as long as you want, my dear. But you must not have such thoughts..."

Cecilia had already closed herself in her impenetrable silence; she was once again unreachable. But they would not leave before the thaw.

When spring arrived, with its lapping of water dripping and slipping away in endless festive rivulets, Emilio had the hotel grounds and much of the surrounding woods and meadows scoured, all the way to the lake and to the tip of the peninsula, into every nook and cranny, not knowing what to hope for. On the one hand, he thought that finding little Leo dead would somehow rid Cecilia of his ghost. On the other, he feared that such a thing would drive them apart forever. Perhaps Cecilia needed hope to continue living together with him, to love him, for them to be happy as he had always wished.

In any case, Leonardo was not found.

When Cecilia consented to leave, it was April 20, 1945. The war would be over in a few days.

Emilio was under the illusion that returning to Milan might bring Cecilia to her senses. But it did not. Cecilia somehow reopened herself to life, but it was a lonely life of which Emilio was not a part of. Or rather, he was just an extra.

Even the arrival of their second child, Manfredi, in 1950 did not bring her back to her old self, the vivacious woman he had fallen in love with. She was a diligent mother and wife. Manfredi never lacked anything. She found him the best schools and organized little parties and snacks without missing a beat. She ran the big house on Corso Venezia with mastery, managing the service staff impeccably. From 1952, Cecilia returned to Sils yearly for very long periods.

But to Emilio, she never really returned. Or, perhaps, he eventually told himself, she had never been his.

He let her go, though, alone, because only up there did she seem to find that part of herself that he missed so much. A little colour, a little life. Right there, where it was impossible for him to really reach her.

Emilio would die in 1985, alone, in Milan.

It was summer, and Cecilia was in Sils as usual.

CECILIA AND SAMAR

12

Engadine, 2010

It was the first time I had entered the yellow library. There was no one there that morning; the room was silent, the woods outside still glistening with the rays of the morning sun. But the landscape could not give me peace. I turned on the computer screen and connected to the Internet. I typed in the address Mehdi had given me and looked at the time at the bottom right: 8 o'clock. My eyes were swollen with tears when I saw Cecilia, my grandmother, enter the yellow library. In Algiers, it was only 7. I brought the little white arrow to the green button and listened for a few moments to the tones as if of the telephone or an old radio. And then Mehdi's face appeared, with dimples on his cheeks, long eyelashes, and his big, off-white smile. It was still him, my irreplaceable friend, whom I would never know how to thank. He had gone back to Algeria for a few weeks to his family but would soon return to Paris. When I had told him the story of Cecilia and my father and that I wanted to organize my grandmother's trip to Algiers, with the practical sense that had always distinguished him, he had told me that it was not possible to risk it, that those two had been looking for each other forever. It would be absurd for him to die before seeing her or for her to get sick during a rather demanding trip, calculating that there were no direct flights from Zurich and it was necessary to have a stopover of several hours in Paris.

I had been a little uncertain. It seemed to me that seeing each other on a screen could never really bridge that distance that required an embrace, a genuine embrace of skin, tears, hands, and bodies. Besides, Dad didn't even have a computer or an Internet connection. I had always used computers at the university.

With his easygoing air, Mehdi teased me a little and said to stop making unnecessary trouble and try it out. Then maybe I would even be able to get them to meet directly. He had convinced me.

And there he was, smiling, in our home in Algiers. I could distinguish the plates my mother kept hanging on the room wall in the background. The one on the left had broken, and it seemed like yesterday that my father had reassembled it by glueing the fragments together to reconstruct its design. That detail made me cry; nostalgia melted something inside me; missing that home, my father's unconditional love and even misunderstandings with my mother overwhelmed me. Then, Mehdi moved, holding the laptop in his hand. I saw some indistinct movement until my father appeared. He was in bed, leaning on many pillows to stay up. His bright, curious look was the same as always, but it now seemed to contradict the rest of his face and body. His face was as pale and hollowed out as I had seen; his hair seemed sparser. If not for the eyes, I might not have recognized him. "Hi, Dad, I have a flight tomorrow night to Paris and tomorrow morning at dawn to Algiers. Sorry, I took so long."

"Stop apologizing." His voice broke, "Thank you, Samar. I don't need anything else." The screen filled with vibrant anticipation, dense and suspended time.

At that moment, the door opened, and Matteo entered; tall as he was, he had to bend down to give his arm to Cecilia, who suddenly looked small and bewildered, as if all the energy I had always seen on her had vanished.

The grandson accompanied the grandmother with unspeakable tenderness. My father stood in silence, eyes fixed on the screen. I got up from the chair and pushed it aside to sit Cecilia.

She let herself fall, clutching the pommel of the stick in her right hand. She stared at the screen.

The instant their eyes met, the distance, time, and coldness of those circuits and that virtual space ceased to exist. Cecilia reached out her hand and brushed her fingertips over the luminescent surface. Her face was still, and heavy tears began to flow from her eyes. The silence of the library was total.

My father spoke first, "Hello." He said it in a hushed French voice.

"I'm sorry, I'm so sorry," Cecilia said, struggling with tears. Leo, it was my fault." She burst out that name, "Leo," which, I saw, reached my father in the centre of his heart.

He seemed to study every detail of that woman's face, his mother, whom he was seeing for the first time. "Leo," he repeated that name almost under his breath to make it his own. Cecilia nodded slightly but could not speak, as if the words were choking in her throat. "It's not time to think about blame, only to close the circle of our lives. Just to find each other," my father said fiercely, as if he did not want to waste time.

The screen had been pierced by the newfound name; now, it was no longer a filter between them; now, it was as if it had vanished.

"You look like your father. The same dark, good eyes, the same features." Finally, my grandmother had found her words again. Then, as if she felt she owed Emilio the loyalty she had denied him, she continued, "His name was Emilio. He died years ago, but he loved you very much, though he barely made it in time to meet you."

"And you are like my Samar, my little blond girl, Samar." He searched for me with his gaze behind his mother and then returned to rest it on her.

At that moment, I realized the meaning of "recognize." Cecilia's eyes were moving to observe every angle. At the same time, my father was still, almost astonished, as if in front of the unthinkable. Their tears flowed silently, and I imagined them joining in another dimension, in lost possibilities, in the space of mistakes and regrets.

I heard a sigh coming mixed with a sob. Cecilia had put her hand in front of her mouth as if to stifle a cry. He sketched a crooked smile. The realization that they now found each other seemed to overwhelm them. "Leo, Leo..." she repeated, still touching the screen with her fingers, as if she could go through it, sinking her hand into that virtual space, cracking the glass, and finding the lost warmth of her son, of the child lost so many years before. She took to smiling and crying together. "Forgive me, forgive me."

"Mother," my father said softly and firmly at the same time, delivering his ultimate forgiveness to that word.

Time around us in the yellow library seemed to stand still. Or perhaps it had turned back. I noticed that even my cheeks were now streaked with silent tears.

I had succeeded.

Cecilia broke the silence, "You don't know what it means to me to have found you and, with you, to have found this granddaughter of mine. And yes, she looks like me; she is like a bridge between us, a perfect bridge."

A thread connected those two distant places, those lives that had been lost too soon and too late found again. I felt like the connecting link, the missing piece that made it all clear.

There were not many words to say. Cecilia lowered her hand but not her gaze. Now, it was my father who was crying.

"I had a happy life, another mother, Nour, who loved me, and now that I know everything, I can die in peace." He smiled with his usual smile, which did not belong to someone about to die, a happy smile that involved his gaunt face.

I was breathing hard, straining not to sob. With my thoughts, I went to my room in the basement: I had to get everything ready, stuff my few things in my bag and trolley, and run to Zurich, Paris, and Algiers.

I had to go to my parents' room, hug my father and mother, and be with my family.

They looked at each other silently, and then Cecilia said, "Thank you." It was a thank you to my father for finding her and accepting her story without judging her.

"Thank you for looking for me, for knowing how to wait for me there, where everything began, where my life began."

Cecilia put her hand over her mouth as if to contain too much emotion. Then I saw my father raise his hand in a final nod of greeting; Mehdi lifted the computer, and the image crunched into a thousand pixels and disappeared.

Cecilia stood staring at the black screen for a few seconds; neither Matteo nor I dared to speak. Franciszka had entered and approached her friend. She encircled her shoulders with strength and tenderness. Cecilia stood up and, without a word, clutching her cane, began to walk toward the exit and the elevator. She looked frail as if she would fall at any moment. But I knew she would not fall.

Shortly afterwards, Franciszka asked Matteo and me, who had remained in the library, staring at each other without speaking, to go to Cecilia's. We went in together and sat on the small sofa across from her, who was in the usual armchair. She was tired, her eyes were puffy, and she looked even paler and thinner than usual. She began to speak at once, without greeting us, without preamble, with a peremptory tone that clashed with what she wanted to tell us: "Matteo, you are not as fragile as your father Manfredi nor as shallow as your mother. I know I have not given you much; I have never been able to give anything to anyone. But you have my strength. Allow yourself to love, Matteo. Never stop yourself from loving. Only then can you have much from life. It is late now for me, but for you, it is not; you are young. I would like you and Samar to continue to care for each other, even after I am gone, and to get to know each other." She paused momentarily and then said, "I'm glad Matteo has found a piece of family. We were never very good at having big, solid families." She smiled wryly. "Now I know you have to go; I can't make it on this trip; maybe I wouldn't get there in time, and I wouldn't have time to build anything with my son anyway, and what we have lost, is lost forever. Go, Samar, fly home now." I approached and held her close to me; she seemed to be made of air. When I was at the door, she called me again, "Samar, don't let Dr. Charlier get away; trust me." She smiled mischievously and then, with her hand, beckoned for me to go.

Left alone in the dim hallway, Matteo and I looked at each other, smiling. He nodded to endorse his grandmother's last sentence about Dr. Charlier. "What a story you brought us, Samar!" Matteo broke the silence by shaking his head as if he could not believe what had happened in those days. "Your flight is tomorrow night, right?" I nodded, "I have to go as soon as possible; I can't waste time," I thought back to my father's face during the video call, and my voice broke on the last word.

Meanwhile, we arrived on the second floor, opposite Matteo's room. "When you leave, I won't be there, I'm going to the Corvatsch glacier soon, and I'll stay there in a hut at three thousand meters for the night. I need to think about many things." He smiled and squeezed my arms affectionately. "But I hope to see you again soon; you will come back, won't you?" I shrugged, not knowing what I would do in the future. "I wasn't fortunate as far as family is concerned; my father left early, and even before that, he wasn't there anyway; my mother... never mind. In the library, I sensed a change in Grandma: I saw her more serene but at the same time more fragile, as if she had finished fighting all her battles. And I fear that soon I won't have her either. But here you come, an unexpected piece of family." He looked at me amused, his eyes shining as if at a surprise.

"I, too, am glad to have found all of you here, and I don't think I will ever lose you." Our eyes met, and perhaps we both thought of Albert.

We hugged briefly on the threshold, and then he took his cell phone out of the side pocket of his hiking pants and showed it to me. I don't know how much it's going to take up there. I'll talk to you when I return, and you'll already be home! After that, he opened the door and disappeared into the room to pack his backpack.

The following day, I got up at dawn to pack my suitcase. That evening, I would leave for Paris, but I did not want to give up my usual duties until the last: I would go to the village for the day's orders one last time. I walked the path I loved so much. After the latest discoveries, I did not sleep a wink that night. I was happy I understood and even had the privilege of meeting my father's mother and grandmother. However, I was also stunned and incredulous. I waited for dawn by hugging myself in Madame Gourmand's sweater. Meanwhile, I shivered in the coolness of the night air that came in lightly through the room's open window.

As I walked down the downhill path, the image of Albert passed through my mind. He was at the bottom, waiting for me, as he had that day a few weeks earlier. I watched the edge of the forest, where the dark fir trees opened to give way to wind-mowed meadows reaching the blue lake. I felt foolish, hoping to see Albert: he was in Zurich, and I did not know when he would return. So, I would never see him again. Before returning to Algiers, I would not even be able to say goodbye. As I wondered whether to send him a message on his cell phone, something unusual came into my field of vision, like a discordant note on a perfect score I knew by heart.

It was something white and wet, like a sheet, perhaps left there by someone, by a distracted camper.

Suddenly filled with a profound uneasiness, I quickened my pace and approached. When I reached the end of the narrow path, just at the point where it led onto the dirt road around the lake, I recognized her. She stood there, half on the shore and half in the slight ripple of the lake water.

It was Cecilia, my grandmother.

I knelt beside her, my heart pounding in my chest. I brushed her with my fingertips, but there was no doubt that she was dead. I noticed a little further on the slippers, laid neatly on the shore.

I rummaged through the large canvas bag and grabbed my cell phone. I called Matteo; his cell phone was off. I tried Albert, but he was also disconnected. I then frantically searched for Franciszka's number, which she answered on the second ring. I heard myself say between sobs, "Cecilia is dead. In the lake."

Franciszka did not seem surprised. She asked me to wait for her and arrived shortly thereafter, accompanied by the hotel bus. She was wrapped in her large coat and came toward me with her arms wide open as if to contain me all in her embrace even before she had reached me. She held me tightly but briefly and then crouched down beside Cecilia. She gently caressed her face and spoke as if her friend could hear her, "You have found the answers you have sought for so many years, solved the riddle of your child's disappearance, you are done, you are done in your own way." She smiled, tightening her lips with liquid eyes. She also immediately tried to call Matteo, but he was unavailable. Then, even though it was clear that there was nothing to be done, she called an ambulance, which arrived quickly. Franciszka asked they take Cecilia to the hotel chapel, then stood beside me, watching her leave and go back up the hairpin bends.

When we returned to the hotel by bus, Franciszka took my hand and invited me to follow her. This time, we went through the front door and climbed the stairs to room 225. It was not locked, so we went in. Franciszka felt authorized to do so; she knew Cecilia would not blame her. And, indeed, she found exactly what she was looking for. On the small desk, there were two envelopes. One was for me, the other for her.

Franciszka opened her own and found a note written in Cecilia's round, irregular handwriting inside it. She clutched it to me with her right arm, holding the message with her left hand. She read it aloud in the firm voice of one who has suffered so much:

> *I don't know if I could forgive myself, as you always hoped.*
> *This pain of mine wanted eternity.*
> *Like our friendship.*
> *Yours, Cecilia*

It was written in German, and Franciszka was moved and smiled wistfully. She knew that, even in pain, it would amuse her...

She sighed at length with the air of feeling fulfilled as when a circle unexpectedly closes.

After a few seconds, she handed me a handkerchief and told me to take my envelope.

I unfolded the paper and read.

> *Don't feel guilty about this act of mine. I simply no longer have a reason to be in the world. The past has come full circle. I die with great remorse, but at least I know that my son had a happy life and a daughter who loves him. It was a pleasure to meet you, Samar.*
> *Your grandmother, Cecilia*

I burst into tears of unstoppable crying, not only for Cecilia but also for my father, for the two of them and for all those who had been lost and never found again, while Franciszka held me close, stroking my hair like the sweetest of mothers.

Between sobs, I vividly imagined Cecilia going down to the deserted hall wearing only her white silk nightgown, pressing the button to open the door, hoping that the slight buzzing would not wake anyone. Then, going out into the frosty mountain night air and, without stopping, entering the woods descending into the lake. Walking the first part of the path illuminated by the two dim streetlights at the hotel entrance, which were always lit, and then walking into the pitch blackness. Thinking back to the many times she had walked that land, first with James, then with little Manfredi, who trotted beside her to get her attention, then with Matteo, her grandson. I thought of her alone, with the knowledge that would be the last time for those trees, for the rustle of that grass, for the flowers that dotted it and which, now, in the darkness, she could not see. I could almost see her walking slowly, groggy from the tablets, brushing her fingers now over a fir tree, now a rock, feeling the dampness of the bark and moss, slipping on the stones in that still night. And then, there she was at the end of the path, in front of the pitch-black lake, apart from the twinkle of the nearly full moon that night, slipping off her slippers and beginning to walk slowly, her bare feet, into the icy water.

EPILOGUE

SAMAR

That afternoon, I left the uniform hanging on the closet door, just as Franciszka had when I started working there. As I slipped Cecilia's letter into the green bag, there was a knock. It was Matteo, who had just returned from the peaks. He had found a series of calls in a spot where there was signal; he had phoned Franciszka, who had told him everything. We embraced each other with transport. There was no need for words. We both knew how tangible Cecilia's absence was between us at that moment. When I turned away, I noticed his eyes were shiny, his hair dishevelled, and his clothes worn out: he looked like a tired child after an afternoon in the park. He sat on the bed, and as soon as he began to speak, I noticed that he really felt like a child. He told me about when, as a child, he used to spend long afternoons at his grandmother's when his father was at work and his mother at the hairdresser's or, perhaps, he said bitterly, at some lover's. Of course, Cecilia had never been the grandmother who made snacks or baked cakes, nor was she the grandmother who played on the carpet with her grandson. Matteo had always felt loved by her, though. She had protected him from his mother's superficiality and his father's weakness. She had read fairy tales and modified them as she saw fit with her colourful and whimsical imagination. She could have left him to some of her maids, but she had never done so. She had scolded him, and he was terrified of his grandmother's scolding. Still, she had also helped him with his French homework and often spoke to him in German, which, she had explained to him, had been taught to her by a Jewish friend during the war years in Sils. She had not been an affectionate grandmother in the classical sense. Still, Matteo had sensed since childhood in that subtle and somewhat algid woman, at least, a genuine desire to love him. Perhaps she had not succeeded as other grandmothers would have done, but undoubtedly, she had tried.

He paused to cry silently. Then, he pulled up with his nose and wiped his eyes with his shirt sleeve. "It may sound silly to you, Samar, but when I'm in the mountains, I sometimes feel the sensation of my little child's hand clasped in Grandma's during the long walks where there was no shortage of forks in the road. She always told me that it was important to learn to choose, and I was the one who had to decide which path to take."

I was happy about that moment of intimacy that had formed between us. I approached him, but at that point, he had stopped crying. The easygoing Matteo had returned, "We need to notify Albert. Will you take care of it?" He shot me with an amused look, but I suddenly bravely replied that yes, I would call him. We said goodbye with one last hug, and as soon as Matteo was out, I pressed the little green handset on my cell phone and dialled the doctor's number.

I had heard that for Albert, those had been intense days: he had become the director of the Zurich Cardiology Centre, one of the world's most famous in that field. The phone rang free for a long time until he answered it just as I was about to give up.

"Doctor, Mrs. Alesini is dead; she threw herself into the lake," I told him immediately, without introducing myself, without greeting him, assuming he had identified me by the number.

"Samar..." he hesitated momentarily, "I'll come right away, leaving tomorrow morning at dawn."

"You will not find me, Albert," I continued, again switching to calling him by name. I am leaving shortly; I have a flight to Paris from Zurich tonight and tomorrow at dawn from there to return to Algeria."

I heard a light rustling as if he were taking off his gown or a coat. "I have just returned from celebrating my promotion, and yet in that whirlwind of colleagues, friends, acquaintances, I could not be truly happy, as if I had a foreboding… From my study window, where I am now, I can see Lake Zurich." I remained silent; those words did not seek answers, only a place where we could be together. "Stay, Samar," he whispered lightly, almost to himself.

"No, Albert, I have to go."

"When do I see you again?" he continued, with a note of impatient anticipation.

"I don't know, I don't know. I promise I'll get in touch from Algiers. If you want." In that instant, I heard on the other side the sound of footsteps, someone walking in heels, probably.

"What's going on?" asked a female voice that made little effort not to be heard by me. It had to be Agnes.

"Cecilia Alesini died," he answered her, briefly apologizing to me for the interruption.

"Albert, are your eyes shining? My God, Albert, you are a doctor, and Mrs. Alesini was over ninety years old, wasn't she?" Agnes said this in a shrill voice without dissimulating her nervousness, not caring that he was on the phone.

"Yeah, but I'll miss her," he answered her dryly and then, letting go, turned back to me, "Call me as soon as you can; I'm counting on it."

I did not have time to stop too long to think about what had been said with Albert. I had to go to the library, where I would say goodbye to Franciszka one last time and then leave Switzerland for Paris.

"Come, Samar, stay for a few more minutes," Franciszka motioned me to sit on the small sofa beside her.

"I'm tired, Samar," she said, letting go against the backrest. "There are still many things I want to tell you about when your grandmother was here during the war. All I can think of is Cecilia and James, who strolled in these woods at the time of their love, and Emilio, who loved Cecilia so much that he forgave her even the most serious betrayal and carelessness. Then I am reminded of the beautiful Béa, who finally got what she wanted, and Louise, who was guilty of horrible sin, tearing a child away from her own mother out of weakness, stupidity and envy. I seem to see again here, in this room, the people of that time, dear Marco..." and in saying that name, her voice trembled a little, "and the Brunnes, with their strange lives, all spent in this strange and enchanted world of the hotel. Who knows what happened then to Anna and David Zeller, with their children, who probably grew old in Israel. And the Klimos, with their dullness? I wonder if all those people ever thought about Cecilia and her child again."

I would have liked to know so much more about those far-off days and those who had been, for better or worse, protagonists in the incredible story of Cecilia and her child, my father. But I could not linger any longer. Franciszka noticed my being on tenterhooks and redeemed herself from her thoughts, "Of course, you must go, dear; I had a cab called for you; it will be here any minute." She kissed my head and said with impetus, "Now go, run to your father."

As the car drove down the hairpin bends, I wondered whether or not to tell Dad that Cecilia had taken her own life. Indeed, I would tell him that his mother had always loved him, and that he had been taken from her by people who hated her while pretending to be her friend – people without scruples. I decided never to reveal to the Vernet twins the truth about their brother; it did not seem right to spread more poison in their lives, casting a further terrible shadow over that mother they had never loved.

As the cab pulled away from Sils, I watched the lake glisten in the cool morning air. The peninsula stretched out over the blue lake, as it always had, forever. For eternity.

Then, my thoughts went to Paris and the little bistro of Madame Gourmand, who, even then, warmed my heart with her cashmere sweater. I would see her again a few hours later and felt she would forever be a part of my life.

My mind reached the sea of the Côte d'Azur, and from there, like a bird's flight across that blue expanse, to my Algiers, to the whiteness of the streets of a city that, suddenly, I felt belonged to me and missed once more. I would soon re-embrace my parents and be able to tell my father all the details of my adventure: he had spoken to me in the firm tone of someone who will not let go before he has untied all the knots. I realized I would soon be alone with Mom, but I felt I could now build a new relationship with her. Because I was a new version of myself.

I slipped my hand into the canvas bag in search of cigarettes. As soon as I arrived, I would smoke one. I realized I had forgotten them at the hotel. Maybe I could quit. I smiled at that thought; I felt strangely strong.

Having left Sils, the car had set off toward the hairpin bends of Maloja and was now driving along the last stretch of the lake. The colourful sails of windsurfers furrowed the blue glaze of the rippling water. I thought I saw a blue and yellow one and thought again of Albert. Suddenly, I was sure I would return to him someday. I would find him again on the shores of that lake. And we would write our future, where I had met my past.

THANKS

Every time I get to the end of a book, I realize how many people have contributed to making it what it is.

I must thank my mother for the sensitivity with which she reads my stories and my father, who always spurs me on.

My husband, who has long asked me why I don't self-publish, and my boys, who really enjoy following their mom's publishing adventures.

Thanks to Richi and Veronica, who, with little Arianna, made a challenging year beautiful.

Thanks to the many friends. Those at school, Alessia, Benedetta, Chiara and Federica, who always follow me, those in Milan, especially from the unforgettable Panda class, and those around the world. I have met many thanks to the Expatclic community, and there are so many; here I mention only Claudia and Federica to include them all. Thank you to the incredible women who participated in my podcast "Unconfined" and those who listened. Each of them has a space in my heart. A big thank you to the Italian friends I met here in Bucharest, particularly Angela, Eleonora, Gaia, Giovanna, Venusia and Ursula: your stories, strength and sensitivity are a great inspiration to me. And then there are the foreign friends who were not able to read this book because they do not speak Italian, but who pushed me to write it, first, Ayşin and Nino.

In Samar, there is a little piece of each of you.

Thanks to Andrea and Michi, who know how to be there for me like no one else.

Thanks to Antonella, because she can make me laugh.

Thanks to Riccardo, Sara, Beatrice and Rossana, who have always been rooting for me.

Thanks to Karina, with the freshness of her eighteen years and her dreams, she has taught me more than I could have taught her.

As with each of my books, I'd like to thank Alessandra, whom I consider a bit of a mentor, and Annamaria, whom I don't know personally but who loved this story from the first draft.

And finally, thanks to Gianluca, the studio pym and the people I was lucky enough to meet there: Marcella, for her editing with her magic touch, and Cristina, who made the perfect cover in a flash.

Each book carries within it the magic of connections and the power to create new ones. In the end, the reason I keep writing is all here.

Giuliana Arena lives in Bucharest. When she was in Milan, she edited a blog on mammeamilano.com; now, she teaches Italian to foreigners, contributes to Expatclic's Human Library and writes, edits and narrates the podcast *Sconfinate, Storie di altri Mondi*. She has published with Francesca Santarelli *Mamme no Panic* (Sperling & Kupfer), *Il Nido di Vetro* and *Dopo le Nubi, il Sole* (both for San Paolo Editore) and the short story *La Casa Azzurra* in the anthology *Voci in Fuga* (Prospero Editore).

Printed in Dunstable, United Kingdom

66776582R00180